Readers love
ARIEL TACHNA

Dance Off (with Nessa L. Warin)

"In short, this is a really great read!"

—MM Good Book Reviews

"…an enjoyable book! If you are looking for a light read, this is a good one."

—Love Bytes

Home for Chirappu

"This was a cute story… sweet, wonderful, and can't help but make you smile."

—Crystal's Many Reviewers

"…if you're looking for a holiday read full of Christmas spirit, no matter which faith is leading the celebrations, then you will probably like this short novella as much as I did. I think it is a fantastic story."

—Rainbow Book Reviews

Cherish the Land

"The writing is evocative and seamless. The images deeply moving and sometimes emotionally shattering."

—Scattered Thoughts and Rogue Words

"…a great addition to the series."

—The Blogger Girls

More praise for
ARIEL TACHNA

Château d'Eternité

"…this is a very romantic, passionate story… Thanks, Ariel, for the stimulating visit to the past."

—Rainbow Book Reviews

"I found this to be a very engaging story of self-discovery and love."

—Live Your Life, Buy the Book

Testament to Love

"I can count on Ariel to give me a fantastic story; she does wonderful things with big intense novels, and sweet little ones like this."

—Love Bytes

The Path

"…never have I felt so connected, so involved in the past and present as I did here in The Path… I read this book twice, and each time its magic grew as did its hold on my imagination and heart."

—Scattered Thoughts and Rogue Words

"This story is one of growth, of passion, and of two men who are so right for each other that words cannot do it justice. The Path is just a really excellent read."

—Joyfully Jay

By Ariel Tachna

At Your Service
Best Ideas
Château d'Eternité
With Nessa L. Warin: Dance Off
Fallout
Her Two Dads
Highland Lover
Home for Chirappu
In Search of Fireworks
The Inventor's Companion
The Matelot
Music of the Heart
Once in a Lifetime
Out of the Fire
Overdrive
The Path
Rediscovery
Revelations in the Dark
Rose Among the Ruins
Seducing C.C.
Stolen Moments
A Summer Place
With Madeleine Urban: Sutcliffe Cove
Testament to Love
Why Nileas Loved the Sea

GAMES LOVERS PLAY
Amorous Liaison • Best Behavior • Ride 'em Cowboy

HOT CARGO
Healing in His Wings
With Nicki Bennett: Hot Cargo • Something About Harry

LANG DOWNS
Inherit the Sky • Chase the Stars • Outlast the Night
Conquer the Flames • Cherish the Land

Published by DREAMSPINNER PRESS
www.dreamspinnerpress.com

By ARIEL TACHNA (CONT.)

PARTNERSHIP IN BLOOD
Alliance in Blood • Covenant in Blood • Conflict in Blood • Reparation in Blood
Perilous Partnership • Crossroads in Blood • Reluctant Partnerships • Lycan
Partnership • Partnership Reforged • Partnership Reborn

With Nicki Bennett
All For One • Checkmate
Under the Skin

THE EXPLORING LIMITS SERIES
Exploring Limits • Stretching Limits • Refining Limits
Breaking Limits • Transcending Limits • No Limits

Published by DREAMSPINNER PRESS
www.dreamspinnerpress.com

AT YOUR
Service

ARIEL TACHNA

Published by
Dreamspinner Press

5032 Capital Circle SW, Suite 2, PMB# 279, Tallahassee, FL 32305-7886 USA
www.dreamspinnerpress.com

At Your Service
© 2016 Ariel Tachna.

Cover Art
© 2016 L.C. Chase.
http://www.lcchase.com
Cover content is for illustrative purposes only and any person depicted on the cover is a model.

ISBN: 978-1-63476-851-1
Digital ISBN: 978-1-63476-852-8
Library of Congress Control Number: 2015952975
Published March 2016
v. 1.0

Printed in the United States of America
∞
This paper meets the requirements of
ANSI/NISO Z39.48-1992 (Permanence of Paper).

For Elizabeth and Zahra, who shared many a special dinner with me.
And to Maurice, Paul, and Florent
—whatever their real names might be—
for making those nights that much more memorable.

CHAPTER 1

ANTHONY MERCER walked out of the Salon du livre, feet dragging with exhaustion. He'd gotten used to doing seven- or eight-hour days at BookExpo America and the other trade shows he attended for Along the Spectrum Press, the publishing company he worked for, but they hadn't prepared him for the ten hours of frenzy that was the Paris event. He'd reveled in the energy in the hall, readers lined up in every aisle to meet authors, discuss issues, or buy books, but even as extroverted as he was, ten hours was a *long* time to be on. They'd know better for next year—assuming they came back to exhibit a second time—and would have a second French-speaking person on hand to allow for longer breaks. Every time he left the booth, even to run to the restroom, he felt guilty for abandoning Patricia, his boss, to a crowd she could barely talk with.

"Put your feet up for half an hour, Anthony," Patricia said as they parted in the hotel lobby. "I'll check with the concierge and get a recommendation for a restaurant so we can eat and then sleep. We have three more days of this."

Anthony groaned theatrically at the reminder.

Patricia grinned at him unrepentantly. "Half an hour," she repeated.

Anthony nodded and caught the elevator up to his hotel room. He toed off his shoes and flopped on the bed. It would be so easy to fall asleep and skip dinner, but then he'd be awake in the middle of the night starving, with no way to do anything about it. He could take a shower. That would wake him up and save time before bed, because he felt grimy enough from the day in the exhibit hall that he wouldn't be able to sleep without a shower. He could only imagine how hard Patricia was struggling. She'd arrived just the day before. He'd come in last weekend to visit friends in Lyon first, so he only had exhaustion from the day to deal with, not jet lag.

The shower and clean, casual clothes instead of the shirt and tie that had strangled him all day made a world of difference in how he felt when he went down to the lobby to meet Patricia for dinner. Patricia wore fresh clothes as well, looking far more like the friend he spent most of his days with than the corporate executive she became at events.

"Ready?" she asked.

"Always." He flashed her a cheeky grin and dodged her swat. "Where are we going?"

"To a little family place around the corner. The concierge said they use all organic, mostly regional products. Whatever's fresh and in season instead of stuff that's been shipped in from who knows where."

"Sounds good to me. You know where it is?"

"Around the corner," Patricia repeated. "Really. It's half a block up rue de Vaugirard."

"You can't beat the location." Anthony felt better, but he hadn't been looking forward to a long walk to dinner. His feet hurt even in tennis shoes instead of his dress shoes.

They walked around the corner and down to the little restaurant, Au cœur du terroir. An older gentleman—bald on top, with a ring of gray hair around the sides of his head and a smile as bright as the lights overhead—greeted them as they came in.

"Two for dinner, please." The French rolled off his tongue as effortlessly as English did, maybe even more so after speaking French all day every day in the week since he'd arrived.

"Do you have a reservation?"

It was Friday. Anthony hadn't even thought about that when they'd talked about the restaurant. "No, we don't. Can you squeeze us in?"

The man pursed his lips for a moment, then nodded and gestured for them to follow him. He led them to a little booth toward the back of the restaurant. Every other table they passed was either full or had a Reserved sign sitting on it. That boded well for the quality of the food, as far as Anthony was concerned.

"Enjoy your meal."

"Thank you." Anthony slid into the booth across from Patricia. "They're a popular place."

"So it seems. What's on the menu?"

Anthony turned his attention to the menu and to translating it for Patricia. He looked up when their waiter approached the table with a grin that punched Anthony hard in the gut. He wore jeans and a white button-down shirt with an elegance that American men never managed. Anthony had spent years trying to put his finger on what made the difference, that ineffable something that made a man French, but he still hadn't managed to put it into words, only to recognize it when he saw it. Their waiter had it in spades.

"Bonsoir. Puis-je vous servir quelque chose à boire?"

Anthony had a weakness for sexy men who spoke French. He had accepted that about himself years ago, but it did nothing to soften the effect the waiter's voice—deep and a little gravelly—had on him.

"Do you have sparkling water?" Patricia asked in English while Anthony recovered his composure.

"Of course," the waiter replied, and his voice in English, with that delectable French accent, undid all of Anthony's hard work. He was going to be a puddle on the floor by the end of the evening, just from listening to their waiter talk. A shiver of anticipation trickled through him. It had been a while since he'd felt the need to indulge in a fantasy, and now one stood before him in the flesh. "And for you, *monsieur*?"

"Un kir, s'il vous plaît." Anthony appreciated the waiter's willingness to speak English with Patricia, but he was in Paris. He wanted to speak French. Even more than that, he wanted to hear the waiter speak French.

"Of course, sir." The waiter switched back into French with a warm smile. Anthony knew what he'd be dreaming about tonight.

"Oh, I want one of those too," Patricia said, breaking the moment. "Only the one with bubbles."

"A *kir royal* for my boss," Anthony translated for her in case the waiter hadn't understood. If it gave him the chance to make clear Patricia was his friend, nothing more, he'd count that as a bonus. The waiter glanced at Patricia with a nod, but he turned back to Anthony almost immediately with what looked like extra interest in his expression.

"We have two specials not on the menu tonight—halibut with potato pastry and white asparagus, and duck breast in a red wine and balsamic vinaigrette sauce. And of course, the house-made ravioli stuffed with foie gras are always a favorite."

"It all sounds delicious." Anthony let his gaze linger on the waiter. Patricia wouldn't care if he flirted a little. She'd probably encourage him. She was always after him to date more. Especially since…. Anthony pushed the thought away. He had better things to do than dwell on the past. Like gathering as much fodder for his fantasies as he could. "What's your favorite?"

"The duck," the waiter said immediately. "Everything that comes out of the kitchen is delicious, but the duck is exquisite."

Feeling bold, Anthony gave the waiter a thorough look before smiling. "Everything certainly seems delicious."

"I'll let you look at the… *menu*. If you have any questions, I'll be happy to answer them when I bring your drinks."

"He's cute," Patricia said as soon as the waiter disappeared around the corner.

"He certainly is. That doesn't make him gay or available, though." He needed the reminder for himself. Fantasies were all well and good, but that was all this could be.

"If he's straight, I'll buy you dinner," Patricia retorted.

"You're buying me dinner anyway."

"Exactly."

Anthony chuckled, as she'd no doubt intended. "There's a halibut special as well as the salmon on the regular menu if you want fish. There's a duck with red wine and balsamic vinegar if you're in the mood for that. Or he mentioned a homemade foie gras ravioli. Can you read the rest or do you need me to translate it?"

"I think I can figure it out. I'll ask if I have any questions."

They spent the next few minutes in companionable silence as they studied the menu. Anthony already knew he'd order the duck simply because the waiter had recommended it, but he was famished, having skipped lunch in favor of staying at the booth to talk to the line of people waiting for them. "The charcuterie platter looks tempting. Do you want to split it with me?"

"You know I'll eat anything you put in front of me," Patricia replied. "Order it if you want and I'll share it with you, and find a bottle of wine for us to share too."

"I'm trying to convince him we aren't on a date," Anthony teased. "You're not helping."

"Sharing an appetizer or a bottle of wine doesn't mean we're on a date. Now if we were holding hands or something…."

Anthony snatched his hand out of reach before she could grab it. He didn't know when the waiter would be back, and he didn't want to ruin his chances, no matter how small, because the waiter saw Patricia holding his hand.

"What do you want me to order for you?"

"Is that lamb?" Patricia pointed to one of the items on the menu.

"Yes, seven-hour lamb, they call it. Slow-cooked and served with potato mille-feuilles. It's like a pastry, only with potato slices instead of pastry dough."

"I'll have that."

The waiter reappeared a few moments later. He set Patricia's drink in front of her with a gallant little bow. When he turned to Anthony, he skipped the bow, but his gaze lingered as Anthony lifted the glass to his lips for a first sip. It was tart and dry from the Aligoté with just the slightest hint of sweetness from the cassis.

"Just the way I like it," he said, hoping he managed to convey more than his approval of the drink.

"I live to please." The waiter's voice deepened as he spoke, the husky timbre rubbing over Anthony's nerves like a caress. He might have imagined the earlier interest, but he wasn't imagining this. He couldn't be. The moment stretched almost to the point of discomfort before the waiter smiled and asked what they wanted for dinner. The routine of placing their order—including a bottle of Hautes-Côtes de Beaune at the waiter's recommendation—settled Anthony.

His equilibrium disappeared again when the waiter took the menu and his fingers brushed against Anthony's. It could have been an accident, but it didn't feel that way at all.

Patricia let out a low whistle. "Isn't he a bold one?"

"It's not just me reading the situation that way?" Anthony didn't see how it could be, but it never hurt to have a second opinion. Not when his pounding heart made it difficult to think clearly. He didn't do things like this, but damn, he was tempted.

"It's not just you. If you can stay awake until he gets off work tonight, he's yours for the taking."

"That's the problem, though, isn't it? We're already dragging from today, and we have another ten-hour day ahead of us tomorrow."

"The morning was slow today. I can manage until lunchtime. Some of the translators said they'd drop by the booth. I can get one of them to help me if I need it."

"I'm not that desperate to get laid," Anthony protested. "I'm here for business."

"You did plenty of business today, and you'll do plenty for the three days that are left, but I haven't seen you feel such an instant attraction to someone in a long time. Take him up on what he's offering. Consider it your declaration of independence: a no-strings-attached spring affair in Paris. Exactly what you need to finish getting over the douche bag."

Anthony smiled as she'd intended, but the reminder still hurt. It had been six months since Doug walked out on him. Anthony thought they'd built something real and worth holding on to, not a temporary thing to be abandoned at the drop of a hat. He'd been wrong.

Maybe Patricia was right. Maybe it was time to stop feeling sorry for himself and get on with his life. The waiter was certainly attractive even before he opened his mouth. With his voice added to the equation, he could probably talk Anthony to an orgasm without touching him at all. He'd be upfront about the fact that he was only in Paris for five more days. If the waiter could live with that, Anthony would take him up on the offer implicit in his gaze.

THE FOOD tasted as wonderful as Anthony could have asked for, and Paul—Anthony had finally learned his name—got more flirtatious with every visit to the table. By the time he'd cleared the last course away, Anthony was convinced this could work.

"Do you have a pen?" he asked Patricia after Paul brought the check.

Patricia smirked as she passed it across the table. Anthony wrote his cell number on the back of one of his business cards and slid it under Patricia's credit card on the tray that held the bill. He couldn't be any clearer than that. If Paul was interested, the next move was his.

"I'll head back to the hotel, shall I?" Patricia said. "You can sign the credit card slip too. Your name is on the business account. That way you can talk to him without an audience."

"Are you sure?"

"Yes, and make reservations for tomorrow night before you leave. The food was incredible, and the prices were surprisingly reasonable. I wouldn't mind eating here the rest of the nights we're in Paris. Especially if that makes things easier for you."

"I guess that'll depend on him."

"He'd be a fool not to take you up on your offer." Patricia gave him a quick hug and left the restaurant.

Paul reappeared a moment later. "Your boss left?" he asked.

"Yes, she was tired and ready for bed."

"And you?"

"I'm ready for bed," Anthony replied, fingers tingling at the illicit thrill of what he was about to do, "but I'm not the least bit sleepy."

"Now that the boss is away, the mouse will play?" Paul asked with a wink. He picked up the credit card and smiled when he found Anthony's card underneath.

"Something like that," Anthony said. "If I'm not being presumptuous."

"Not at all, but I don't get off work for another hour."

Anthony's pulse thudded in his ears. He was actually doing this. He was going to take Paul up on his offer. He was going to have a fling in Paris. His friends would tease him for falling into the stereotype, but this chance—this man—embodied years' worth of fantasies all rolled up into one lithe bundle of sex on legs. He took a deep breath and flashed Paul his most inviting smile.

"Why don't you use that card to pay for dinner and open another tab for me? I'll have a cognac while I wait."

"I'll be right back," Paul said. "I still have to take care of my other tables. I don't want my father annoyed at me. He's been known to make us stay late if he thinks we've been slacking off."

Anthony nodded. Of course he couldn't have Paul's undivided attention while the restaurant was open. He'd take what he could get now in exchange for being the sole focus of Paul's attention later.

Paul returned a few minutes later with Patricia's credit card and a cognac for Anthony. He took a sip and closed his eyes in delight at the slow, smooth burn down his throat.

"I wonder what else would put that look on your face." Paul leaned in close as he spoke, giving Anthony a whiff of his cologne. Anthony didn't claim to be an expert on perfumes, but the fresh citrusy scent over sandalwood drew him closer.

"You'll have to find out."

Paul's gaze turned heated. "I plan on it."

Anthony's cheeks burned at the promise in Paul's words, but he wanted it. Oh, how he wanted it! It had been so long since someone looked at him that way, like he was worth taking the time with.

"Good." His voice sounded funny in his ears, like he hadn't quite gotten the word out around the lump in his throat, but Paul didn't seem displeased. He leaned in a little closer, and Anthony had to resist the urge to kiss him right there.

"Are you a sweet little bottom waiting for a big dick to fuck you open? Or are you the one doing the fucking?" The words were barely a whisper against Anthony's ear, but they left him trembling with the sudden rush of need. A strangled sound escaped before he could bite it back. He tried to breathe, to summon a coherent thought, but before he could think past the desire swarming through him, Paul stepped back at the sound of someone calling his name. "I'm coming, Papa. I was just bringing a drink to one of my tables." He turned back to Anthony. "Think about it."

Anthony watched him walk away, gaze glued to his ass until he was out of sight. Holy shit, what had he gotten himself into? He adjusted himself surreptitiously below the table. A few lingering looks and that voice, and his brain had already short-circuited. Paul had told him to think about it. Like he could think about anything else. If only he knew how to answer, because both scenarios had their appeal. It had been six months since he'd had sex of any variety, so either would be a welcome respite. Maybe he'd leave it up to Paul, although his offer alone suggested he didn't have a strong preference. Which did he want more? Paul had a self-assurance about him that would surely carry over into bed, meaning he'd give Anthony a night to remember if Anthony chose that route. Then again, he'd always enjoyed being the one to take apart a strong man's self-control, something far easier to do if he was the one on top.

"Have you decided?" Paul's voice rubbed along Anthony's nerves. He took a sip of his cognac for courage and to buy himself a little more time. He didn't do this. He'd never done this, but he was going to do it tonight.

"House rules. You decide."

Paul's smile widened, and his gaze went dark. "You won't regret it."

Anthony didn't doubt that for a minute.

CHAPTER 2

RUE DE Vaugirard was a busy, vibrant street, even at midnight, exactly what Anthony had come to expect from a commercial area of Paris. Almost as soon as they left the thoroughfare for the side streets, though, they left the bustle behind for the quiet of a residential neighborhood. Another block away to rue du Hameau and Paul guided Anthony toward the front door of an eighteenth-century building in pale stone, white or yellow—he couldn't tell in the light of the streetlamps.

"Do you ever feel like you can't get away from work, living so close to the restaurant?" Anthony asked as Paul dug in his pocket for his keys.

"It's the family business," Paul replied with a smile. "Unless I quit the restaurant and never went to family gatherings, I wouldn't be able to get away from it, no matter where I lived."

"There is that."

Paul got the heavy wooden door unlocked and ushered Anthony inside with his hand low and hot at the small of Anthony's back. Anthony stood in pitch darkness for a moment until Paul found the light switch that illuminated the entry hall. The inside of the building matched the outside, buffed stone floor shining in the bright light and wrought-iron railings with a wooden banister leading up a curved staircase.

"We'll take the elevator unless you really want to walk," Paul said, following Anthony's gaze. "I live on the fourth floor."

Which meant they'd have to walk up four flights of stairs, not three. He'd had too much wine at dinner for that. Not to mention how ready he was for the promise implied in the hand that had returned to his back. "We can take the elevator. I can admire the architecture another time."

Paul grinned at him. "Does that mean there will be another time?"

Anthony swallowed hard. "I'm in Paris for five more days. I have to be at the Salon du livre during the day, but Patricia made it pretty clear my evenings were my own when she left without me tonight. I don't see why this has to be a one-night thing, as long as we both understand that I'm leaving on Wednesday."

Paul pulled open the elevator door and herded Anthony inside. The tiny cabin, probably a century old, barely held both of them, but Paul didn't seem concerned as he punched the button for the fourth floor and crowded Anthony against the wall. Anthony leaned into him, letting their bodies touch in as many places as possible. Paul tilted his head and mouthed at Anthony's jaw, his lips catching on the stubble Anthony hadn't bothered to shave away before dinner.

"I'll shave tomorrow before I come to the restaurant," Anthony gasped.

"Don't bother. I don't mind a little beard burn." Paul worked down Anthony's neck to the collar of his sweater. He nudged the cloth aside and nipped at the skin beneath. "Do you?"

"It can't show tomorrow." His voice sounded wrecked to his own ears, but he couldn't be bothered to care. Paul was taking him apart, and he didn't want to be put back together anytime soon. "Beyond that, no."

The elevator dinged and the interior door slid open. Paul pulled Anthony out of the elevator with him and spun him around so his back hit the wooden door behind him. The doorknob dug into his back, but he ignored it in favor of running his hands over Paul's shoulders and arms. Beneath the simple shirt, he could feel solid muscle, tribute to all the heavy trays Paul carried around the restaurant. He yearned to see as well as feel, but he'd wait until they were inside for that. Paul's wasn't the only door on that floor, and he didn't want someone coming out and seeing them half naked.

Paul didn't seem to share Anthony's concern about his neighbors, given the way he ran his hands under Anthony's sweater.

"Fuck," Anthony grunted.

Paul laughed and pulled away. "Should I be pleased I have you so worked up that you speak in English instead of French?" he teased.

Had he spoken English? He hadn't even realized. "Ouais," Anthony replied, consciously switching back to French. He didn't have to think to speak French these days, but exclamations were always the last thing to come naturally in French, and Paul had muddled his brain thoroughly already.

"What did you say?" Paul asked.

Anthony considered his reply for only a moment. He could translate it as a simple expletive—*putain* or *merde* or something like that since he couldn't imagine Paul not knowing the word fuck—or he could get what he really wanted. "Baise-moi."

Paul's eyes widened momentarily before a grin spread across his face. "With pleasure." He unlocked the door and ushered Anthony inside, the hand that had rested so conscientiously above his waistband in the foyer and elevator now squeezing his ass provocatively. Anthony shivered. He hadn't realized how badly he needed this.

Paul didn't bother with the lights as the door latched shut behind them. He simply pulled Anthony back into his arms and waltzed him down the hall and into his bedroom. Light spilled through the window from the moon and a streetlamp outside, enough to let Anthony see Paul's captivated expression—a match, he was sure, for his own. He reached for the buttons on Paul's white shirt just as Paul pulled his sweater up. Laughing, Anthony raised his arms to let Paul divest him of the sweater and T-shirt he'd thrown on after his shower. As soon as his hands were free, he returned to the task of undoing Paul's shirt. He wanted them both naked as soon as possible.

Paul shrugged out of his shirt the moment Anthony got it unbuttoned, letting it fall unheeded to the floor. Not wanting to wait, Anthony reached for the buckle on Paul's belt. Paul's grin widened, if that was possible, as he toed off his shoes and pushed out of the rest of his clothes in one practiced move. "Your turn."

Anthony nodded and undid his own jeans. He didn't manage the rest with the ease Paul had, but Paul didn't seem bothered by his awkwardness—there was no graceful way to take off socks.

Paul embraced him from behind as he straightened, his cock slotting perfectly into the crease of Anthony's ass. Anthony moaned as heat washed over his skin. The room was cool, but the goose bumps on his skin had nothing to do with the temperature and everything to do with the way Paul's hands roamed over his body.

Anthony arched into the caress, reveling in Paul's obvious desire. If Paul was thinking of someone else, it didn't show in the way he lavished attention on Anthony, and being the center of an attractive man's attention did wonders for Anthony's bruised ego. Doug could go fuck himself for all Anthony cared. *He* was in Paris, enjoying a night with a sexy Frenchman who couldn't get enough of Anthony if the way he sucked and nibbled on Anthony's shoulder was any indication. Anthony tilted his head to the side, inviting Paul to continue his explorations.

He tensed when he felt Paul's lips move up his neck, but before he could protest, Paul nipped at his earlobe. "No marks where they'll show. I won't forget."

The tension faded from Anthony's muscles, and he leaned back against Paul more fully. Paul took his weight without difficulty, settling one hand across Anthony's sternum while he ran the other over Anthony's belly. Anthony canted his hips, inviting Paul to move lower, but Paul ignored him and circled his navel with one long finger instead. Anthony moaned at the suggestively innocent caress, trying and failing not to imagine that same finger teasing another orifice.

He sucked in a deep breath when Paul probed a little, tickling him. "Careful," he warned. "You wouldn't want to ruin the mood."

"Ticklish?" Paul asked.

Anthony nodded.

"A little laughter during sex never bothered me, but I'd rather you squirm because you feel good than because I tickled you. Do you want me to stop or just use a firmer touch?"

Anthony's abdomen had always been exquisitely sensitive, sparks shooting through him at any touch, but he could usually keep from squirming away from a lover's hands if they were careful to keep a steady contact with his skin. "A firmer touch," he replied. "It feels good."

"I want it to feel more than just good," Paul murmured. He urged Anthony onto the bed. "Let's see what I can do to make you scream."

Anthony lay back against the pillows and watched with anticipation curling in his gut as Paul crawled up his body on hands and knees. He stopped when his face was level with Anthony's stomach. Anthony's skin tightened as he waited to see what Paul would do. Would he move up for a kiss, pinning Anthony to the bed with his weight? Would he stop midchest and lick and bite at Anthony's nipples? Or would he move lower instead and suck Anthony's dick? He wouldn't complain about any of those options. Paul just needed to hurry up and decide already. The waiting was killing Anthony.

Paul winked at him, firing Anthony's nerves, and buried his face against Anthony's abdomen to rub his stubble back and forth over the sensitive skin. Anthony gasped and writhed beneath the caress. It bordered on tickling, but Paul kept the contact firm enough to avoid that. Anthony closed his eyes beneath the erotic intimacy of the moment. He was a sure thing—Paul had to realize that—yet Paul was taking the time to seduce him anyway. He cupped Paul's head, encouraging him to continue. When Paul flicked his tongue over Anthony's navel, a jolt went through Anthony's system, leaving him desperate for more. "Please."

Paul lifted his head enough to meet Anthony's gaze in the dim room. "Please what? What do you want?"

Anthony could have answered that question a hundred different ways, but that would require putting words to desires he didn't know how to express. He dropped his hand to the duvet, giving Paul complete control over whatever came next. "You."

Paul's smile softened. "You have me."

For a few days at the most, but it would be enough. Anthony would go home with a week's worth of memories and it would be so worth it.

Anthony's thoughts blanked out completely when Paul returned to what he'd been doing. He gave himself into Paul's care, lost in the sensation Paul evoked with his hands, his lips, his beard, his tongue. Heat surged through him in ever-strengthening waves. Anthony gasped and moaned and undulated on the bed, begging wordlessly for everything Paul would give him.

When Paul urged him to roll over, Anthony went eagerly, moving up onto his knees in preparation for the fast, quick fuck he was expecting. They weren't lovers after all, just fuck buddies out for a bit of fun and release. Any second now, he'd feel lubed fingers getting him ready. It would feel good—everything Paul had done to him felt good—and then it would be over and he'd go back to his hotel so he could return to work in the morning. He spread his knees a little wider in silent invitation.

Instead of using his fingers, Paul gave Anthony's back the same attention he'd given his front, rubbing his stubble over Anthony's skin. Anthony slumped onto the bed, head spinning at the unexpected turn the evening had taken. He'd accepted the first bit of foreplay as natural to get them both worked up and ready for the main event, but he'd passed that point some time ago, as had Paul judging by the hardness prodding Anthony's knee, yet Paul seemed in no hurry to bring things to a head. Had the rules for hookups changed? Granted, it had been a while since he'd last picked a guy up purely for sex—probably since he was in college—but he didn't think things had changed that much in fifteen years.

Maybe it was just that French men were more considerate? If so, he didn't want to go home. He'd had long-term lovers who hadn't paid as much attention to him as Paul was doing!

"You smell good," Paul murmured against Anthony's skin.

"I showered before dinner," Anthony replied. "I needed it after the day at the book fair."

Paul nipped at Anthony's shoulder blade. "Good. Then I can do this."

Anthony jerked beneath Paul's teeth, then let out a hoarse shout when Paul moved between his cheeks and licked up his crease. His thighs trembled as he spread them even wider. He hadn't dreamed Paul would…. The prickle of Paul's stubble left him panting as Paul settled in to feast. Babble poured from Anthony's mouth, some mixture of pleas and curses in French, English, or just nonsense. He couldn't think, could barely breathe. Paul was driving him wild with every pass of his tongue. Sweat dripped down his forehead where it pressed against his forearms. He rocked back against Paul's mouth, desperate for more. Then Paul reached between his legs and surrounded his cock in a tight grip, and Anthony screamed.

Paul stroked him leisurely, like he had all the time in the world, but Anthony had run out of control. He bucked into the caress, his hips jerking as he chased his release. Paul tightened his grip even more, creating a channel for Anthony to thrust into. He plunged into it, all thought gone as his desire built. Electricity shot up his spine as Paul pressed his tongue past Anthony's sphincter and ran his thumb over the tip of Anthony's cock. His whole body shook as he climaxed.

He vaguely registered a grunt behind him before a hot spurt of fluid sprayed across his ass. Fuck…. Paul had come from tonguing him open and jerking him off. That was almost enough to turn Anthony on again, but exhaustion was catching up with him, and he still had to walk back to the hotel, not to mention take another shower either before bed or in the morning. Patricia wouldn't appreciate him working the stand smelling of sex.

He rolled to the side, intending to get up and make his excuses, but Paul stopped him with a tender hand to his hip. Anthony turned to look at him, but Paul just smiled. "Don't move. Let me clean you up."

Anthony subsided, bad idea though it was. It would be so easy to read something into Paul's consideration, but Anthony pushed the thought aside. This was a hookup, not the start of a relationship, even if they wanted it to be. He was leaving on Wednesday. Paul returned a moment later with a warm washcloth. He wiped up the mess across Anthony's backside, then reached around to clean Anthony up.

That was more intimacy than Anthony could handle at the moment. He took the cloth and dealt with the wet spot and the stickiness still coating his cock. "Thank you."

"You're welcome," Paul said. He set the cloth aside and stretched out beside Anthony. Anthony waited for some clue as to what happened next, but Paul simply rested his hand on Anthony's chest and played idly with his chest hair.

"What time do you have to be at the Salon tomorrow?" Paul asked eventually.

"It opens at ten, although Patricia said I didn't have to come in until noon if I was too tired," Anthony replied.

"I have to be at the restaurant by ten thirty since it's my morning to open," Paul said. "You're welcome to stay if you want, but I'll understand if you'd rather go back to your hotel."

Anthony hadn't even considered staying, but he was tired and sated, and the thought of getting dressed and walking back to the hotel in the cold and dark didn't appeal in the least. "I shouldn't stay."

"You shouldn't have come back to a stranger's apartment and had sex with him either," Paul replied easily. "I didn't hear you complaining about that."

"There wasn't any reason to complain about that."

"And there's a reason to complain about sleeping in my bed? It's surely more comfortable than the one in your hotel room. Hotel beds are never truly comfortable."

Paul's mattress was soft and welcoming, and if Anthony stayed, he might get a second round in the morning. "If you're sure you don't mind."

"I wouldn't have offered if I did." Paul snuggled closer and draped his leg over Anthony's thighs as his head came to rest on Anthony's chest. "Mmm. Perfect."

Anthony was far from perfect, but the night had been the closest thing to perfection he'd felt in a long time. He would relax and enjoy it rather than look a gift horse in the mouth. If it all went to hell tomorrow, he'd deal with it then.

CHAPTER 3

SUNLIGHT STREAMING through the floor-to-ceiling windows woke Anthony the next morning. He pulled the pillow over his eyes with a groan. He wasn't ready to wake up yet.

"I'm sorry," Paul said. "I forgot to close the shutters."

Anthony yawned and scrubbed at his face. "It's fine. Shutters that actually close aren't a luxury I have in the US. The sun wakes me up all summer at home." He stretched, feeling his back pop, and slumped back onto the bed. "I should get out of your way so you can get ready for work."

"If you want," Paul said, "but I can make coffee as easily for two as I can for one. Do you want a bath while I'm getting breakfast together?"

"How are you real?" Anthony asked. "You don't even know me."

"It doesn't cost me anything to treat my lovers with courtesy, whether we have one night or years together," Paul replied with a shrug. "It's up to you. You don't have to stay."

"No, I'm sorry. I've had boyfriends who didn't treat me as well as you have. I didn't expect it from a casual affair, but I'm not going to refuse. It feels good," he admitted.

"And that's why I do it. I like making my lovers feel special," Paul said.

It showed. "I'll take you up on the offer of a bath, then. Thank you."

"There's an extra towel on the radiator. Help yourself to anything you need. I'll start the coffee."

Paul's bathroom was the size of a postage stamp, just a tub, a sink, and the toilet. Anthony plugged the tub and turned the water on hot. He hoped he remembered the trick of using the shower attachment because the tub had no curtain to keep the water inside. When it was hot, he climbed in and sat down, bracing the nozzle between his knees. It splashed a little, but he didn't spray water everywhere like he had the first time he tried to take a bath in France. He chuckled a little at the memory as he washed his hair and body. He'd assumed Paul's scent had come from a cologne when he'd smelled it last night, but the body wash by the tub had the same distracting fragrance. Oh fuck, he was screwed. He was going to spend the whole day smelling like Paul. He'd never be able to concentrate on work. He only hoped today was mostly selling books rather than trying to conduct business. He'd never manage to discuss print runs and distribution options and bookstore orders in the state he was in now. He briefly considered jerking off in the tub, but Paul was waiting for him and they had to get to work. He'd have to hope Paul was interested in a repeat—maybe a less selfish one on Anthony's part—tonight. Paul hadn't seemed anything but delighted by the evening's outcome, but Anthony would enjoy the chance to return the favor.

He pulled back on his jeans and sweater. He'd only worn them a few hours the night before. They'd get him back to the hotel, where he could change into a suit for the day. Finished with his ablutions, he left the bathroom to be greeted by the welcome smell of caffeine. Real coffee, not the watered-down stuff so many Americans preferred. He followed his nose through the apartment to the kitchen. Paul leaned against a granite countertop with a bowl of coffee in his hands.

"I eat at the restaurant almost every night," Paul said when Anthony looked around for a table. "I don't have a dining table."

"It's fine," Anthony said. "I can drink my coffee standing up."

"I started to pour it for you, but I realized I didn't know how you like it. There's milk and sugar if you want. And there's a croissant, a *pain au chocolat*, and a *chausson aux pommes*. Help yourself to any or all of them."

"You didn't have to get all that for me," Anthony protested.

Paul leaned over and kissed him, the taste of coffee strong on his breath. "You're in France, remember? The patisserie down the street charges less the more you buy. I paid five euros for both our breakfasts."

"Which patisserie?" Anthony asked. "I should get something for Patricia on my way in to the Salon du livre."

"Your boss?"

"Yes. She doesn't speak French very well, as you noticed last night. Not that she lets that stop her. But since she'll have to open the booth without me this morning, I figure the least I can do is bring her breakfast."

"You should have told me. I would have set an alarm," Paul said.

"She told me not to rush. She… well, she approved of me coming home with you last night. She thinks it's time for me to move on with my life."

"Is that what last night was?" Paul asked, his voice warm with amusement. At least Anthony hoped it was amusement. Certainly the way his eyes twinkled supported that interpretation. "Your declaration of independence?"

"More like me seeing a very attractive man and having the good sense not to pass that up," Anthony replied. He didn't want to talk about Doug. That was over and he didn't want to spend the morning talking about him.

"I can think of worse things to mean to a man," Paul said. "We have four more days to celebrate your freedom."

Something in Anthony's chest uncoiled. Paul wasn't offended, and he wasn't pushing Anthony away. "I'd like that. We'll come in for dinner, and I'll come back here with you when you get off work." He dug in the pastry bag and pulled out the *pain au chocolat*. It was every bit as flaky and buttery and bittersweet chocolaty as he could have hoped. "What's in the water over here? I can't find pastries like this at home."

"It's not the water. It's the air," Paul replied with a grin.

"No, I think it's the lack of sugar," Anthony said after a moment. "Even if they get the pastry dough right, they're always too sweet."

Paul smiled. "I have the perfect thing for you when you come to the restaurant tonight. Dark chocolate, definitely not sweet. Here, drink your coffee."

"Sounds decadent." Anthony took the bowl Paul handed him with both hands. He missed this too. No matter how big the mug, it was never a whole *bowl*. The coffee, like everything else, was rich and dark.

"I won't offer you sugar, but do you want cream?" Paul asked.

Anthony shook his head. "No, it's perfect like this. Everything has been perfect since the moment we walked into the restaurant last night. I'm already looking forward to tonight."

He paused.

"But?" Paul prompted.

"But maybe tonight you'll let me take care of you too? I feel a little guilty you had to get yourself off."

"Don't," Paul said. "You had me so worked up I couldn't wait. But I won't say no to mixing things up tonight. I like sex in all its forms."

Anthony smiled at that and took another sip of his coffee. Paul set his bowl in the sink and pulled out a packet of cigarettes. "I'm going to smoke, if that's okay."

"It's your home." Anthony lived in North Carolina. The smell of tobacco didn't bother him, although he hadn't noticed the smell in Paul's apartment.

"Oh, I don't smoke in the house. I'll go out on the balcony. My mother didn't let me smoke inside. Even here, I still can't do it."

Anthony popped the last bite of pastry in his mouth and picked up his bowl of coffee. "Do you have a good view from the balcony?"

"Not really," Paul said. "Just the street, and it's not a very interesting one. No monuments or historic buildings or anything."

Anthony stepped out onto the stone ledge with a wrought-iron rail that passed as Paul's balcony. He couldn't see Sacré-Cœur or the Eiffel Tower from that vantage point, but it was still a view of Paris, and that made it a good view as far as he was concerned. Paul lit his cigarette and leaned against the casement.

"I know you're here for the Salon du livre, but so are thousands of people. What do you do in the publishing world?"

"Anything Patricia tells me to," Anthony said with a chuckle.

Paul laughed. "Including flirting with your waiter at dinner?"

"Even that, although that was Patricia the friend, not Patricia the boss, giving those orders. I'm allowed to ignore those."

"That's good," Paul said. "You didn't answer my question."

"Patricia runs a genre publishing house called Along the Spectrum," Anthony said. "Mostly sci-fi and fantasy with a bit of steampunk thrown in when it's really good. What sets her apart is that all her books—by which I mean all the books we publish—have one main character who falls into at least one diversity category. Maybe they're an ethnic minority, real or fictional. Maybe they're on the LGBTQ spectrum. Maybe they have a physical or mental disability. Maybe it's a class or caste system that puts them outside the majority. It's pretty much up to the author to sell their sense of diversity to her, but it isn't all rich, white, able-bodied straight men in positions of power. Something has to break that mold. In a lot of cases, the characters break many of the molds."

"It sounds like quite the undertaking. Are you an editor? Or maybe one of the authors?"

"I started out working as an editor for her," Anthony said, "but while I'm a decent editor, it's not my strength. I'm in charge of expansion, as Patricia puts it. She wants to see our books in as many different markets as possible, whether that's in English, in translations we do ourselves, or in translations we sublicense out to partners. My job is to determine what will work best in the different markets and then make that happen."

"And she's looking at the French market? Since you're here, I mean."

"We've had some interest in our content from some small French presses, but no one had a business plan Patricia was completely comfortable with. They're even more start-ups than we are. We're still looking at options with them, but we also have done some translations in-house. The problem is we're based in North Carolina, not in France, and this is still a very print-driven market. It's hard to publish print books when you don't have someone on the ground to manage inventory, approach bookstores, and everything else that goes into a successful book launch. We're hoping to put enough things in place while we're here this week to get things up and running. We had some productive meetings yesterday as well as some less productive ones. We have more scheduled for Monday. Today and tomorrow are mostly about meeting our readers."

"It sounds fascinating," Paul said, and Anthony actually believed him. He'd bored more than one person to tears with the details of his job, but Paul seemed genuinely interested. "I especially like the diversity angle. In some ways, France deals better with diversity than America— look at when we approved marriage for all as an example—but in others we struggle still. Many places are not accessible or only with great difficulty if you're in a wheelchair. And then you have the struggles with race and religion we have in France right now. What acknowledgment of diversity is the right amount? What is too far? It's the question on everyone's mind right now, or it should be. There are Muslims who want to impose halal in all schools so that their children can eat in school cafeterias. On the one hand, it isn't good that children should be denied access to the food at school if they need to eat there, but we don't provide special meals for children with allergies or with other dietary restrictions. They can ask if certain dishes fit their restrictions and buy only those that do or they can go home to eat or bring their lunch with them. Why shouldn't Muslim children do the same? Or maybe it doesn't matter. Maybe we wouldn't even notice the difference if the cafeteria food was all halal. After all, I have eaten in *Maghrébin* restaurants that were surely halal and not cared because the food was so good."

"Thinking of going into politics?" Anthony asked.

"It is the responsibility of all citizens of a country to be involved in politics," Paul said. "If you are not, you have given permission to those involved to make decisions for you. We are fortunate to live in a country with a widely varied political structure. Whatever your beliefs, there is a party for you. We don't have a two-party system that lumps people together as conservative or liberal. We have a system that allows for all different shades and variations, but it only works if people are involved. That's the biggest problem in France now, more than all the questions of religion or race or diversity. Apathy is allowing fringe elements to have more of a voice than they should based on their size." He paused and flushed. "Sorry. I get a little worked up about it."

"Don't apologize," Anthony said. "It's wonderful that you're so passionate about it. It's the same thing that drew me to Patricia. Get her started on what it means to be part of a minority population, and she'll keep you there for hours. The publishing industry is still dominated by white men. They see a black woman walk into the room, even if she's in a business suit, and assume she's someone's secretary or she's one of the staff of the meeting venue or some such thing. Unless they've met her before, of course. No one underestimates her twice."

Paul finished his cigarette. Anthony looked down and realized he'd finished his coffee while they were talking. "I should let you go so you aren't late to work, and I still need to go back to the hotel. The Salon closes at eight, so we'll be at the restaurant no later than eight thirty. Save us a table?"

"I will," Paul promised. "Let me get my coat and we can walk out together. Which hotel are you staying at?"

"Le Mercure across from the parc des expos," Anthony said.

"Then we can walk all the way to the restaurant together. You have to go that way to get back anyway."

"I'd like that," Anthony said. He could find his way back, but as ridiculous as he felt, he wasn't ready to say good-bye, even for the day. He'd decided to stay an extra day in Paris after the book fair before flying home, and now he was glad of it. "What are you doing on Tuesday?"

"Working. Why?" Paul asked.

"Because the Salon du livre ends Monday evening, but I don't fly home until Wednesday. I'd planned to spend Tuesday being a tourist. I thought maybe if you were free…."

"Let me check the schedule," Paul said. "Papa takes Monday off. Florent, my brother, usually takes Tuesday off, and I usually take off on Wednesday. But Florent might switch days with me. Or maybe this week I got lucky and Papa gave me Tuesday off instead."

Anthony wouldn't get his hopes up. He wouldn't. That would be foolish. He'd already used up more than his share of good luck in meeting Paul in the first place. Asking for more would be pushing it.

Anthony checked his pockets to make sure he had his wallet and hotel key while Paul finished getting ready.

"Here," Paul said, handing Anthony the bag of pastries as they left the apartment. "Take them for your boss. That way you won't have to make an extra stop and they won't go to waste."

The elevator was just as crowded with the two of them on the way down as it had been on the way up, but the heat of the night before had given way to an easy familiarity Anthony was at a loss to explain. He hated morning-afters. It was one of the reasons he'd stopped with the casual hookups back in college. He never knew how to extricate himself afterward, but he didn't feel awkward with Paul. He could have stood on his balcony and kept talking for hours. He was already looking forward to tonight, and not just for the chance of another round of damn good sex. He wouldn't say no to the sex, but if they ended up talking all night, he wouldn't complain either.

Paul didn't reach for Anthony's hand as they walked down the street toward the restaurant together, but he stayed close enough that their shoulders brushed. Anyone seeing them would surely guess they were together because even with the smaller sense of personal space most French people had, they didn't usually stand quite *this* close unless they were a couple. When they reached the restaurant, Paul pushed open the flap to the plastic tenting surrounding the terrace and tugged on Anthony's hand. When Anthony stepped closer, Paul leaned in and kissed him. "Thank you for last night and this morning. Have a good day, and I'll see you tonight."

If anything, Anthony ought to be thanking Paul. "I'm looking forward to it," Anthony said because an argument over who should be thankful to whom wouldn't get them anywhere. "I'll see you tonight."

He was dragging his feet and he knew it, but it didn't make it any easier to turn and walk the rest of the way down rue de Vaugirard or into the hotel. The interior of his hotel room felt even more sterile after his night in Paul's bed and his morning in the brightly lit, very lived-in apartment. Anthony glanced at his watch. Ten thirty. Patricia had said not to come before noon, but he'd go stir-crazy sitting in the hotel alone for an hour and a half. He changed quickly into his suit, grabbed the bag of pastries, and headed for the book fair.

"Well, well, well," Patricia drawled when Anthony walked up to the booth. "Look what the cat dragged in."

"I'm an hour earlier than you told me to be," Anthony retorted, smiling despite himself, "and I brought you breakfast. Be nice or I'll keep it for myself."

Patricia held out an imperious hand for the pastries. "Good night?" she asked as she looked inside.

"Good night, even better morning," Anthony replied.

"Ooh, baby," Patricia said with a leer. "You stayed over? I didn't think you had it in you. Or did you have *him* in you?"

"Patricia," Anthony protested. "Don't be vulgar."

"That wasn't anywhere close to vulgar," she said. "I have three sailors for brothers. I know what vulgar sounds like. That was… mildly suggestive."

"Mon œil." Anthony shook his head at her.

"You didn't answer my question."

"And I'm not going to. My sex life isn't open for discussion in public. We have dinner reservations at eight thirty. Paul said he'd save us a table."

"In his section?"

Anthony hoped so, but Paul hadn't specified. "Probably. It's not like it's a big restaurant. He invited me back to his place again tonight."

Patricia's eyebrows shot up. "You've been busy. I've never seen you like this, and I've known you for fifteen years. You sure this is a good thing?"

"Last night you were telling me to go for it."

"And I'm glad you did, but you don't do casual sex as a rule, which is all this can realistically be. You leave on Wednesday."

"I haven't forgotten," Anthony grumbled. "Paul's going to see if he can switch days off with his brother so we can spend Tuesday in the city together before I leave. I know this is a fling, but it feels good. I'm not expecting it to last beyond my flight home, but just for once, it's nice to be wanted. He's not looking at me and wishing I were someone else." He wouldn't have taken the time to seek out Anthony's sensitive spots like he had if he'd been dreaming of someone else. "I spent eighteen months living in the shadow of a man half a world away and failing to measure up. I think I've earned a week with Paul."

"As long as he doesn't break your heart when you leave."

"I'm the one leaving. If my heart gets broken, I'll have no one to blame but myself."

Patricia looked like she had something to say about that, but a customer at the booth took Anthony's attention before she could say it, and when Anthony had finished, she didn't bring it back up.

CHAPTER 4

PAUL LINGERED on the terrace as Anthony walked away. Damn, the man could fill out a pair of jeans. The thought brought a smile to his face. It had been a good night. A great one, even. Much better than his recent string of bad luck where men were concerned. A frisson of remembered pleasure skittered along his skin. Anthony had been warm and heavy in his arms, ass pressed against Paul's groin all night long. And he already had the promise of tonight to look forward to. Maybe he'd get even better acquainted with Anthony's ass. Paul had never been a selfish lover, taking delight in making his lovers feel good, and Anthony's reactions last night had made Paul all the more eager to lavish more pleasure on him. When Anthony finally turned the corner out of Paul's sight, Paul forced his mind to focus on the day ahead. Au cœur du terroir had the reputation it did because of the family feel and the quality of the service. He might flirt with the occasional customer the way he had with Anthony, but he never let it upset the way he did his job.

"You're smiling," Florent said when he went inside.

"And this is worth commenting on why?" Paul asked with a repressive glare for his younger brother.

"Because you hate mornings. You never smile before the first customer comes in."

Paul shrugged. "I had a good night."

"Don't let Papa hear you say that. He hates it when you pick up a guy at the restaurant."

"It doesn't have to be someone I picked up here."

Florent rolled his eyes. "It always is."

Paul grabbed a pile of cloth napkins and started folding them for use at lunch. "I'm not that bad."

Florent sat down opposite him to help with the napkins. "When was the last time you had a date with someone you didn't meet here?"

Paul opened his mouth to answer, then closed it again. "I'm not interested in dating. I'm not ready to settle down," he said finally. Gilles had seen to that.

"Fine. When was the last time you had sex with someone you didn't meet at the restaurant?"

"Where else would I meet people?" Paul asked. "I'm here six days a week."

"You just proved my point."

"I don't know why Papa gets so upset about it," Paul said with a sigh. "I do my job. I don't push. I just respond to interest that comes my way. And I don't do it that often. Once or twice a month at the most."

"He wants you to be happy," Florent said, "and he doesn't think anonymous sex makes you happy."

"Nobody would put up with my schedule."

"Maman did."

"Maman was a saint," Paul replied.

"Good morning, Paul, Florent," Papa said as he walked in, his arms full of baguettes from the bakery down the street. He bent to kiss Paul's and Florent's cheeks despite the load in his arms. "Is Nicolas here yet?"

"He's in the kitchen getting everything ready for lunch," Florent said. "We would have been in the way in there."

Nicolas, their chef, was a whirlwind in the kitchen, and Paul had learned years ago that everyone was happier if he was left to work in peace. The sous-chefs would trickle in shortly, but Nicolas did all the prep work himself.

"I'll go ask what the specials are for today," Paul offered. As expected, Nicolas turned the air blue with curses the minute he walked through the doors.

"I won't get in the way," Paul promised when Nicolas paused for a breath. "Just tell me what the specials are so I can put them on the board."

"Filet of sole with capers and lemon butter," Nicolas snapped. "If I can get it ready. Out!"

Paul shook his head and headed back to the front. Florent was setting the tables already, so Paul pulled down the black slate board where they recorded the daily specials and changed out last night's halibut and duck for the sole. His handwriting wasn't nearly as artistic as his mother's had been, but it was still far more legible than Papa's or Florent's. He hung the chalkboard back in its spot over the bar and ran his hand over the smooth wood. So many memories tied up in the scarred mahogany. He wondered what Maman would think if she could see them now. She had been as invested in the restaurant as any of them, before the cancer that stole her from them far too soon. Some nights he could still smell her perfume mingling with the aromas from the kitchen and the cigarette smoke on the terrace. He'd learned to walk holding on to the table legs.

"Paul, did you restock the bar with clean glasses?"

Papa's voice tore Paul out of his memories. "I'm working on that right now," he called back. He hefted the tray of clean glasses from behind the bar and started hanging the stemware each in its place. They served far more wine and champagne than they did mixed drinks, but they were prepared for anything.

Henri and Romain, Nicolas's assistants, arrived as he was putting the last of the glasses away. "He's in a mood today," Paul warned them.

"He's always in a mood," Romain replied. "We're used to it. Do you need any help out here?"

Paul glanced around the restaurant. He'd prepped the bar and Florent had the tables set. "I don't think so. We'll let you know if we end up swamped." Saturday was hit or miss. When there was an event going on at the parc des expos, they got more traffic than when there wasn't, but a lot of the attendees grabbed a bite to eat inside rather than having to come out and then wait in line to get back inside. They'd be crazy busy that night, but lunch was usually quieter on Saturdays.

Henri and Romain disappeared into the kitchen, leaving Paul to finish the last-minute preparations. He set out the menus so Papa could seat their patrons easily and filled a couple of carafes of water. That done, he grabbed his cigarettes and stepped outside for a quick smoke before the restaurant opened.

The nicotine hit his system almost immediately when he took a deep drag, a rush of energy and heat infusing him along with the smoke. He was running on even fewer hours of sleep than usual, what with having stayed up late with Anthony and then risen early so they'd both have time to bathe, so the jolt was a welcome one. He'd be fine if the restaurant was busy at lunch. If not… well, if not, he could step back outside for another smoke if he started dragging. Maybe he could slip away during the afternoon, when the restaurant was closed, and take a quick nap, because he couldn't be tired later. Anthony was coming home with him again.

He let his mind wander back to the night before, to having Anthony in bed with him. That had been a far more potent adrenaline rush than anything he could get from a cigarette, and the thought of what else they might get up to heated his blood enough that he loosened the light scarf around his neck. He'd put it on against the nip of the early spring morning, knowing he wouldn't need it once they got busy in the restaurant, but he hadn't taken it off yet since the radiators hadn't defeated the chill from overnight. He smiled at the memory of Anthony insisting Paul not leave marks where they'd be visible. He didn't think he'd left any beneath the collar either, an oversight he'd be sure to remedy as soon as he had Anthony back in his bed. He pulled another deep breath of smoke at the thought of his love bites covering Anthony's torso. His heart beat like a boy with his first crush, a ridiculous reaction given his age and variety of experience, but the thought didn't settle his racing pulse.

A day pass to the Salon du livre was only ten or fifteen euros, if he remembered correctly. He could justify that amount for an afternoon of wandering among books and checking out what Anthony's company put out.

Florent's voice interrupted his musings. "Paul? Papa is looking for you."

"Coming."

He stubbed out his cigarette and followed his brother back inside. "Yes, Papa?"

"You added a reservation this morning?" Papa asked.

"Yes. The couple from last night. They want to come back tonight, and I forgot to write it down before I went home. I put it in the book this morning," Paul said.

Papa's eyes narrowed like he wasn't entirely sure he believed Paul's story, but Paul gave him his best innocent look and prayed Florent would keep his mouth shut. Papa would probably see right through the story when Anthony arrived tonight, but it would keep the peace until then.

"PAUL, WE'RE completely out of lemons and a few other things. The delivery truck from the farm didn't get here this morning. I need you to go to the market and see what you can find. At least three dozen lemons plus any other vegetables that look good. Nicolas can replace what we served with the dishes last night as he runs out as long as he has something to replace them with."

"Wouldn't it be better to send Henri or Romain?" Paul heard the whine in his voice and hated himself for it, but he'd been looking forward to going to the Salon du livre and seeing Anthony. He couldn't do that if he spent his afternoon off at the market. "They'd have a better idea of what would go with what Nicolas has planned."

"They're busy helping him adjust the menu for tonight based on what we have in stock," Papa said. "They can't be spared. You know what fresh vegetables look like." He handed Paul the restaurant credit card. "Take my car so you can bring everything back."

Paul smothered a sigh as he took the credit card. The downside of running a restaurant with an insistence on fresh, local products was that sometimes they ran out of things at the last minute. He'd spent his childhood watching his mother adjust menus and replan dishes to make use of what they had rather than what they'd expected to have. As much as he'd wanted to be elsewhere that afternoon, he could hardly refuse his father's request. "I'll be back as soon as I can so they'll know what they're working with. Is there anything we don't need?"

"Potatoes," Papa said. "We have plenty of those. Nicolas is already figuring out how many ways he can prepare them so each dish doesn't have the same sides tonight, even if they all have potatoes. Anything else will be welcome."

Paul nodded and headed out the back door to the alley where Papa left his car. Sometimes Paul wondered why he kept it when he lived upstairs and took the Métro everywhere else he needed to go, but then something like this happened. The old *deux chevaux* still ran like it was new, and it held a surprising number of bags in the backseat and open trunk area. Paul figured that was worth the cost of insurance on it.

The morning rush at the market had died down when Paul got there, but that also meant the stands had been well picked over. He spent far more time than he'd hoped poking through the produce. Papa would fuss over how long it took, but the other option was spending money on vegetables that were bruised or not yet ripe or otherwise unusable. His mind wandered as he made his selections. He wondered what Anthony was doing, if he'd had a chance to eat lunch or if they'd been too busy for him to get away from the booth. Anthony hadn't mentioned anyone else from the company being in Paris, and his boss didn't speak French. If they were swamped, he'd be trapped there all day with no way to grab a bite. Paul made a mental note to buy a sandwich tomorrow morning when he went to get breakfast so Anthony would have that much lunch. He loaded up the car and headed back toward the restaurant. He'd make sure to add a little extra to Anthony's plate tonight when no one was looking.

Papa and Florent met him at the car as soon as he pulled back into the alley. They unloaded his purchases into the kitchen. Nicolas hemmed and hawed and complained, but he whisked the vegetables away to begin preparing them, so Paul chalked that up to his natural irascibility. The only person he had ever talked to without snarling was Maman, and she'd been gone nearly fifteen years.

"Do I have time to go home and change shirts?" Paul asked Papa when the car was completely unloaded. "It was warmer at the market than I expected. I'd like to be fresh for tonight."

Papa stared at him for a long moment before sighing and waving him off. "Be back by six. Your brother and I can't do all the preparation for dinner alone."

Paul glanced at his watch. It was not quite five, which gave him over an hour. Not enough time to duck into the Salon du livre, but definitely enough time for a bath if he wanted one. "Thank you, Papa. I won't be late."

He checked to make sure he had his keys and dashed out the back door, down the alley to the street, and toward home. He ducked into the pharmacy to buy another bottle of lube and more condoms. They hadn't gotten around to needing them the night before and maybe they wouldn't tonight either—Paul could think of plenty of things he wanted to do to Anthony that wouldn't require them—but he saw no harm in being prepared.

He climbed the steps to his apartment because it was faster than waiting on the elevator. His thighs burned from the exertion, but it kept him fit. He let himself inside the cool, dim space and set his package down on the table by the door. He'd put it away when he went into the bathroom, but he headed into the kitchen first. The bowls from the morning coffee still sat in the sink. He ought to put those in the dishwasher before he left so Anthony wouldn't think he was a complete slob. He set another pot of coffee to brewing while he cleaned up the kitchen. When it was done, he took it and his cigarettes back out to the balcony. He wished he could put his finger on what intrigued him about Anthony. The sex had been fantastic, and Anthony had agreed to stay, which set him apart from most of the men Paul hooked up with these days, but that didn't explain the fact that Anthony had been in his thoughts all day.

It might have something to do with the slightest hint of an accent, although, really, if he hadn't heard Anthony speaking English with his boss, he probably wouldn't have picked up on it. Certainly the square-cut jaw, blond hair, and blue eyes didn't hurt either. He wasn't the most handsome man Paul had ever slept with, but he was no slouch in the looks department. He'd been so earnest in his reactions to Paul, gratifyingly eager for everything Paul chose to do to him. And then this morning, he'd listened when Paul talked, and he'd answered honestly when Paul inquired about his career and interests. That was the real difference. Anthony might have come home with him for the sex, but he'd been interested in more than just the physical. He'd treated Paul like a person, not just a good lay.

Maybe Florent was right. Maybe he needed to get out more and meet people for more than just sex if a simple conversation was enough to have him hung up on a man who was leaving town in four days.

He finished his cigarette and downed his coffee. He'd think about that later. Right now, he had four days he could spend with Anthony. He wasn't going to waste them on what-ifs. He bathed carefully and changed into clean clothes. Last night Anthony had showered before coming to the restaurant. Paul wanted to be ready if he did the same again tonight. And if he didn't... the tub was big enough to fit two if they didn't mind squeezing in together.

CHAPTER 5

BY SEVEN thirty, Paul was already swamped, only the tables that had Reserved signs on them still empty. Even Papa was helping serve, something he rarely did these days. Many of the patrons were regulars—Arnaud and his team celebrating their victory on the rugby field, Eric and Emmanuel having dinner before going out to the clubs, Marc, who lived down the street, and whichever colleagues he could convince to come out with him—but at least half the tables were filled with faces Paul didn't know.

He put on his best professional demeanor and tried to pretend he wasn't watching the door for Anthony's arrival as he served drinks and carried out appetizers and dinners. He didn't want Papa asking why he was so distracted. It was Saturday night. They couldn't afford distractions.

Anthony and his boss arrived at precisely eight thirty, and this time Anthony was still wearing a suit, although he had loosened the tie. Papa brought them to their table in Paul's section, and Paul's mouth watered as Anthony peeled off his jacket before taking his seat. He'd be lucky not to jump Anthony before they got back to his place.

He grabbed a bottle of Badoit and headed to the table as soon as Papa left them.

"Paul," Anthony said with a smile as he approached.

"You brought sparkling water," Anthony's boss said before Paul could reply. "You're my new favorite waiter."

Paul laughed along with Anthony as he poured the water into their glasses. "Welcome back," he said, addressing Anthony's boss. She knew about them, but he had to keep up appearances. "A *kir royal* again tonight, *madame?*"

"Yes, please. And call me Patricia. As well as you know Anthony, there's no reason to stand on formalities."

Paul's cheeks burned. She'd encouraged Anthony to stay the night before, and she'd told him he could be late this morning so he could enjoy his night, but hearing her talk about it was unexpected. "Of course, Patricia. Anthony, what would you like?"

"Just a kir," Anthony said. "I don't need the bubbles."

"I'll bring those while you look at the menu and decide on appetizers." Paul beat a quick retreat, far more flustered by the exchange than he should have been. Why did it matter what Patricia knew or thought she knew? He'd talked to Florent about Anthony that morning, and from everything Anthony had said, Patricia was as much friend as boss. Anthony had no reason to hide his evening's activities from her, and Paul had no right to expect him to do so. And yet, it felt more like Papa finding out than Florent. He took a deep breath and went to the bar to mix their drinks. He wasn't much of a bartender, but he could make simple things like kirs.

He set the drinks on the bar and checked on his other tables, but they were all eating. He'd walk by after he took Anthony and Patricia's order and make sure they didn't need anything, but he could indulge his need to be near Anthony a little more first.

He set their drinks down on the table with a flourish, winning a smile from Anthony and a peal of delighted laughter from Patricia. The sound relaxed something inside him. Whatever she knew, she wasn't bothered by it. "Before you decide on anything, the special tonight is sole with lemon butter and capers. I only have six servings left, so if you want it, tell me quickly."

"Yes, please," Patricia said immediately.

"That sounds really good," Anthony agreed. "Make that two."

"And a bottle of wine," Patricia added.

"What would you recommend?" Anthony asked. "You gave us such a good suggestion last night."

Paul considered the contents of the wine cellar for a moment. They had good wines in a variety of price ranges, but he didn't think either Patricia or Anthony was looking to impress anyone with a high-priced bottle. "We have a nice, crisp Chablis or a slightly rounder Saint-Véran. Either would go very nicely with the fish tonight."

"The Saint-Véran," Anthony said. "We can get Chablis at home, but Saint-Véran is harder to find."

Paul pondered a world without easy access to his favorite wines for a moment before deciding it didn't bear thinking about. "You'll have to come back so you can enjoy it here."

"The wine isn't the only thing worth enjoying," Anthony said with a soft smile, making Paul very glad Patricia didn't speak French.

"Save your flirting for after the food comes. I'm starving," Patricia said.

Anthony turned a particularly stunning shade of scarlet all the way up to the roots of his blond hair. At least Paul wasn't the only one embarrassed.

"Would you like an appetizer or just the sole?"

"You said you wanted to try escargots while we were here," Anthony said to Patricia. "They have them on the menu."

"Six or twelve?" Paul asked.

"Twelve," Patricia replied. "I told you I'm hungry."

"Twelve escargots, two sole, and a bottle of Saint-Véran," Paul said. "I'll bring it out as soon as it's ready."

He placed the order with Nicolas and went to check on his other tables.

"Is that your new guy?" Florent asked when Paul walked by the bar to get the Saint-Véran for Anthony and Patricia.

"I wouldn't call him my 'guy' when he's only here until Wednesday, but yes, that's Anthony. Oh, that reminds me. Switch days with me this week so I can spend Tuesday with him before he leaves?"

Florent frowned. "Are you sure that's a good idea? Not the switching days. I don't care about that. I mean spending all this time with him when you know nothing can come of it."

Paul shrugged. "I like him. I like spending time with him. I know nothing's going to come of it, but there's no harm in enjoying the time together while he's here. He makes me feel good, okay?"

"Okay," Florent said. "I'll tell Papa you agreed to switch with me. That way he won't hound you about why you need a different day off this week."

"Thanks," Paul said. He grabbed the bottle, checked that he had a corkscrew, and nipped two glasses off the shelf. "I owe you one."

He brought everything back to the table and opened the wine for Anthony to taste. If he flipped the corkscrew with a little more flair than usual, Florent wasn't there to see him and tease him about it, and it made Anthony smile.

Anthony took a sip of the wine, darting his tongue out to lick the last droplets off his lips, and Paul had to look away before he embarrassed himself. The jeans he had on weren't tight, but if he popped an erection, it would be noticeable, and with him standing while Anthony was seated, it would put the bulge at eye level. He needed to stop that train of thought because eye level wasn't all that far off from mouth level and—

"The wine is perfect. Thank you for the recommendation."

Anthony's prosaic words were so at odds with Paul's randy thoughts that he had to blink a couple of times to focus back on the present. Damn, he had it bad. Florent might have reason to worry after all.

"You're welcome," Paul said. "I'll go check on the escargots. They shouldn't take much longer." He fled the table before he embarrassed himself, hoping he hadn't spoiled his chances for the rest of the evening. He couldn't remember the last time a simple flirtation flustered him this much.

That was the difference, though, wasn't it? For all that Anthony was leaving in a few days, their conversation that morning had taken it outside the realm of his usual simple flirtations. He rarely got to know the men in his bed beyond the physical. In some cases, they weren't interested. In other cases, he wasn't, but one way or another, he watched most of them leave without a second thought. Anthony had been interested and interesting. If he lived in Paris, they could be friends. Friends with benefits, but friends. And because he didn't, Anthony wouldn't have time to get fed up with Paul's schedule and leave. He'd be leaving anyway, so Paul could relax and enjoy the camaraderie and the sex while it lasted without worrying about when the sword would fall.

Romain plated up the escargots just as Paul walked into the kitchen, leaving Paul without that as an excuse to avoid Anthony for a few minutes. He mustered his best smile, pushed down his misgivings he couldn't quite will away, and brought the plate out to their table.

"Don't leave yet," Anthony said as Paul set the plate down between them. "You should wait while Patricia tries the first bite."

Paul hesitated, but none of his other tables needed him, and Anthony was looking at him expectantly, so he smiled at Patricia and waited while she scooped one of the escargots out of the little trough filled with garlic butter. He could see the steam rising from it as she lifted it to her mouth and blew on it. Finally deciding it was cool enough, she took a bite. The delighted look on her face was worth every bit of discomfort on his part. He smiled for real and turned to Anthony. "Your turn."

"I've had escargots before."

"Not ours," Paul replied. Anthony looked skeptical, but he took an escargot as well and blew on it. Paul refused to let his mind wander down fantasy paths this time. He wanted to see Anthony's face when he finally tasted it. The moment he put the escargot in his mouth, his eyes closed and a look of sheer bliss crossed his face as he chewed. Paul fully intended to put that look back on Anthony's face before the night was over, but for the moment, he simply appreciated the sight.

"I stand corrected," Anthony said. "These are amazing."

Paul smirked. "Next time you'll listen to me."

Anthony's eyes darkened. "Anytime, anywhere."

Putain.

He needed to kiss that look off Anthony's face—or else kiss him until his pupils were so dilated the blue didn't show at all. He'd take either one. "I'll let you enjoy your appetizer," he said, his voice sounding strangled to his own ears.

One of his other tables caught his attention, and he let himself be drawn into a conversation with them. They weren't regulars, so they didn't know his usual demeanor or tease him about his distraction the way some of their customers would have done. He'd take whatever small blessings he could get.

He craved a cigarette, but all of his main courses would be ready to serve soon. He took a smoke break most evenings, but not until later, when things had calmed down and everyone was settled in with their food. Then it wasn't a problem for Florent to cover for him for a few minutes and for him to watch Florent's tables in turn. He'd just have to suck it up until he could get away without putting undue strain on anyone.

The next thirty minutes passed in a blur of serving dishes, either to his tables or helping Florent with his large parties. He laughed and joked with the regulars, cheering with Arnaud's team over their victory and commiserating with Eric over a bad week at work. At least being busy kept him from dwelling on Anthony and what might happen when they got back to his apartment that night.

Finally all the main courses had been served with no one ready for dessert yet, and he had a chance to breathe. He checked the bar out of habit, only to see that they were running low on a couple of different bottles of wine. He ran down the stairs to the wine cellar to grab some to refill their stock. He met Anthony in the narrow hallway that led first to the restroom and then on to the wine cellar as he came out with his hands full.

Anthony looked him up and down slowly, a leer on his face. Then he smiled and leaned over the box in Paul's arms to kiss him, all teeth and tongue and heat and need and….

"I'm going to drop the bottles, and that will bring everyone running," he gasped.

"So set them down," Anthony said. "I can wait that long."

Merde. Anthony was going to be the death of him. "I have a better idea. Let me take them upstairs and tell Florent I'm going on break…." He let the rest of his suggestion go unspoken, but Anthony's eyes widened as he stepped into the restroom.

"The last door."

Paul swallowed hard and raced back up the stairs. He set the box behind the bar and called for Florent. "I'm taking my break," he said as soon as Florent came into view. Florent waved him off with a smile. Paul hoped that was just Florent being Florent and not that he suspected something, but he didn't care enough to check. He made himself walk down the steps like he wasn't in any hurry. Not that anyone would think it odd to see him rushing down the steps since he regularly took the steps at a run, but he didn't want to give anyone a reason to wonder why he was rushing when he was on break.

He stepped into the restroom area and checked the room quickly. The sink area was empty and three of the four individual restroom doors were ajar. The fourth—the last—was closed but not locked. His pulse pounded in his ears as he tapped softly on the door before opening it. Anthony reached for his shirt and pulled him inside, not that Paul put up any resistance.

Paul reached behind him and locked the door so the occupied sign would show on the outside. Then he pushed Anthony against the wall and took his mouth with all the lust that had been simmering in him since Anthony had walked in still wearing his suit and tie. Anthony met him with matching eagerness, opening his lips beneath Paul's amorous assault. Paul delved as deeply as he could, chasing the taste of wine on Anthony's tongue.

Anthony sucked on Paul's tongue, making him wonder what it would feel like to have Anthony's mouth elsewhere. Not here—they didn't have the time or space for that—but later tonight. Or tomorrow. Or on Tuesday when they had the whole day to spend together. They could spend part of it in bed.

He worked a hand between them and rubbed over the placket of Anthony's slacks, finding a bulge to match his own. He closed his fingers around it and relished the way Anthony gasped into his mouth.

"Chut," he warned. "There could be people outside."

"You put your hand on my dick and you want me to be quiet?" Anthony asked. "Not happening. You'll just have to keep kissing me so no one can hear the noises I make."

Paul could do that. He could *so* do that. He captured Anthony's mouth again as he tugged on the zipper of Anthony's trousers and slipped a hand inside. Anthony moaned into the kiss, the sound egging Paul on. He popped the button and pushed Anthony's pants and underwear down out of the way. They had to be presentable enough to go back upstairs when they were done, and he didn't want to have to explain a wet spot on the front of his jeans to his father.

He angled his body so he wouldn't rub his jeans against Anthony's bare skin and broke the kiss long enough to take in the picture of pure debauchery Anthony made as he stood there against the wall, chest heaving beneath his white shirt. The slightest hint of hair peeked out of the vee of the open collar and loosened tie, and Anthony's cock, already hard and red, poked out beneath his shirttails, his trousers and underwear pushed down around his thighs. Briefly Paul considered dropping to his knees. It would solve the issue of a mess, but while the cleaning service had mopped the floors that morning, he didn't trust they were still clean twelve hours later. He'd have to make do with his hand.

He teased the tip of Anthony's erection with one finger for a moment, but the clock on his break was ticking. As much as he wanted to take his time and enjoy every second of taking Anthony apart, he'd have to save that for later. Anthony bucked into the caress, urging him to continue. Paul closed his fist around the hard shaft and stroked. Anthony groaned loudly, reminding Paul of the potential for an audience listening in. He caught the next sound with his mouth as he settled on a rhythm designed to send Anthony flying as fast as possible. In a matter of moments, Paul's hand grew slick with the fluid that spurted from the tip with each pass, just enough to ease the way. They didn't have unlimited time, but they could afford to take a little time for foreplay.

Anthony fumbled with the button on Paul's jeans, breaking the kiss to curse sharply when he couldn't get it undone. "Get your pants off," Anthony ordered. "We aren't having a repeat of last night. I'm going to make you come this time."

Paul tore open his jeans and pushed them down to give Anthony uninhibited access. The heat of Anthony's palm seared through Paul as he bucked into the bold caress. Anthony had been such a greedy bottom last night that Paul hadn't expected him to take quite so much initiative now. He should have known better than to assume.

He matched his movements to the rhythm of Anthony's hand so that they stroked each other in tandem. Anthony moaned almost constantly into their kiss. Paul remembered those noises from the night before and wished he could hear them more clearly now, but the sound of a toilet flushing reminded him where they were and how easily they could be caught. He didn't want to know what Papa would say about it if they were, so he swallowed all the delicious sounds and consoled himself with the fact that he wouldn't have to muffle them later that night when they got back to his apartment.

Laughter pealed through the outer area of the restroom, and Anthony froze beneath Paul's hand. Paul broke their kiss to nuzzle Anthony's ear, never pausing in his caress. "Don't make any noise," he whispered before nibbling on Anthony's earlobe. "Not a sound. They're caught up in whatever they found funny. They won't think anything of a closed door if you don't give them a reason to."

Anthony trembled beneath his touch, biting down hard on his lower lip to silence his reaction to Paul's words and continued caress. Paul swiped his thumb over Anthony's lip, soothing the abused flesh. Anthony whimpered softly and sucked Paul's thumb into his mouth. Paul bit back a moan of his own and worked Anthony's cock faster. "Come for me," he whispered. "I didn't get to see your face last night."

"I can't," Anthony said hoarsely. "They'll hear."

"They'll be jealous," Paul replied. "Come for me."

Paul claimed Anthony's mouth in another torrid kiss. He wanted to see Anthony's face, but he needed Anthony relaxed enough to climax more than he needed to see his face, and that wouldn't happen if he was worried about being overheard. A toilet flushed again, followed by the sound of water running in the sink and then footsteps receding up the stairs. Almost immediately, the tension in Anthony's shoulders eased and he moved more easily into Paul's touch. Paul deepened the kiss and sped up the movement of his fist. Anthony jerked into the caress and spilled all over Paul's hand and hip. Paul kept his grip tight and his strokes fast until Anthony eased completely beneath him, only then gentling the caress to the point of simply holding Anthony in his palm.

"You made me come first again," Anthony grumbled.

"It's not a question of first and last," Paul said. "I like making you feel good."

Anthony didn't look convinced. "Maybe so, but now it's my turn."

Paul grinned at him and leaned against the wall with his arms outspread. "Do your worst."

Anthony grinned back. "How about if I do my best instead?"

CHAPTER 6

PAUL LOVED sex. He loved everything about it—the shape of a lover's body, the smell of musk, the sounds of anticipation and release, the feel of skin against skin, the taste of another man's body, the intimacy of the moment, however fleeting. He especially loved making his partner feel good. As he stood there against the restroom wall, jeans around his knees and his cock hard enough to pound nails, he thought it might be okay this time to let his partner take care of him too. Anthony took him in a firm grip and leaned in to kiss him. Paul ceded control and let himself feel. No pressure, no expectation, just the heat of Anthony's skin against his own. Anthony could hardly accuse him of being selfish when he'd already come.

Anthony set a rapid pace, stealing Paul's breath. He bucked into the channel formed by Anthony's fist, fucking it the way time and space wouldn't let him fuck Anthony's ass. They'd have time for that later. For now, he strove for his release, chasing it with the same determination he'd brought to bear on Anthony moments earlier. The cold of the tile wall bit at his butt when he rocked back to thrust forward again, a sharp burst of sensation in counterpoint to the heat consuming the rest of him. Every muscle in his body clenched as he raced toward his climax. He moaned into the kiss and pulled Anthony toward him, wanting the press of his body. Anthony shifted to Paul's left, curling along Paul's side.

"Now it's my turn," Anthony murmured in Paul's ear. "I want to see your face this time."

Gooseflesh raised all along Paul's arms, beneath the sleeves of his shirt, and prickled down his stomach. He shook with the force of it, needing more in a way he didn't understand and couldn't explain. He threw his head back and bit his lip to smother the shout building in his throat. Anthony caught his nape and pulled him into a deep kiss, filling Paul's mouth with his tongue. He delved into every nook and cranny, leaving Paul feeling as thoroughly claimed as if he'd been fucked into next week.

He gasped into the kiss as his orgasm took him. His vision whited out and even breathing seemed like too much of a chore. He rested there against the wall, caught between its chill and the heat of Anthony's body for several long moments. "*Fuck*," he said when he could muster enough coherence to make his mouth work. "Maybe I should let you be in charge all the time."

"Where would the fun be in that?" Anthony replied before kissing him again. "But I'll take turns."

Paul could hardly wait for the restaurant to close.

"We should get back," he said regretfully. "I only get a fifteen-minute break, and after that, I need a cigarette."

Anthony grinned and reached for a wad of toilet paper to clean his hand and Paul's cock. "Go on. I'll clean up when you're done and wander back upstairs in a few minutes so your father doesn't suspect anything."

"What about Patricia?" Paul asked as he zipped his jeans and tucked his shirt back in.

Anthony shrugged. "I'm not working right now. She may tease me, but she's done that all day anyway."

Paul's cheeks burned at the thought that she would know—or guess—what they'd been up to, but he couldn't bring himself to regret sneaking into the restroom with Anthony. They only had three more days. He didn't want to waste a single moment they could have together. He gave Anthony a quick kiss that lingered despite his awareness of the passing time. Tearing himself away, he unlocked the door and slipped out. He washed his hands thoroughly and checked his watch. The cigarette would have to wait. He'd spent his entire break with Anthony.

Paul checked on his tables, speaking to all the regulars and his father's friends even if they weren't in his section, clearing dishes, taking dessert orders, whatever they needed. It did nothing to diminish the craving for a cigarette or the promise in Anthony's words, but it did help the time pass.

"Paul," Papa called, "take this out to the terrace, the last table."

Paul grimaced. He'd been avoiding the terrace, knowing the smoke would only exacerbate his desire for a cigarette, but he could hardly explain his craving to his father when he'd just come back from a break, ostensibly a smoke break. He grabbed the tray full of desserts and carried it outside. The heat lamps provided light as well as warmth in the chill of the Parisian night. Fortunately for the patrons seated outside, the air was calm, no breeze coming to chase away the warmth, but that meant the smoke hung heavily over the terrace.

Paul smiled and pretended his hands weren't shaking as he passed out the plates. He had turned to head back inside when a patron on the other side of the terrace looked up and waved.

"Paul, how are you?"

Paul's smile felt brittle as he crossed the wooden boards to the other side of the terrace. "Ludovic, I haven't seen you in a while. How have you been?"

"Good. I was hoping I'd see you tonight, but you've been inside all evening." A tendril of smoke curled up from the cigarette between his fingers.

"It's Florent's night for the terrace," Paul said automatically, "although I'd have come to say hello if I'd realized you were out here."

Ludovic's smile broadened, making Paul curse silently. He hadn't actually meant to encourage the man. They'd hooked up a few months ago. It had been fun, but nothing had come of it. Neither of them had wanted anything to come of it, or so he'd thought.

Paul's nostrils flared when Ludovic took a puff of his cigarette and exhaled with a plume of smoke. Ludovic smiled sympathetically and offered the cigarette to Paul. He should say no. He shouldn't encourage Ludovic, but he needed a hit. He took the butt and inhaled deeply. "Thanks. I needed that."

"Anything else you need tonight?" Ludovic asked with a leer.

Any other night, Paul would have said yes without hesitation. He never turned down sex when it was offered, but tonight was different. "Not tonight. I already have plans for the evening. Sorry."

Ludovic shrugged. "That's what I get for not coming to find you as soon as I came in. I'll know better next time."

Anthony was leaving in three days, and he'd enjoyed the couple of nights he and Ludovic had spent together. "Next weekend? If you're free, of course."

"Making plans ahead of time?" Ludovic teased. "I'm honored."

This was a bad idea. "I need to check on my other tables, but if you make it in next weekend, come find me and we'll see how things go." He escaped back inside before Ludovic could reply.

When he got back to the kitchen, Romain had plated up desserts for two more of his tables. He served those and then went to check on Anthony. Hopefully enough time had passed that Patricia would be done with any teasing.

Anthony's smile was so bright as Paul approached that Paul felt even more guilty for the exchange with Ludovic on the terrace. He hadn't done anything wrong. He and Anthony weren't dating. This was as much of a hookup as any night he'd spent with Ludovic or any other man in recent memory. Paul pushed the feeling aside and smiled back. "Have you decided on dessert?"

"I think Anthony's had his already," Patricia said with a smirk. "I will have the crème caramel and a *verveine*."

"Just an espresso for me," Anthony said. His cheeks were nearly as flushed now as they'd been in the restroom earlier when he'd come apart under Paul's hands. The sight did nothing good for Paul's composure.

"No cognac tonight?" Paul asked.

Anthony shook his head. "I don't want to be too drunk to enjoy the rest of the night," he said in French. Patricia gave no sign of having understood that, much to Paul's relief.

"That's not likely to be a problem after the appetizer downstairs," Paul replied. "She may call it dessert, but for me, it was just the first course."

"Let me finish the coffee first. Then I'll see how I feel."

Paul nodded and left to place their order. Florent cornered him as he came out of the kitchen. "I didn't see you in the alley during your break."

"Spying on me?" Paul asked.

"Trying to keep you out of trouble," Florent replied. "Just watch yourself, okay? I don't want Papa angry at you again, especially over a guy who won't be here to help you bear it."

"It wouldn't be any different than any other time he's angry at me," Paul said. "They never stick around, even if they live in Paris."

Not that he ever asked them to, but that wasn't the point.

"Because you never give them the chance," Florent retorted. "Or else you deliberately pick ones you know aren't interested or, like Anthony, can't stay. You're setting yourself up to be alone, and that's just stupid."

It was a familiar argument, and one that Paul dreaded each time it started because he didn't have an answer Florent would accept.

"Mind your own business," Paul said when it was clear Florent was waiting for an answer. "I can handle myself just fine without your help."

He pushed past Florent and made his rounds of the restaurant again, dropping off checks and taking payments from most of his tables. By the time he was done, Florent had already delivered dessert and coffee to Anthony's table. Paul glared at him because he'd wanted that excuse to go back and talk to Anthony again, but he knew how it would have gone. Papa had seen the tray waiting to be delivered and had certainly sent Florent to take care of it rather than leave customers waiting without their food. Paul would just go make sure they were enjoying it.

"How is the crème caramel?" Paul asked Patricia when he reached their table.

"Delicious," Patricia said. "Very different from crème brûlée, more than I was expecting, but still very good."

"People confuse them because they both start with crème," Paul said with a nod, "but as you say, completely different preparation."

"That's one of the things I love about traveling," Patricia said. "I get to try all kinds of new dishes. I've already decided what I'm ordering tomorrow night. Unless you end up with another special like you had tonight. I eat fish a lot, but that was exceptional."

"We won't know what tomorrow's specials are until we see what comes in from the farm in the morning. What have you decided to try tomorrow?"

"The stuffed chicken," Patricia said. "I love spinach and mushrooms, and it sounds delicious."

"It is a good choice," Paul said, "but if you love mushrooms, you should try the cannelloni too. It is stuffed with mushrooms instead of with cheese. It's very light, very fresh, and definitely not typical of what you would find in most restaurants."

"That does sound like something worth trying. I have tomorrow and Monday left. I have to leave on Tuesday instead of staying an extra day. I'll have the chicken one night and the cannelloni the other night, and if you have a special that tempts me, you'll have to tell me which one to choose."

Paul smiled at her. "Have you decided what you're having tomorrow?" he asked Anthony in French.

Anthony's eyes glittered up at him. "The same thing I'm having tonight," he replied. "If I'm invited back again."

"I think you can convince me," Paul said.

Patricia finished the last bite of her dessert and stood up. "Anthony, you can pay the bill. No need for me to wait. The booth opens at ten tomorrow. I'll see you then." She leaned in and kissed Anthony's cheek. "Take good care of him for me," she told Paul as she left.

"I hate it when she does that," Anthony grumbled.

"When she does what?" Paul asked.

"When she deliberately embarrasses me. 'Take good care of him for me,' like I need a keeper."

"I think it's wonderful that you work with someone who cares about you," Paul countered. "Not a lot of people can say that."

"You work with your family."

"I do, and believe me, the only reason my brother hasn't said the same kinds of things to you is because he's spent the whole evening picking at me," Paul said. "They embarrass me plenty, but they never do it out of spite."

"No, it's not out of spite," Anthony agreed. "It's just the way she is. The way she's always been. Most of the time, I ignore it, but I'm not having a lot of luck with that this time around."

Paul wanted to ask why, but he'd lingered longer at Anthony's table already than was wise. Papa hadn't said anything, but he was standing at the bar now, his friends having left for the night, and Paul saw the beginnings of a frown on his face. "I'll be back soon," he promised and went to check on his other tables so Papa would relax and stop staring at him.

He'd closed out three of his remaining tables when Papa caught his arm. "Your new friend…."

Paul was tempted to play dumb and give a facile answer until Papa chose to ask his question explicitly, but it wouldn't change anything.

"Anthony and Patricia," he said. "They're here for the Salon du livre. They go home on Wednesday."

"Are they planning on coming in again tomorrow?"

"I haven't asked," Paul replied. He assumed they would, based on Patricia's comments about what she'd order the next time, but he hadn't actually asked. He ought to do that, although Sundays were usually quiet enough that they wouldn't need a reservation if Anthony didn't know what Patricia wanted to do.

"You should. We had two large parties reserve for tomorrow night. If they want a table, we should put them down for one tonight."

"I'll check with Anthony and see if he knows what their plans are," Paul said. "I only have two tables left. Do I need to stay after I close them out?" Usually he'd linger and help out even when it was Florent's night to close up, but with Anthony waiting for him, Paul didn't want to stay any longer than necessary.

Papa sighed. "No, you can leave with your friend, but I expect you in early in the morning to make sure everything is ready for lunch."

The sigh was a punch in the gut strong enough to offset the elation of Papa's words. He hated disappointing his father, and despite his attempts at being discreet, he'd managed to do it anyway.

"Thank you, Papa. I won't be late in the morning."

"See that you aren't. I'm going upstairs. Tell Florent to lock up when he leaves."

Paul flinched at the bite in Papa's words, but at least he wouldn't have to walk out with Anthony under his father's disapproving stare. Talk about a mood killer.

"Sleep well, Papa. I'll tell Florent."

He watched until Papa disappeared through the kitchen, where the steps to the apartment where he had grown up connected with the restaurant. When he was out of sight, Paul took the check to his last table and grabbed Anthony's bill as well. "I have one table left, then we can leave. I don't have to stay until close tonight. I just have to tell my brother we're leaving."

"Then I'm glad I didn't order a cognac," Anthony said as he drained his espresso. "Otherwise we'd have to sit here while I finished it."

"I can think of better ways to spend our time," Paul said with a smile.

Anthony winked at him. "So can I."

CHAPTER 7

SUNLIGHT STREAMING through the window woke Paul from hazy dreams to a far better reality. Anthony lay curled up against him in bed, as he had the past four mornings, warm and pliant and naked in Paul's arms. Paul nuzzled Anthony's neck and inhaled the scent of sex and sweat that clung to his body. Anthony stirred in his arms and pressed back against Paul's erection. It would be so easy to reach down and coax Anthony fully awake into another round of sex. They had time. Neither of them had to work so nothing was forcing them out of bed and in different directions today. As much as his fingers itched to feel the smooth skin of Anthony's cock, he refrained. It was Anthony's last day in Paris. They shouldn't spend it in bed. He traced the dips and curves of Anthony's chest instead, enjoying the chance to simply touch without it having to turn into more.

"What time is it?" Anthony murmured without opening his eyes.

"Does it matter?" Paul pressed a kiss to Anthony's jaw. Anthony turned his head to meet Paul's lips, and the temptation to forget about everything else and keep Anthony in bed with him all day increased. "We don't have anywhere we have to be today, even if we really shouldn't spend your last day in Paris in bed," he made himself say.

Anthony rolled to face him and rocked against his cock enticingly. "I could think of worse ways to spend it."

"Can you think of better?" Paul asked, his voice sounding strangled to his own ears. He had promised to spend the day in Paris with Anthony. Spending it in bed didn't count. "We could go to the Louvre or the Eiffel Tower or—"

"Nothing touristy," Anthony interrupted. "I've done all that. I want to do something I wouldn't know to do without a Parisian at my side. What do you usually do with your day off?"

Paul flushed and shifted uncomfortably on the bed. He had accepted having no life outside of the restaurant, but that didn't make admitting to the fact any less embarrassing. "I spend all my time at the restaurant. On my day off, I clean my apartment, do my shopping, and catch up on my sleep. I don't exactly have an exciting life."

"There has to be something we can do," Anthony said.

"We could go for a walk along the Seine," Paul suggested. People—Parisians—spent days in Paris all the time. There were things to do that didn't involve crowds and monuments. He just had to think of some. "We'd pass a lot of the tourist sites, but it would get us outside and not necessarily in a huge crowd of tourists. Or we could head to the Marais, the gay district, and wander through the shops."

Anthony shook his head. "I'm not much of a shopper, at least not for the sake of shopping."

"Then the Quartier Latin is probably out too, although there are supposed to be some really interesting little restaurants if we wanted to stop in one for lunch," Paul mused. He didn't mind missing the shops. He wasn't much of a shopper himself, and he wanted to be the center of Anthony's attention rather than sharing it with shopkeepers all over town. "What do you do with your free time at home?"

"I spend a lot of time outdoors," Anthony said. "I don't have a house, so there isn't that kind of work to do, but Winston-Salem is near several state parks where I can go hiking or camping."

Paul filed away the name of Anthony's town. He wasn't familiar with it, not that he would have been familiar with much outside of New York, Chicago, and Los Angeles, but it was still a little detail he could store up for when Anthony was gone. He could easily imagine Anthony hiking in the woods. It fit him.

"Not a lot of hiking in Paris, but we could go by the charcuterie and buy some meat, get a loaf of bread, and wander through one of the parks. Paris has some lovely, out-of-the-way parks that tourists would never think of visiting."

"That sounds more like something I'd enjoy," Anthony said. "Just a day spent together outside."

They could go all the way out to the bois de Boulogne, but if they stayed in one of the city parks, when they were done with their picnic, they could wander into the surrounding neighborhood. Paris had plenty of residential quarters with interesting little streets and nothing remotely touristy on them. And if they ended up spending all day in the park, well, there was nothing wrong with that either. "There's the jardin du Luxembourg on this side of town. There's a little park near the Eiffel Tower where a lot of people who work in the area eat lunch. Or we could hop the Métro and go up toward Montmartre to the parc Monceau. If we did that, we could wander around Montmartre later in the afternoon and maybe head toward Sacré-Cœur to watch the sunset. It's quite the view over the city, if you've never seen it."

"I've been to Sacré-Cœur, but I've never been there at sunset," Anthony said.

"Then it's a plan," Paul decided. He scratched at the matted hair of his belly. "After we take a bath."

THEY FINALLY left the apartment an hour later—Paul's bathtub was *not* meant for two despite his earlier thoughts on the matter, but that hadn't stopped Anthony from dragging Paul in there with him and delaying their departure with the leisurely round of morning sex Paul had intended to skip in favor of the city. Almost immediately, Paul shed the light jacket he'd donned against the possible chill in the air. The sun shone brightly overhead with not a cloud in the sky, and while the breeze still had a hint of winter in it, spring had firmly sprung in Paris. He didn't suggest they go back to drop off their jackets, though. If they spent the whole day outside into the evening, they'd be glad of the extra layer when the sun went down.

They bought pastries at Paul's usual shop to eat on the Métro on their way north toward Montmartre, where they would change lines to get to the Monceau station. The treats would hold them over until they could find a charcuterie or crémerie near the park to buy meat and cheese for their picnic. The trains were mercifully uncrowded, but Anthony sat close to Paul anyway. Paul suspected anyone looking at them would assume they were a couple out for a day together. He might not have much personal experience with that kind of life—his last attempt at a relationship had ended around the same time his mother died—but he'd grown up seeing the way his parents stood together. He knew what it looked like when he saw it. He just hadn't wanted it for himself since Gilles left.

"What a perfect day!" Anthony said as they climbed the stairs to street level at their destination. "I'm not sure I've ever been in Paris on a day like this."

"Have you ever been in Paris in the spring?" Paul asked. "Because this is not unusual for this time of year."

"No, it's either been in the summer when it was hot and not a breath of air to be found in the city or in the winter when it was cold and gray.

Before I came in the summer the first time, I used to joke that the pictures on the postcards with blue skies behind the monuments were staged, with a huge blue cloth hung behind the buildings. I'd seen the buildings, but never the blue sky."

"Then I'm glad we decided to spend the day outside," Paul said. "You can visit the museums on cold, rainy winter days or the hot summer ones when you have to escape to somewhere with air-conditioning."

"I've done plenty of escaping both kinds of weather, but not today. Come on. I want to see the park."

"Let's find food first. We can carry it with us until we're ready to eat, but otherwise we'd have to come back out of the park when we get hungry," Paul suggested, although the eagerness on Anthony's face made him want to hurry so he could see Anthony's reaction to the park. He didn't come all the way across town often, but he had attended a cousin's wedding several years ago and remembered well the manicured lawns and ornate stonework of the follies. They could easily spend hours wandering through the park, and this way they could do it undisturbed.

They found a charcuterie nearby and stocked up on prosciutto and thinly sliced sausage, and the bakery next door netted them two baguettes to share. They walked back to the main entrance of the park through the wrought-iron gates tipped with gold leaf. "Even away from the center of town, everything is so ornate," Anthony commented.

"It was a royal park," Paul said. "One of the king's cousins, I think. We'd have to find a marker. I don't remember all the details."

"It doesn't matter," Anthony said. "It was an observation, nothing more. If I get curious, I can look it up later. I'd rather spend the day enjoying the time with you."

The words brought a smile to Paul's face despite the reminder that this was their last day together. Anthony's flight left at ten the next morning. "Me too. Come on, let's wander. There are some amazing vistas. The park's designer was very creative."

They made their way deeper into the gardens, past the reflecting pool with the Greek columns along one side and the willow in the middle until they found the stream that bisected the park. If memory served, the trees grew wild along the waterway, the one area of the park not manicured into submission. They could find a bench along the path and sit out of the direct sun with the illusion of more privacy than if they sat together on the open lawn.

They had nearly reached the classical bridge that crossed the stream before they found a bench that matched Paul's image of their afternoon together.

"How's this?" Paul asked.

"Perfect," Anthony said, taking a seat on the bench. "Are you hungry? I didn't think I was, but suddenly I'm starving."

"Then let's eat," Paul said. He unwrapped the paper around the charcuterie they'd purchased and tore off a hunk of bread to offer to Anthony. Anthony took it with a smile and grabbed a piece of prosciutto to go with it.

Paul peeled off a thin slice of sausage and folded it bite size, stuffing it into his mouth with a bit of bread. It wasn't any different than any other time he'd grabbed a bit of bread and meat for a quick lunch, but somehow it tasted better.

"I don't know if it's the company or the location or what, but I swear prosciutto never tastes this good at home," Anthony said.

Paul laughed. "I was just thinking the same thing, so it must be the company."

Anthony reached for another piece of meat and stole a kiss as he leaned close. "Best company I've had in a while. I'm not the type to pick someone up at a restaurant, but I'm so glad I took the chance with you."

If Paul was the best company Anthony had had recently, he was keeping poor company indeed. Paul was no catch, but he wouldn't spoil the mood by telling Anthony that. "I could say the same about your company," Paul said. "Most people don't have the patience to deal with my schedule for long."

"Their loss," Anthony said after he'd finished his next bite of lunch. "But I'm not going to complain. If they weren't so blind, I wouldn't have had this week with you."

"You never did tell me how a great guy like you ended up single long enough to have a fling in Paris," Paul said. "If it's not too personal, that is."

Anthony shrugged, but he hunched in on himself, leaving Paul cursing for ruining the good mood. "I made the mistake of falling for a man who was still hung up on his ex. When his ex decided he wanted him back, I was suddenly unnecessary. That was six months ago."

"His loss, my gain," Paul said firmly. "Even if it was just for a few days."

"Best few days I've had in years," Anthony insisted. That had to be an exaggeration, but Paul didn't question it further. He'd already pushed more than he had any right to given the transitory nature of their relationship.

"Your turn," Anthony said. "How did I get so lucky?"

"I told you: my schedule. Guys who work normal hours aren't interested in a lover who doesn't get home until after they're asleep and who isn't up yet when they leave in the morning."

"Not everyone in Paris works normal business hours, surely," Anthony teased.

"Maybe not, but I work every Friday and Saturday, no matter what, and most Sundays, because the restaurant is too busy to spare me then. It doesn't leave a lot of possible overlap for couple-type things," Paul said. "It's never really bothered me. I'm not cut out for relationships." He'd tried once and it had been a spectacular enough failure that he hadn't tried again since.

"Has the restaurant always been in your family?" Anthony asked.

"My parents started it forty years ago," Paul said. "We lived upstairs, and Florent and I grew up in the kitchen and bar. We were washing vegetables at five, carrying plates at ten, and working there after school well before we were legal. It's the only job I've ever had and the only one I've ever wanted. It may have started as their dream, but it's become mine too."

Anthony reached over and squeezed Paul's hand. When he would have pulled it back, Paul didn't let go. He didn't open up this way, not even to Florent or his father. They knew he was committed to the restaurant—they had to know—but it wasn't something they talked about. They'd never needed to.

Anthony scooted a little closer so that their thighs touched as they sat on the bench. The contact settled Paul enough that he relinquished Anthony's hand so they could finish their lunch.

Eventually they finished the meat and bread. Paul balled up the trash and tucked it in his back pocket. They'd pass a trash can at some point, and he'd get rid of it then. For now he was content to sit next to Anthony in the shade of the overhanging trees and listen to the brook babbling behind them.

"Do I have to go home?" Anthony asked. "Can't I just stay here?"

"You wouldn't be the first person to take a trip to Paris and never go home," Paul replied, determined to keep his response light despite the sudden desire to suggest that Anthony stay. He couldn't get invested more than he already was. As much as it might be fun to imagine, Anthony had a job and a life in America, and nothing in France. He couldn't really stay.

"I could miss my plane," Anthony said. "No one would ever have to know it was intentional."

"That would only delay the inevitable," Paul said. "As nice as it is to imagine, you have responsibilities."

"I know," Anthony said. "If nothing else, someone has to feed my fish. I only paid for the aquarium service to take care of them through tomorrow."

"Not your job or your family or any of that? It's your fish you're worried about?"

"My job is almost completely portable," Anthony said. "I go into the office once a month at the most, and that's as much to get out of the house as because Patricia and I need to discuss things face to face. The rest of the time, I work from home. My family lives in Michigan. I see them at Christmas and that's about it. My mother is too ill to travel and only knows I'm there half the time. I never knew my father. My fish, however, require more regular attention. Saltwater aquariums are more finicky than freshwater ones."

Maybe Anthony really could drop everything and move to Paris, but Paul wasn't about to suggest it. He didn't want to be the reason Anthony uprooted his life, only to have it all come tumbling down when Anthony realized just how burdensome Paul's schedule really was. It had been fine when Anthony was in town on business and had to eat in a restaurant every night. It would be another thing entirely if he lived here and wanted to eat at home with his boyfriend from time to time. His parents had made it work, but his mother had spent as much time in the restaurant as Papa did until cancer stole her away without a second thought.

"What kind of fish do you have?" Paul asked, because that seemed the safest thing to say.

"I don't know the names in French," Anthony replied. "I've never needed to tell someone before."

Paul laughed. "As much as we've talked about leaving, you speak French so well that it's easy to forget that it isn't your first language."

"I love hearing that," Anthony admitted. "I worked so hard the year I was a student in Lyon to get to the point that no one had to ask themselves the question of whether I'd understand or even, ideally anyway, if I was French.

I'm out of practice now, although I try to visit with my French professors at Wake Forest once or twice a month so I don't lose all my fluency."

"I wouldn't have known if I hadn't heard you speaking English with Patricia that first night," Paul assured him.

"Thanks," Anthony said, leaning into Paul's side. Paul stretched his arm around Anthony's shoulder and relaxed into simply being together.

"Shall we walk?" Anthony asked after some time. "I want to see the rest of the park."

Paul nodded and stood. Anthony rose next to him and slipped his hand into Paul's. They wandered over the bridge and on through the rest of the park, stopping here and there to admire the features. The tulips were a riotous burst of color against the green lawn and flowers peeked out from green leaf buds ripe almost to opening. It was everything perfect about spring in Paris, and Paul breathed deeply, enjoying the absence of noise and pollution in the secluded corner of the park. Elsewhere the city was full of the honking of horns and smog, but not here.

They wandered for an hour or more—Paul saw no need to keep track of time—until they finally reached the far gate. "We can turn around and walk back the way we came or we can head into Montmartre," Paul said. "Do you have a preference?"

"I should probably find something to take back to my mother," Anthony said. "Even if she won't remember I was gone or know why I'm giving her a gift, I'll feel better if I bring her something back."

"Montmartre is more famous for its sex shops than it is for its tourist kitsch, at least around place Pigalle, but we can surely find something," Paul said. "What were you thinking about?"

"Maybe a scarf," Anthony said. "She always complains about being cold."

"We'll find something," Paul promised. They left the park for the neighborhood streets around the park. Paul turned them in a general northwesterly direction so they would eventually end up in the heart of Montmartre but without any rush. The tourist shops frequently carried pashminas, but Paul wanted something nicer than that for Anthony's mother. He didn't know what they'd find in this area, but if they didn't see anything they liked, he would suggest the Monoprix on rue de Vaugirard. It wouldn't be high fashion, but it would be authentic in a way anything bought in a tourist shop could never be.

They walked through the neighborhood streets, but nothing jumped out at Paul as a good place to find what Anthony was looking for. As they drew closer to place Pigalle, the stores changed, becoming the sex shops the neighborhood was famous for. "I know we said nothing touristy, but we're going to walk right past the Moulin Rouge," Paul said. "Sorry."

"We're in Paris," Anthony said. "I'm not sure you can walk more than three blocks without passing something touristy. The difference is passing it on your way to somewhere else instead of being in the area specifically for that purpose. I don't mind."

They crossed place Pigalle and started up the hill toward Sacré-Cœur on a little back street away from the tourist bustle of the main thoroughfares below. Anthony murmured something in English that Paul didn't understand. "What was that?"

"Oh, nothing really," Anthony said. "A memory from my first visit to Paris. I was sixteen, here with a group of classmates and our French teacher. She'd painted a very vivid picture of what France was like, with the small shops, each with its own specialty frequented by the locals, far away from the big chain stores that are so common at home. We joked about it before we got here. The butcher, the baker, and the candlestick maker, we'd always say when she started talking about it. It's part of a nursery rhyme. Then we got here. Probably not this street exactly, but one very much like it, and suddenly it wasn't a joke. It was exactly what she'd described to us."

Paul paused for a moment to look around him at the little shops that lined the street level of the buildings. A chocolatier, a bakery, a café, a crémerie, a shoe store, another café… a perfectly typical neighborhood street, as far as he could tell. "If this was what she described, I'd say she gave you a pretty accurate image."

"She told us about all the monuments, of course. We studied them as part of our units on French history. She expected us to recognize them, know when they were built and what they represented, then and now, but she also insisted we see that France was more than a collection of old buildings. It's a living, breathing entity that can't be summed up by any one image. It's the monuments *and* the neighborhood streets. It's the *premier arrondissement and* the *banlieue*. It's big cities *and* tiny villages." He broke off suddenly and flushed dark red. "Sorry. That must have sounded really arrogant coming from a foreigner like me."

"No, on the contrary," Paul insisted. "It's like I said that first morning. The biggest threat to our country, to any country, really, is apathy. If more people were as passionate about France as you are, we wouldn't have the same troubles we do now."

They walked on a little farther and turned the corner. Two shops down was a little maroquinerie. "I bet we'll find something for your mother in there," Paul said. "You'll have to pick, though. I don't know what she likes."

"At this point she doesn't even know what she likes anymore," Anthony said sadly. "But yes, I'm sure we'll find something that works."

They browsed through the selection of leather purses, bags, wallets, and more until they found the section of other accessories. Anthony lingered over the silk scarves in the back, fingering the cloth gently as he looked at the different patterns.

Anthony nodded decisively and picked up the scarf he'd first touched and then set aside. It was one of the simpler ones, but Paul knew enough to recognize the quality of the silk. "That's a nice one. It will keep her warm in the winter."

Anthony paid for the scarf with such a look of melancholy on his face that Paul wrapped his arm around Anthony's waist as soon as the transaction was finished. "Come on. Let's go the rest of the way up the hill. We can sit and watch the sunset and then decide what we want to do for dinner."

Anthony let Paul lead him along the street and out into the open area in front of Sacré-Cœur. Anthony leaned against Paul when they found a spot to sit. Paul took his weight and accepted his silence, providing what support he could. After a few minutes, Anthony shook himself. "Enough feeling sorry for myself. I should take some pictures. Patricia will want to know what we did today, and if I don't have proof, she'll insist we spent the day in bed."

"Go stand over there," Paul said. "I'll take a picture so she can see you're here."

Anthony stood up obediently and went where Paul had pointed. Paul pulled out his phone and waited for the camera app to load. He snapped a couple of pictures of Anthony with the sun beginning to set behind him, shining through his hair and giving him a golden halo. Paul moved a little to the side so the sun didn't glare directly into the camera and took a few more.

"Enough," Anthony said through his laughter. "I'm not some supermodel at a photo shoot."

"This way you'll be able to choose which one you like best," Paul said. "What's your e-mail? I'll send them to you."

Anthony rattled it off as Paul typed it into his phone and hit Send on the pictures.

If Paul planned to keep copies of the pictures for himself as well, he figured he was allowed his memories too.

CHAPTER 8

PAUL WAS quiet as they left the crêperie near St. Michel. It had been everything he could have hoped for in a day spent with someone special, and therein lay the problem. Despite all the promises they'd made and the knowledge that Anthony was leaving in the morning, he'd still become someone special. And now they had fewer than twelve hours left together before Anthony caught a cab to the airport and went home to a life that didn't include Paul.

Anthony seemed to share his melancholy mood, reaching for his hand in silence as they walked toward the Métro stop that would take them back to Paul's apartment and their last night together. Paul tried to map out the hours to follow the way he would any seduction, but he couldn't reduce Anthony to a collection of attractive parts he'd like to explore. He had no doubt they'd end up in bed doing wonderful and wicked things to each other, but it wouldn't be like it usually was. Oh, on the surface it would be more typical than ever because Anthony would leave in the morning with no plans to return, but usually Paul's lovers left without a second thought, exactly the way they both wanted it. Paul didn't want to send Anthony on his way.

They found seats on the train, squeezed in together on the narrow bench. Anthony's body was a line of heat against Paul's side, a reassuring weight. He might be leaving in the morning, but he hadn't left yet. Paul still had a few hours left to wring every drop of memory from. He switched Anthony's hand to his other one so he could put his arm around Anthony's shoulders. Anthony rested his head against Paul's arm and squeezed his hand.

Paul glanced quickly around the subway car, but at this hour it wasn't crowded and the few people on the train with them were lost in their own occupations, listening to music or reading. He kissed Anthony's temple where his blond hair met a day's worth of stubble. "You should grow a beard," he murmured. "If a little bit of scruff looks this good on you, I can only imagine how good you'd look with an actual beard."

Anthony laughed. "Long and scraggly."

Paul smiled and relaxed back against the seat. "Not that kind of beard. Still short and trimmed, but grown in all the way. It's up to you, of course. I wouldn't be around to appreciate it even if you did, but it certainly is a nice thing to think about."

"Tell you what," Anthony said. "If Patricia decides we're coming back to the Salon du livre next year, I'll let it grow in before we arrive so you can see it. How does that sound?"

The chances of Anthony still being single a year from now were probably too miniscule to calculate, but Paul pushed that thought aside. He'd gotten lucky this year. Maybe his luck would hold. "That sounds perfect."

"I hope we'll get to come back. It's been really interesting from a business perspective, and I've had a wonderful time with you." Anthony leaned closer to Paul as he spoke. Paul pressed another kiss to his temple and allowed himself one moment to wish that Anthony didn't have to leave the next day. He knew better than to get attached. He limited himself to one-night stands and casual hookups for precisely this reason, but he couldn't regret it.

"You'll have to let me know if you're coming back," Paul said on impulse. "Maybe I can use a few of those vacation days I never take except when Papa closes in August. If you can come in a few days early or stay a few days late, that is."

"I have a few vacation days stored up too," Anthony said. "As long as I pay for my own hotel and food, Patricia won't care if I come over a week early or stay a week late. The airfare is the same either way."

"It's a date," Paul said, even knowing it would probably never happen. He'd deal with the disappointment later. For now, he clung to the illusion of seeing Anthony again.

They changed trains at Montparnasse, keeping their fingers entwined the whole way. The train leaving Montparnasse was a little more crowded, so Paul refrained from kissing Anthony the way he wanted to, but he stood close enough to keep an arm around Anthony's waist in the gently swaying car. A rough curve knocked them both off balance and into the door. Anthony laughed and kissed Paul full on the mouth as they righted themselves.

"How much longer until we get back to your apartment?" Anthony murmured against Paul's lips. "Because I really want to kiss you with less of an audience."

Paul took a moment to get his bearings. "The next stop is ours. Then a five-minute walk."

"I bet we can make it in less than that if we hurry," Anthony replied.

Paul couldn't decide whether it would be better to hurry so he could have Anthony to himself—and preferably naked—that much sooner or to take their time because if they rushed, the time would pass that much more quickly. In the end, though, Anthony's urgency was contagious, and when they left the Métro station, they walked as quickly as they could down the sidewalk toward his apartment. He could only imagine what picture they presented, but the side streets were mostly empty with no one to see them as they hurried to his door and inside.

Out of the wind and encased in darkness, Paul stopped trying to resist the temptation Anthony represented. He pulled Anthony close and slid his hands into Anthony's soft hair. He mated their lips tenderly, taking his time now that they were alone. Anthony's lips parted beneath his, but Paul didn't take the invitation immediately. He wouldn't rush tonight, not now that they were here. This might be the last time he ever got to do this with Anthony, if Anthony didn't come back for the Salon du livre next year, or if he came back but was involved with someone else. If this was to be the last time, he would have it be such a powerful moment that it would live in both their memories, no matter what the future held.

He brushed his mouth over Anthony's once, twice, a third time, reveling in the softness broken by the one rough spot where Anthony sometimes bit at his lip. It was an odd thing to cherish, perhaps, but it was proof that he was kissing Anthony, not some random stranger he'd picked up at the restaurant or elsewhere. He used his grip on Anthony's cheek to tilt Anthony's head to the side ever so slightly, improving the angle of the kiss. He half expected Anthony to resist, to try to take control—or share it—but Anthony hung there between his hands, letting Paul lead the kiss. Paul flicked his tongue over the chapped place, eliciting a huff of laughter from Anthony. Paul kissed the sound away and then stayed, exploring Anthony's lips and teeth with tender care. He committed every whisper of sound, every hint of reaction, to memory. He didn't know what the future would bring for either of them, but he would have this one night, and he would make the most of it.

Anthony leaned against him pliantly, every line of his body proclaiming his willingness for whatever Paul proposed next. He could pin Anthony against the wall and rut against him until they both came in their pants like horny teenagers. He could push Anthony's pants down to his knees and swallow him whole. He could spin him around and rim him open.

Or he could take him upstairs and make love to him.

The thought shocked Paul to his core. He fucked anyone who was willing and interested, but he never let it go beyond that. He never let it mean anything, but it had snuck up on him this time. He broke the kiss and caught Anthony's hand in his once more. "Let's go upstairs. There's a bed waiting for us. Much more comfortable than the wall of the entrance hall."

Anthony laughed. "True, although that wouldn't have mattered, the way you were kissing me."

Did Anthony feel it too? Paul wouldn't hope for it. He couldn't. Anthony had a plane ticket with tomorrow's date on it and a life and livelihood in North Carolina.

"Come upstairs and I'll kiss you some more," Paul promised.

"I hope that's not all you'll do."

The husky tone of Anthony's voice grabbed Paul by the throat and squeezed so hard he couldn't find his voice. Instead he pulled Anthony into the elevator and pushed the button for his floor.

Anthony dove back into their kiss immediately. Paul met him halfway, but he gentled the contact. Tonight was not about fire and heat and speed and force. They had done that, and it had been magnificent, but tonight Paul wanted more. He wanted tenderness.

Paul cradled Anthony against him with one arm, using his other hand to steady Anthony's head at the perfect angle for a long, lingering kiss. Anthony moaned softly, encouraging Paul to hurry up, but Paul ignored it. Instead he brushed his lips over Anthony's cheekbones, the bridge of his nose, his closed eyelids, his temples, exploring every inch of Anthony's face with his mouth. The elevator bounced and jerked to a stop as it always did. Paul eased out of the kiss to find his keys so they could go inside.

Anthony crowded close as they crossed the hall to his apartment door, but he didn't try to raise the stakes as he had their other nights together.

Good. He'd caught Paul's mood and was playing along.

Paul opened the door and gestured for Anthony to go inside. The door secured behind them, he pulled Anthony back into the same tender embrace, only this time, he set his lips to wandering over Anthony's jaw and neck. He'd eschewed a coat, making it easy for Paul to brush aside the collar of his shirt and suck lightly on his collarbone.

"When's the next time you have to go into the office?" he murmured against Anthony's skin.

"Not for a month," Anthony said. "Patricia and I will talk, but I won't drive down to see her until early May, probably. Why?"

"Because if you don't have to go to the office, I can leave marks," Paul replied. He nipped at the curve of Anthony's shoulder and relished the full-body shiver that went through him.

"As many as you want." Anthony's groan made the words nearly incomprehensible, only adding to Paul's desire to leave Anthony covered in love bites. He bit a little harder, trying to find the perfect pressure, but Anthony's shirt kept getting in the way.

"Come on." Paul got them into the bedroom and pulled Anthony's shirt over his head swiftly. "Tell me if it's too much."

Anthony nodded and lay back on the bed, his head tilted to one side in silent invitation. Paul stretched out next to him, propped on one elbow, and lowered his head to the juncture of neck and shoulder. He inhaled deeply, letting Anthony's cologne invade his nose, another memory to store away.

Anthony reached up and cupped the back of Paul's head, pushing him toward his neck.

"Patience," Paul teased, his lips moving against Anthony's skin as he spoke.

"I don't have any left," Anthony replied.

Paul grabbed Anthony's hand, kissed the knuckles tenderly, and pinned it to the mattress with a firm grip. "Then I'll just have to have it for you."

Anthony moaned again and undulated on the bed. Paul paused to appreciate the sight before he returned to the spot on Anthony's neck. Everything about Anthony appealed to him, from the scruff on his jaw to the patch of hair on his chest. Paul sucked at Anthony's skin hard enough to win a gasp and a groan from him. It wouldn't raise a mark just yet, but he had all night. Given their relative heights, it was the perfect spot to plant his teeth as he drove into Anthony from behind.

And if that wasn't how the night ended, he could leave a mark in other ways.

He took his time licking and kissing across Anthony's collarbone, lingering especially at the hollow of Anthony's throat where the scent of cologne was strongest. Anthony kept his head back, giving Paul uninhibited access to the tender skin and taut tendons. Paul mouthed at them gently as he slid his free hand down Anthony's side to his hip, steadying them both. The feel of denim beneath his palm reminded him that Anthony was still half-dressed, but that could wait. Paul had barely begun to enjoy Anthony's undressed half.

Anthony's skin tasted slightly salty, testament to all the walking they had done as they wandered the city. Paul found Anthony's nipple, peeking out of its nest of hair, and sucked it into his mouth. Anthony had been responsive to that caress before, but they'd always been in a hurry for more. Paul refused to hurry tonight. He wanted to make the most of every second they had left, greedily hoarding memories and sensations for after Anthony went home.

When he could no longer taste the sweat from the day, he worked his way over to the other side, latching on and sucking that nipple clean as well.

Anthony panted above him, his body bowed up against Paul's mouth. Paul wondered idly what else would make Anthony react that way. He reached for Anthony's hand and sucked two long fingers into his mouth.

Yeah, that did it. He settled in to tend to Anthony's hand, working his tongue over each knuckle and against the thin webs at the base of each digit.

Anthony gasped and groaned and twisted beneath Paul, rubbing their bodies together delightfully. "Fuck, what you do to me."

Paul smiled and moved on, kissing his way across Anthony's palm to the soft skin of his wrist. Anthony shivered and goose bumps raised across his body, so Paul lingered, licking and sucking on the sensitive spot. He craved this knowledge even more than he craved release. He could find release with anyone. Only with Anthony could he learn these secrets.

Anthony's fingers curled around his ear as Paul continued to tease. Paul chuckled and moved on, seeking other places that would make Anthony gasp and curse and writhe. The inside of Anthony's elbow, the curve of his bicep as it inched toward his armpit, the hollow of Anthony's collarbone, the base of his throat, as he'd already learned.

He lost himself completely in his worship of Anthony's body, every caress a sonnet to Anthony, every gasp he won in return an accolade he stored near his heart. He managed to strip them both when he could stop touching Anthony long enough to deal with their clothes, but pulling away even long enough to deal with his jeans was almost too much for his self-control. Anthony lay waiting for him, gaze fixed on his every movement but not making any effort to guide their lovemaking.

Paul rolled Anthony to his side, sliding in behind him so he could find the spot on Anthony's neck he had promised to mark. Anthony moaned and angled his head to give Paul easy access to it. He rocked against Anthony's ass as he sucked hard on the spot. Anthony bucked back against him, adding to Paul's sudden desperation. He'd imagined taking his time prepping Anthony and slipping inside him, smooth as silk, but he'd never last that long now. Keeping his teeth latched firmly onto Anthony's shoulder, he urged Anthony to lift his upper leg, making space between his thighs for Paul's cock. Anthony caught on, reaching back to draw Paul into the narrow channel created by his legs. Paul moaned when the position drew his cock right over Anthony's balls. The friction from hair and skin nearly tipped him over the edge right there, but he couldn't let go yet. He *had* to take Anthony with him. He thrust experimentally, making sure the position would work for both of them. When Anthony moaned and pushed back to meet him, Paul reached around and pumped Anthony's erection in time with the movement of his hips.

Anthony shivered and moaned sweetly. That was all the encouragement Paul needed. He set up a lazy rhythm at first, determined to keep the hazy tenderness for as long as he could manage. He continued to lick and suck at the darkening bruise but held back from biting down hard. He didn't want to hurt Anthony, just entice him.

Anthony closed his hand around Paul's wrist, not guiding him, just stroking the back of Paul's hand in time with the rest of their movements. Paul trembled at the simple touch, somehow more intimate than all the fucking around they'd done over the past four days.

When Anthony spilled over his fingers, Paul's control deserted him. He rutted hard between Anthony's thighs and bit down sharply on Anthony's shoulder, all the pent-up tension of the day and week and Anthony's impending departure pouring out of him in great, shuddering waves. He collapsed against Anthony's back, panting for air.

Anthony snuggled back against him, making Paul hesitant to get up. He needed to clean them up. He needed a cigarette. He *needed* to not let Anthony out of his arms.

CHAPTER 9

A BURST of cool air woke Anthony from his doze. He reached for Paul to warm himself up but found only cold sheets. Paul wasn't in the bed next to him. He blinked a couple of times to clear his vision and looked toward the window. Paul stood on the balcony, a cigarette in hand.

He cast around for his jeans so he could join Paul outside. It would be cold, but he would do his best to lure Paul back to bed. "Hey. You okay?"

Paul stubbed out his cigarette. "I'm fine."

Anthony took in the way Paul stood with his shoulders hunched. "Come inside where it's warm," he urged.

Paul stepped over the casement and shut the windows behind him, sealing them back in the cocoon of warmth. He kept his distance, though, which worried Anthony a little. Had something gone awry without him realizing it? Paul had driven him out of his mind with a few kisses and caresses, as he'd done every night they'd spent together, but Anthony had felt him come too, between his thighs.

"You don't seem fine," Anthony said. "You've never gotten up after we've gone to bed before. Did I do something wrong?"

"No, of course not," Paul said quickly. Almost too quickly, but pointing that out would only make Paul tenser.

Anthony pulled Paul into an embrace, shivering a little when his bare chest came into contact with Paul's cold T-shirt. "Come back to bed."

Paul shook his head.

"Why not?" Anthony asked.

"Because if I do, I'll fall asleep," Paul replied.

"That's what you usually do in bed," Anthony agreed. He was definitely missing something here. "Why is that a problem tonight? I know you have to work tomorrow."

"It's stupid," Paul said. "You should get some sleep."

"I can sleep on the plane tomorrow," Anthony replied. "And it's not stupid if it's keeping you awake."

Paul shrugged. "You want a glass of wine? Or a cup of coffee? If you're going to stay up with me, you may as well enjoy it."

Coffee would keep them awake, which Paul obviously wanted, but wine might make him sleepy. Paul didn't have a plane ride to provide him a chance to sleep during the day. If he could drink enough to fall asleep, that would be better than staying up all night. "A glass of wine sounds lovely."

Anthony followed Paul into the kitchen. He hoped they'd go back to bed even if they did end up staying awake because it would be warmer, but he wanted to be where Paul was, both because he only had a few hours left with him and because something was bothering Paul. Whatever it was, Anthony could do his best to be supportive, even if he couldn't fix the problem.

Paul pulled a bottle off the wine rack without looking to see what it was, as far as Anthony could tell. Either he didn't care what he drank or he had the entire contents of his wine rack memorized by location. Neither thought was terribly comforting. He hated the idea that Paul had so little to do with his free time that he knew his wine rack that well. The thought that Paul was so bothered by whatever had turned his mood sour that he didn't care what wine he picked was even worse.

"What are we drinking?"

Paul handed Anthony the bottle so he could see it, but the label meant nothing to him. It was a white wine, from the shape of the bottle, but he wasn't familiar with the varietal.

"From the Loire valley," Paul said. "It's a nice drinking wine, no food required. As much as I love my Burgundy wines, they're better with food."

Anthony handed the bottle back so Paul could open it, which he did with a deft hand. Anthony could open a thousand bottles of wine and never achieve the same flourish Paul had naturally. He supposed working in a restaurant would do that. His gaze lingered on Paul's hands as he worked. Paul had touched him so tenderly earlier in the evening. He'd never been too rough, but their first couple of nights together had been fast and needy, all about the heat between them and getting off as fast as they could without neglecting the other. Tonight had been… different. If they hadn't laid the ground rules from the beginning about what was possible between them, Anthony would have said Paul had made love to him.

The way a man makes love to the one he wants to keep.

It was a ridiculous thought, of course. No matter how wonderful their time together had been—and it ranked up among Anthony's fondest memories already—they'd known it was just for a week when they started. Paul wasn't foolish enough to fall for Anthony, knowing he was leaving. That Anthony felt a greater attachment to Paul than was wise was his own business, but it was gratitude for a wonderful week mixed with a healthy dose of attraction, because Anthony wasn't blind, and knowing he was leaving didn't make Paul any less compelling. Even if Paul felt the same way—and he'd felt enough to keep Anthony around more than one night—he was too practical to let it turn into anything more.

Paul handed Anthony a glass. He took a sip and hummed appreciatively. "See, this is why I love France. Well, one of many reasons I love France."

"What is?" Paul asked.

"You pull a bottle of wine out of your rack and it tastes like this," Anthony explained. "Unless that's a really fancy bottle and you grabbed it by mistake, I can easily say no average wine I could get at home tastes like this."

"You just need to move to France," Paul joked. "It would make your life so much easier."

Anthony's heart missed a beat. If he moved to France…. He pushed that thought out of his head. He loved France and could live here easily, but his job and his life were in North Carolina. He wasn't willing to give up his dream job for a few good bottles of wine, or even a few nights of stellar sex. He laughed because Paul expected an answer, but he couldn't make words form.

Paul smiled, but his expression darkened again. He hadn't really expected Anthony to say he'd move to France, had he? Surely not.

"I'll just have to find more reasons to come back to visit," Anthony said. "I have more than enough friends who'd let me crash at their place for a night or two, although not in Paris."

"You're welcome here while you're in Paris," Paul said. "Sex or no sex. I mean, I wouldn't say no to having you in my bed again, but even if you've met someone else or whatever, you'd still be welcome to stay here."

Anthony hid his confusion behind the glass. Paul had mentioned the possibility of seeing each other if Anthony came back to the Salon du livre next year, but that was work, and the proximity of the restaurant to the parc des expos made it logical that Anthony would run into him again. This was entirely different. This smacked of keeping in touch and making plans to come visit specifically for the purpose of seeing Paul again.

"I'd have to look at vacation days and prices and everything," he equivocated. "I don't have a trip planned or anything."

"Of course," Paul said. He took a long drink of wine and topped off his glass. When he tipped the bottle toward Anthony, Anthony extended his glass. He'd need the fortification the wine could offer, the way the conversation was going.

"Do you travel a lot outside of work?"

"Not a whole lot," Anthony said. "I go see my mother a couple of times a year, as I said. I go camping up in the mountains sometimes with friends from college, or down to the beach, but those are usually three-day weekend trips, not big trips. I can get to Asheville in a couple of hours and to the coast in about five hours, so even if I leave after work on Friday and come home on Sunday, I've had a nice weekend away."

"That sounds really nice," Paul said. "Papa always closes for a couple of weeks in August, depending on the dates of events at the parc des expos, but running away for the weekend isn't really an option. I only have one day off a week, and I can't really get anywhere interesting and back in one day."

"Maybe you should come see me, then," Anthony said. "North Carolina has both beach and mountains, and all the college and professional sports you could hope for. The only thing it's missing is a good rugby team."

"You like rugby?" Paul asked.

"What's not to like?" Anthony joked. "A bunch of good-looking men running around in tight shorts and tackling each other."

Paul laughed, as Anthony had hoped he would. "You have a point. If North Carolina doesn't have a good team, who do you root for?"

"Lyon," Anthony said. "That's where I lived when I was studying here. I got hooked on rugby with them and never looked back. There is a rugby league in the US, but there aren't any games close enough to attend."

"You aren't attending Lyon's games either, from all the way over there," Paul said.

"No, but I can find their games on satellite or online. I'd have to care enough about a particular US team to make that effort, and I just don't. Besides, this way I have an excuse to buy the *Dieux du Stade* calendar every year. I'm supporting my players who participate."

"Sure," Paul said. "It has nothing to do with the naked men inside."

Anthony grinned even as his cheeks heated. "Not a thing."

Paul clinked his glass against Anthony's. "My calendar is in the living room."

"You're a fan too?"

"Not of Lyon. I root for Toulouse, but yes, I love rugby. I used to play a little when I was younger. No time for it now."

"I've never played, just watched. At home it's basketball if you want to play a sport with a group of guys."

"Basketball is good, although most basketball players are too tall and awkward off the court," Paul said. "Not nearly as nice to look at as the rugby boys."

Anthony laughed. "Should I be worried about not measuring up?"

Paul shook his head. "They're nice to look at," he repeated, "and from the interviews I've watched, a lot of them are nice guys, but they're a fantasy. You're real, and that's much better than any fantasy."

Anthony could live with that.

"There's a couch in the living room," Paul said. "That'll be more comfortable than standing here drinking."

"Or we could go snuggle in bed," Anthony said. "Warmer and more comfortable, and we can get naked again."

Paul waggled his eyebrows at Anthony. "Up for another round?"

Anthony had been thinking of the comfort angle more than anything else, but if Paul was offering…. "I could be persuaded, but only if that's what you want too. I really was thinking about snuggling and sipping our wine and talking, not more sex."

"That sounds perfect," Paul said. They carried their glasses and the wine bottle back to the bedroom, and Anthony watched appreciatively as Paul stripped down again. He was the definition of willowy with his long, slender frame, not an ounce of extra weight on him anywhere. He wasn't bulked up like so many of the men Anthony saw at the gym, but Anthony had seen the trays he carried. His thinness was deceptive.

"I thought we were getting undressed again," Paul teased as he slipped between the covers. Anthony jerked his jeans off and snuggled beneath the duvet right up against Paul's side.

"Watch it, your feet are cold," Paul said, but he didn't pull away when Anthony tucked his head against Paul's shoulder and burrowed his hands between Paul's thighs to warm them up.

"You never did tell me what was bothering you earlier," Anthony said.

Paul shrugged. "You're leaving tomorrow. And yes, I knew it was coming, but it snuck up on me anyway. I've enjoyed the time we spent together. I'm not ready for it to end."

Anthony snuggled closer, if that was possible, and pulled Paul's head down for a kiss. Paul met him eagerly, devouring his mouth with enough desperation to make Anthony reconsider the second round. "I'm not ready for it to end either. We can keep in touch, though. And I'll be back next year."

The promise sounded empty to his own ears. It was so easy to say, but long-distance relationships were hard work even when the foundation was solid and the separation finite. He and Paul had a few days of hot sex as a foundation, and "until Patricia sent Anthony back" as an end point. Hardly enough to support anything beyond what they'd already shared. He'd still try. He'd had more fun with Paul today than he'd had in a long time, certainly more than he'd had with Doug. He hadn't realized it until spending a carefree day with Paul, but the tension that never left Doug, the resentment that Anthony wasn't the Marine who'd left him to go to war—and for whom Doug had left Anthony when he came home—had tainted everything. With Paul, the only tension between them was the sizzling sexual kind that kept his nerves jumping as he wondered what new treat Paul would have in store for him when they got back to the apartment.

If he lived in Paris…. Hell, if he lived in France, he'd find a way to rearrange his schedule so he could be here on Paul's days off. He'd give them a chance. Maybe it wouldn't work out, but it wouldn't be because of distance keeping them apart.

He reached across Paul for his wineglass and gave it to him. Then he grabbed his own and clinked it against Paul's. "Here's to making new friends in unexpected places."

THE SUN rose far too early, as far as Anthony was concerned. They'd finished off the first bottle of wine and uncorked a second, although he didn't think they'd finished that one before they switched to coffee because Anthony had to be coherent enough to take a taxi and navigate the airport. Honestly, it would have been easier to stay drunk because the alcohol would have numbed him enough to blunt the pain of saying good-bye.

"I should take a bath," he said with a sigh. "Between walking around all day yesterday and having sex with you last night, I'm pretty sure no one will want to sit next to me on the plane today."

"Maybe they won't let you board and you can spend another night with me," Paul said, his words slurring together with fatigue and inebriation.

"I don't think they do that," Anthony said with a shake of his head. "It would be nice, though."

"Probably shouldn't take that chance, should you?" Paul said. "Let's go. I'll help you."

That was a recipe for disaster, but Anthony didn't say no. He refilled his coffee and followed Paul to the bathroom. They fit in the tub if Anthony sat pressed tightly against Paul's body. He wouldn't complain about that, not when Paul smeared shampoo through his hair and started washing it messily. If they were sober, this would probably rank high on the list of most arousing things they'd done together. As it was, they both laughed more than anything else as Paul sprayed water everywhere in his attempt to rinse the suds out of Anthony's hair.

"Okay, maybe this wasn't such a good idea," Paul said when they were done and he surveyed the mess his bathroom had become.

"Next time," Anthony said. "We'll do it again next year when I come back and we're both sober. Then it'll be good."

"Next time," Paul agreed. He handed Anthony a towel and dried off in silence. Anthony did the same and padded back into the bedroom to get dressed. He'd packed his suitcase before he left the hotel Monday night and had only taken out the bare necessities at Paul's, so repacking was the work of a couple of minutes. "We could go get breakfast."

Anthony considered the suggestion, but he wasn't sure he could stomach anything right now between the alcohol and the coffee. "We could. Or we could snuggle in bed until I have to leave."

"We'll fall asleep," Paul said. "Even with the coffee. And that would be bad. I don't want you to go, but I don't want to make you miss your plane either."

"Then breakfast it is," Anthony said. He'd tuck the pastries in his laptop bag and eat them at the airport when his stomach had settled a little. They walked down to the patisserie hand in hand and bought *pains au chocolat* and *chaussons aux pommes*. Anthony managed one *chausson aux pommes*, along with another cup of coffee, but the *pain au chocolat* was too much.

"I know they feed you on the plane, but that's still going to be several hours. You're going to be hungry," Paul said.

"I'll take it with me. I can eat it later if I get hungry." He wrapped the pastry back in the bag and tucked it in the outer pocket of his laptop case. "There, that way I can get to it easily."

"Don't eat in the cab. They don't like it when you leave crumbs everywhere," Paul warned.

"I won't," Anthony promised. The alarm on his phone chimed. "The taxi should be here in five minutes. I should go downstairs and wait for it."

"I'll walk you out," Paul said.

Anthony wanted to refuse because it would be hard enough to get in the cab by himself. If Paul was standing there with him, it would be even harder. But he couldn't do that to Paul. He grabbed Paul in a tight embrace and kissed him deeply. "Thank you. Whatever else happens or doesn't happen, this week was amazing, and I'll never forget it."

"You're welcome," Paul said. "I expect a repeat next year. Only next year I'll know, so I can plan for it. It'll be even better."

If it was any better, it would break Anthony's heart.

"I'll hold you to that."

Anthony took a deep breath and reached for his suitcase. Paul took it from him. "I'll get this. You get your laptop."

They barely fit in the elevator with Anthony's bag, but it gave Anthony an excuse to press close to Paul's side. The sun that had shone in Paul's bedroom window hadn't made it down to street level yet, so they huddled close together in the doorway while they waited. A few moments later a cab pulled up in front of the building. "Monsieur Mercer for Roissy?"

"Yes, that's me," Anthony said. The cab driver took the suitcase from Paul and gave them the illusion of privacy as he loaded the suitcase in the trunk. Anthony turned back to Paul. "Try to get a little sleep before you have to go to work. I don't get in until late this afternoon US time. You'll already be asleep, and I probably won't stay awake long either. But I'll try to e-mail in the morning, just to see how you're doing."

He was trying too hard, and it showed on Paul's face. He stopped the flow of words and gave Paul one last, lingering kiss. He hoped he'd get another chance next year, but if it didn't work out, he would have the memory to hold on to.

He gave Paul's hand a quick squeeze and ducked into the cab before he changed his mind. Paul stayed where he was as the cab pulled away. Anthony waved, but if Paul saw him, he didn't give any indication.

When they turned the corner and Paul disappeared from sight, Anthony slumped back against the seat and wondered if he hadn't just made the biggest mistake of his adult life.

CHAPTER 10

Hi, Paul,

Thank you for the pictures. They turned out better than I expected. It always surprises me what good cameras they put in cell phones.

I made it home, obviously. I was lucky and had a row to myself on the flight, so I was able to get some sleep. I hope the day wasn't too hard for you. I'd say I'm sorry I kept you up all night, but it was your idea. And even if it hadn't been, I wouldn't be sorry because it was a few extra hours spent with you.

It seems strange being in my apartment alone after spending so much time with you in the past week. I didn't expect it to bother me this much. My fish are my pride and joy, but they're not much in the way of company. I've attached a picture so you can see my aquarium. I have a service come in and feed them while I'm gone. They probably don't even notice the difference.

The hamburger and fries I picked up on the way home from the airport were nothing compared to what I ate in Paris. What's the special tonight? If I can't eat there, at least I can live vicariously.

Anthony

Paul read through the e-mail with a smile on his face. The aquarium photo was obviously taken with a cell phone, much like the pictures Paul had sent, but it was good enough for him to pick out eight different kinds of fish in the large tank. Anthony had clearly invested time and money in his setup.

He read the e-mail again, hearing Anthony's voice clear as day in the words. Best of all, it wasn't just a quick "I'm home, thanks for the sex" e-mail. Anthony had put some thought into writing it, with the picture and the comments about his flight and his dinner. Paul hadn't been sure Anthony would keep in touch when he got home. After all, their time in Paris was supposed to be a no-strings-attached fling, a way for Anthony to get over the guy who'd dumped him—Paul never did get the full story out of Anthony, but that could wait for another time. It didn't impact them other than being the reason Anthony was willing to hook up with Paul in the first place.

With a grin on his face, he hit Reply.

> *Hi, Anthony,*
>
> *Wednesday was quite possibly the longest day of my life. I got maybe an hour's sleep before I had to get ready for work—just enough to make it hard to get up. We were busy, which was good, I guess, but it meant I had to spend the break between lunch and dinner doing all the things I couldn't keep up with during lunch. Florent wasn't there since it was his day off, so it was just Papa and me and the kitchen staff, but they were too busy cooking to help. I didn't think I'd make it through dinner. I was too tired to even think about flirting with the customers. None of them were as interesting as you anyway.*
>
> *I haven't been in to the restaurant yet today to see what tonight's special is, but last night's was pork chops stuffed with bleu cheese and bacon. You would have loved it. Definitely better than a hamburger and fries.*
>
> *Your aquarium is beautiful. I couldn't tell what kind of fish you have, but it looks like a lot of different kinds. What made you decide to keep fish?*
>
> *It was strange not seeing you at the restaurant tonight. I know it was only a few days, but it started to feel like a routine, like you were one of our regulars.*
>
> *I'm looking for a new book to read, and I was thinking about looking up one of yours. Recommend one for me?*
>
> *Paul*

ANTHONY IGNORED the leap of excitement along his skin when he saw that Paul had answered his e-mail. He made himself deal with all the messages actually related to work that had piled up while he was in France. Paul wouldn't be at home to read any reply right now anyway, and even if it popped up on his phone, he'd be at the end of the lunch shift and too busy to answer right away. Anthony could be a responsible employee before he answered his… he didn't know what label to give Paul. They'd been lovers for a few days, but that title hardly applied now. He didn't know Paul well enough to call him a friend, although he wanted to. Acquaintance didn't do justice to the intensity of their time together. He shrugged. He could be a responsible employee before he answered Paul.

Two hours later he felt like he'd barely made a dent in all the messages waiting for him, but he'd worked long enough to justify a break. He clicked on Paul's e-mail and started reading.

He immediately felt guilty for having given in to Paul's suggestion of staying up and having wine. Even if they'd stayed up, surely it would have been an easier day without the hangover too. He'd known Paul had switched days off with his brother so they could spend Tuesday together in the city. He should have bought Florent a bottle of wine or something as a thank-you gift, because he cherished the memory of those hours together.

The line about flirting with the customers gave him pause, but he could hardly criticize Paul for it when that's how he and Paul had met in the first place, and Paul did say Anthony was more interesting than anyone who'd been there the night before. Anthony would have to deal with the fact that it might not always be that way, but that was his problem, not Paul's. It wasn't like they'd made any promises other than to keep in touch.

The description of the special made his stomach growl. It was getting close to lunchtime, but that would require either going out or going to the grocery store, because he didn't have anything in the fridge. He would work a little longer and then decide. He had to go to the grocery store before dinner, but he could do it on his way home from the gym if he didn't get there sooner. Nothing he could make would come anywhere close to the food he'd eaten at Paul's restaurant.

He wanted to be one of Paul's regulars, a familiar face who made Paul smile each time he came in. He'd have to settle for being the one whose e-mails made Paul smile, since he didn't know when he'd be back in Paris.

As for the book recommendation, he hadn't the slightest idea where to start. He and Paul had talked about a lot of things, but not what Paul liked to read. He'd have to e-mail him back and ask so he could pick one Paul would enjoy.

> *Paul,*
>
> *Thanks for the intellectual workout. I never learned the names of all my fish in French, but now I know them. I have two damselfish, a dottyback, three clownfish, a handful of wrasse, an anemone, and a green mandarin that I just got. I had an angelfish, but he died a month ago. Now that I'm home, I'll get a new one. I didn't want to get one and then leave right away. Fish aren't as picky as most pets, but I still like to be around for the settling-in stage. I took a marine biology class in high school as an elective and loved it. As soon as I got set up in Winston-Salem after college, I bought an aquarium, and I've been adding bits and pieces to it ever since.*
>
> *I'd be happy to recommend a book for you, but our titles are so wide ranging that I need a little guidance in finding something for you. We don't have any books about rugby players or French politics, the two things I know you're passionate about.*
>
> *Speaking of rugby, I saw that Toulouse won their match yesterday. I have a couple of Lyon's matches recorded, but I haven't had time to watch them yet. Patricia actually expects me to work for a living. I'll watch one tonight while I'm cooking dinner (nothing as good as what I got with you, but better than going hungry). And yes, I saw the scores so I know they won one and lost one, but I want to watch the match anyway. You know, if I manage to come in a few days early next year, we should try to get tickets to one of the games in Paris.*

Anthony debated what else to say. He'd managed to get in enough of a question to keep the conversation going if Paul was serious about a book recommendation. He wasn't going to touch the comment about Paul flirting with a ten-foot pole. He had no grounds to be jealous, no matter how much the green devil raised its head at the thought of Paul picking someone else up at the restaurant. He'd probably run into some of his friends at the gym tonight. They almost always managed a pickup game of basketball on Thursday nights, and it would do him good to get some exercise and stay up long enough to get back on his regular schedule. He could tell Paul about that now, or he could wait and mention that in the next e-mail. He didn't want to run out of things to say too quickly.

He signed his name and hit Send before he could change his mind.

"WHAT ARE you grinning about?" Florent asked, interrupting Paul before he could read more than the first paragraph of Anthony's reply.

"None of your business," Paul said with a scowl. He couldn't explain it to himself; he certainly wouldn't be able to explain it to Florent.

"Yesterday you couldn't keep your eyes open, from what Papa said, so I take it you had a good night with Anthony, but he left yesterday, so that's not what has you smiling now."

Florent was like a dog with a bone. "He sent me an e-mail."

Florent raised an eyebrow. "Really? It's not like you to give your e-mail to a random guy you slept with."

Anthony could have been so much more than a random guy, if they didn't live on different continents. "I took some pictures on Tuesday and sent them to him. He sent me an e-mail to say thanks and to let me know he'd had a safe trip home, and one thing led to another."

"One thing led to another…. How many e-mails have you exchanged in thirty-six hours since he left?" Florent asked.

They hadn't been exchanging e-mails thirty-six hours, more like twelve, but Paul wasn't about to tell Florent that. "This is the second one I've gotten from him. I've sent him two. Not that it's any of your business."

"Two counting the pictures or not counting the pictures?"

"I'm not talking to you," Paul said. "I'm going to read my e-mail, smoke my cigarette, and get back to work. And you should get back to work. Papa can't run things by himself if we're both out here."

"I'm going," Florent said. "Just promise me you didn't do something stupid, like get attached to a man you knew was leaving."

"I didn't do anything stupid," Paul said dutifully. From the look on Florent's face, his brother didn't believe him. Paul shrugged. He'd never been a good liar.

Florent went back inside, leaving Paul to his e-mail, but the burst of happiness he'd felt at seeing it in his in-box was tainted now by Florent's assertion. He couldn't be attached to Anthony, no matter how easy it had been while he was still in Paris. That was a recipe for misery because Anthony certainly wasn't sitting at home pining for a simple waiter when he had a degree and a career and a life of travel and excitement. Paul had been good for a fling, which was exactly what they'd agreed on. The e-mail was a courtesy, nothing more. He needed to get over himself, go inside, and find a cute guy to take home. *If you fall off, get up and get right back on.* His father had told him that every time he crashed his bike. The same applied now. He'd find someone new and forget about Anthony for a few hours. Tomorrow, when he was rested, he'd read and acknowledge the e-mail since it was only polite. He could even keep in touch with Anthony as long as he kept it light and made it clear he wasn't pining for someone he couldn't have. He didn't have to give Anthony a play-by-play to make it clear he'd moved on.

Paul took another deep drag on his cigarette, letting the nicotine settle his nerves. He still had three hours left on the dinner shift, plenty of time to find a target and flirt him into bed. He didn't know what was going on at the parc des expos now, but something was because they'd had men in suits at dinner last night and tonight. It would be easy. Someone in town for the show who would eat there tonight and somewhere else tomorrow night and would be up for anonymous sex. He just had to find the right target.

It was harder with a group, his success with Anthony notwithstanding. Much easier to chat up someone sitting at a table alone.

He ground out the cigarette with the heel of his shoe and tossed the butt in the trash can. With a deep breath, he went back inside and took a moment to study the evening's clientele. Most of the tables had groups of three or four, even the tables that weren't filled by regulars. Two tables had singles sitting at them, but one was Papa's age or older and the other had a wedding ring on. Paul didn't mind a bit of anonymous sex, but he wouldn't knowingly be the other guy. He'd feel out the groups, but it didn't look like he'd get lucky tonight. He'd made tentative plans with Ludovic for the weekend. If he didn't find anyone tonight, he only had to wait another day or two for a sure thing.

"Paul, take this to the table in the back corner," Papa called, pulling Paul from his morose thoughts. He grabbed the tray of appetizers and put on his best polite smile. That had been the table Anthony and Patricia sat at the first night. Maybe he'd get lucky again.

CHAPTER 11

PAUL HIT Send on the e-mail to Anthony, congratulating him on Lyon's upset against Toulouse a week later and rested his head against the back of the couch. He was exhausted, but he needed to unwind a little before going to sleep. He hadn't found anyone interesting at the restaurant tonight, so he had the apartment to himself. A quick calculation told him it was late afternoon, getting close to dinnertime, for Anthony. Probably too late to get a quick reply. He'd have to suck it up and deal with a night with only himself for company. He ought to get a cat. That would be healthier companionship than random hookups, except that would require a commitment, and Paul had never been good at those.

His computer dinged, drawing his attention back to the screen and the chat window that blinked happily at him. He clicked on it and smiled.

AnthonyMercer: Hi, you're up late.

PaulDelescluse: Too tired to sleep. We were really busy tonight. Did you watch Lyon play?

AnthonyMercer: No, I was finishing up e-mails for work when I saw your note. And then your light was green, so I pinged you. I hope that's okay.

PaulDelescluse: Of course! How was work? Not too crazy?

AnthonyMercer: No more than usual. I'm still catching up from being gone, although most of the urgent stuff is done now. It's the daily tasks that piled up. I should be back to a normal schedule by the end of this week.

PaulDelescluse: Good. You work too hard.

AnthonyMercer: You're one to talk. I know how many hours you work in a week. You have tomorrow off, though, right? You can get some sleep and catch up too. I kind of took over your entire day off last week.

And it had been the best day off in recent—and not so recent—memory.

PaulDelescluse: If you were here, I'd spend tomorrow with you too. Did you have a good weekend?

AnthonyMercer: I had a great weekend. I played basketball with some friends on Saturday, and then we ended up going out. I don't even know what time we got home that night. I wasn't the designated driver. ;)

Paul frowned at the thought of Anthony out drinking with friends. He had no grounds for the jealousy roiling through his gut. They hadn't made any promises. Hell, he'd slept with Ludovic on Saturday night while Anthony was out with his friends.

PaulDelescluse: That sounds like a story worth hearing. Did you see any hot men?

AnthonyMercer: There was one, but I'm not sure anything will come of it. The bar's in a neighborhood that's very offbeat, gay friendly without being gay-centric. There were gay couples at the bar, and a couple of twinks who were clearly looking for someone to take them home, but there were also straight couples. It's one of my favorite bars, but the hot men aren't always gay.

It should have been some comfort that Anthony hadn't hooked up with the first guy he met after getting home, but it wasn't. That wasn't Anthony's style, their week together notwithstanding. He'd take his time, get to know a man, and then keep him. That's what Anthony deserved too.

PaulDelescluse: Did you get his number, at least? You can't find out more about him without some way to contact him.

AnthonyMercer: I don't move as fast as you do. It's not the first time I've seen him. If I see him again, I'll work up the courage to talk to him. What about you? I know you had to work, but did you get a break at all?

Paul debated how much to tell Anthony, but Anthony had asked, and he'd obviously already moved on if he was checking out men at a bar. He might not have picked the guy up yet, but that was just Anthony being Anthony. He'd take his time, flirt a little, back away, flirt a little more. Despite the rather direct way he'd approached Paul, the slow approach was much more the way he'd do things.

PaulDelescluse: Actually I did have a bit of fun Saturday night. An old friend came into the restaurant.

AnthonyMercer: That's wonderful! Did you have a chance to visit with him?

PaulDelescluse: If you want to call it that. :D

AnthonyMercer: Oh, so it's like that, is it?

PaulDelescluse: Yep. It was exactly like I remembered.

Anthony could take that however he wanted. It wasn't even a lie. Sex with Ludovic had been exactly like Paul remembered… unfortunately. He wasn't going to tell Anthony that part, though. Let Anthony think Paul had moved on as easily as Anthony himself had.

AnthonyMercer: Will you get to spend some time with him tomorrow while he's in town?

Paul had no desire to spend any more time with Ludovic if he could help it, but Anthony didn't need to know that. Nor did he need to correct Anthony's assumption that Ludovic was visiting.

PaulDelescluse: He has to work. That's the downside of my schedule. When I have time off, nobody else does, and I have to work when they're off.

AnthonyMercer: You need someone with flexible hours. That's one of the things I love about my job. As long as the tasks are done at the end of the week or month, Patricia doesn't care when I actually do them. I could work from midnight to eight in the morning and sleep all day if I wanted.

PaulDelescluse: There aren't a lot of jobs over here with that kind of flexibility. Everyone still reports to the office every day at nine, Monday through Friday.

AnthonyMercer: It's becoming something of a trend here, so maybe it will make it across the ocean soon and it'll be easier for you.

It wouldn't make that much difference anyway, as far as Paul was concerned. Someone with a flexible schedule would want someone with a similarly flexible schedule so they could do things together. Paul was lucky to have his day off. He worked nights, holidays, and weekends, and that wasn't likely to change. As a child, he hadn't thought anything of opening Christmas presents and then going to the restaurant for the rest of the day, but Gilles hadn't approved at all. He'd dealt with it for a few months, but he'd been perfectly clear when he ended things that the biggest reason for the breakup was Paul's schedule.

PaulDelescluse: We can hope. Do you always play basketball on Saturdays?

AnthonyMercer: When I'm in town. We met when we were in college together. We're fraternity brothers and all stayed in town after we graduated. We played in an intramural league back then and have kept it going.

PaulDelescluse: That's great.

AnthonyMercer: They all wanted to know what happened in Paris. They said they hadn't seen me smile like I was on Saturday in at least six months.

PaulDelescluse: What did you tell them?

AnthonyMercer: That I had a relaxing vacation and made a new friend. I don't think they believed me.

Paul wouldn't have used those words to describe the week they spent together, but he didn't know Anthony's friends. Presumably they knew he was gay, but that didn't mean they'd approve of him having a fling in Paris.

AnthonyMercer: I hope you don't mind. It's just we had such a good week together, and I didn't want to reduce that to fodder for their teasing and gossip. We're all in our thirties, but sometimes I swear they're still fourteen.

Relief made Paul smile.

PaulDelescluse: They're your friends. It's up to you what you tell them. And no, I don't mind. I understand not wanting the teasing. Florent is the worst.

AnthonyMercer: The doorbell's ringing. Back in a second.

Paul waited for several minutes, but Anthony didn't ping him back. He yawned once and then a second time. He didn't have to get up early, but it was almost one in the morning. No wonder he was sleepy. He waited a little longer, but Anthony still didn't come back.

PaulDelescluse: I can't keep my eyes open. Have a good evening, and I'll talk to you soon.

He shut his laptop and went into the bedroom to get ready for bed. He snuggled under the covers and wished they still smelled of Anthony.

"HOLD ON one sec, Matt," Anthony said when it became clear his best friend since college wasn't just dropping in for a moment or two.

"Sorry, I figured you'd be done with work by now," Matt said.

"I am. I was chatting with a friend." Anthony grabbed his laptop to tell Paul what was going on. Paul's message blinked at him. He typed a reply quickly, knowing Paul would see it next time he logged on.

AnthonyMercer: Sorry I didn't get to say good night. My best friend dropped by unexpectedly. I hope you sleep well.

With that taken care of, he shut his laptop. "Okay, I'm all yours. I didn't expect to see you tonight."

Matt shrugged. "Robin had her book club tonight, so she won't be home until after nine, and I didn't feel like sitting alone in an empty house."

"It won't be empty much longer," Anthony said. "Before long, you'll be wishing for a night with nothing to do but stare at the walls." Robin, Matt's wife, was six months pregnant with their first child, and they were already eagerly anticipating their growing family.

"If I get to that point, I'll call Uncle Anthony to babysit for the night," Matt said with a grin.

"Have you eaten?" Anthony asked. "I was going to toss something together, and it's easy to make enough for two instead of one. It won't be anything like what I got in Paris, but it'll be better than fast food."

"Speaking of Paris, the others might buy that line you fed us about having a nice vacation, but I know you better than that," Matt said. "What gives?"

Anthony shrugged. "I told you. I made a new friend."

"Uh-huh," Matt said. "You have plenty of friends and none of them put that look on your face."

"This one does," Anthony insisted.

"Why? What's different about him?"

How to explain Paul to Matt in a way that made sense? Anthony didn't even know where to start. "I met him at a restaurant around the corner from the hotel. Patricia and I went there for dinner, and we got to talking, and talking turned to flirting, and Patricia was egging me on, and the next thing I knew, she was leaving to go back to the hotel while I waited for Paul to finish his shift so I could go back to his place. It was supposed to be a night of strings-free sex with a cute guy."

"But?"

"But it turned into almost a week of really amazing sex with a guy who was as interesting as he was cute, and I didn't want to come home," Anthony said in a rush. "We spent my last day in Paris together, and he took some pictures that he sent me. We've been e-mailing back and forth since then. When he e-mailed tonight, I pinged him. I was chatting with him when you arrived."

"What does he think of all this?" Matt asked.

"I don't know," Anthony said. "He's answered my e-mails and every reply of his has asked for a reply from me in one way or another. He seemed happy to chat with me tonight. But then he told me he'd hooked up with an old friend over the weekend. He's a nice guy. I enjoyed getting to know him. I enjoyed sleeping with him. And I'm enjoying e-mailing and chatting with him now."

"That's ambitious of you," Matt said. "People don't usually keep in touch with their flings. Unless there's more to it than that?"

There couldn't be more to it than that, no matter what Anthony might have wanted if circumstances were different. "I don't have any illusions. We didn't make any promises. I was upfront from the beginning that I only had five days in Paris."

"Then why are you keeping in touch with him?" Matt pressed. "I get why you wanted to have the fling in the first place. Doug screwed you over left, right, and center. With your thing for French men—anything French, really, but especially French men—it makes perfect sense the fling would happen there. The guys might buy that explanation, but I'm not 'the guys.'"

No, Matt had never been just one of the guys. They'd hit it off from their first letter exchange when they found out they'd been assigned as freshman roommates. Matt had been the first person Anthony came out to, and he'd been Anthony's biggest supporter through good relationships and bad ones, just as Anthony had supported Matt. When the time had come to pick roommates for the next year—and the years after that—there hadn't been any question. They'd signed up to room together. If he could be honest with anyone, it was Matt.

"I don't live in Paris. I knew that going in. If I'm messed up in the head about it, that's no one's fault but my own."

"If you're messed up in the head about it, why are all the side effects we've seen good?" Matt asked. "I'm not saying you aren't messed up in the head, because Lord knows you are, but you also seem happier than you were before you left."

Anthony took a deep breath and tried to figure out how to put the contradiction that was his current mental state into words. "No matter how it ended or didn't end or whatever you call what we're doing or not doing now, having someone like Paul interested in me enough to want to spend all our mutual free time together while I was there was a huge ego boost."

"Doug did more of a number on you than you want to admit," Matt said. "You keep saying he just bruised your ego a little, but you didn't used to doubt whether you were worth the attention of the guy who caught your interest. If Paul gave you back some of that confidence, I like him already."

"He's a great guy," Anthony said. "If I lived in Paris—hell, if I lived anywhere in France—I'd find a way to keep it going, but I live here. Even if I saved up and flew over there two or three times a year on my own, that's not the way to have a relationship."

"No, it's not. Robin and I did the long-distance thing for a few months, but we always knew it was temporary. There wouldn't be anything temporary about the distance between here and France."

"And there's my problem. I had too good of a time with Paul. I wasn't ready for it to be over, and I'm not ready to let go, but Paul obviously doesn't feel the same way. There's no reason he should. I can't tell you how many times I repeated that it was only temporary, that I was leaving on Wednesday, that I had to go home, et cetera. He couldn't have gotten attached because I didn't stop reminding him it was pointless. It just didn't work on me," Anthony said.

"I'm glad you had a good time in Paris, and I'm glad it gave you a boost to your confidence again," Matt said. "Now we need to find someone here in Winston-Salem who can give you that same confidence boost."

That would be great, if it happened, but Anthony wasn't holding his breath. He'd give it his best shot because his self-respect wouldn't let him do any less, but he didn't expect lightning to strike twice.

CHAPTER 12

As ANTHONY wrapped up his work e-mails, he heard the notification from an incoming Skype conversation. He clicked on it and smiled when Paul's face appeared on the screen for their weekly conversation. They'd started chatting on Skype because it was easier than typing in a chat window. Now it was a weekly occurrence that Anthony looked forward to with as much anticipation as he did the basketball games with the guys or Sunday dinner at Matt and Robin's house where he could spend hours spoiling Baby Layla.

"Perfect timing. I just finished."

"Good," Paul said, his voice crackling a little through the connection. "How are you?"

"I'm good," Anthony said, thinking back to the Fourth of July barbecue at Cary's house and his date with Steve. "Really good."

"That sounds promising." Paul's grin was wicked. "What happened?"

"I had a… date on Saturday. Remember the hot guy at the bar, the one whose number you kept telling me to get? Well, I finally asked him out."

"About time, man. You're slow as a snail. I'm not saying you have to fuck everything that moves, but four months?" Paul teased. "So where'd you take him?"

"Saturday was Fourth of July, our national holiday, and one of my friends, Cary, always has a big barbecue at his house," Anthony explained. "Everyone brings their families, their girlfriends, or a date, so I thought it would be a good first date."

"And?"

"You are a closet pervert," Anthony said.

"Nothing closet about it," Paul replied. "Go on, tell me what happened. You know you want to."

"It was good. We had fun. Cary makes the best hamburgers I've ever tasted," Anthony said.

Paul rolled his eyes. "Was the sex good?"

"I wasn't kidding about the closet pervert bit. I didn't sleep with him. I don't know him well enough for that yet," Anthony said.

Paul looked way too smug for Anthony's peace of mind, but he didn't ask Paul for an explanation. If he did, he'd have to explain how Paul was different, and that would either belittle the time they'd spent together or make it out to be more than it had been. He and Paul had become friends in the four months since Anthony left Paris. Through e-mails, online chats, and Skype calls, Anthony had learned almost as much about Paul as he knew about Matt, Cary, and the others. The only difference was the physical proximity. And the fact that he'd slept with Paul, something he hadn't done with any of his circle of friends in Winston-Salem.

"What do you know about him?" Paul asked.

"His name's Steve, he's thirty-three, he works at Wake Forest in the business department. He's been in Winston-Salem for a year and likes it so far. He laughs at my friends' jokes, and my goddaughter likes him."

"How is Layla?" Paul asked. "You didn't send me pictures last week."

Anthony relaxed immediately at the change of subject. He'd been stunned at Paul's fascination with Layla, but he'd gladly shared all the updates on the last few months of Robin's pregnancy and then on Layla's development since she was born. "She's doing great. She's a month old now and getting more alert all the time. Hold on a second. I'll send you the pictures from the barbecue. I think there's one of Steve too."

"Eh, keep the pictures of the boyfriend. I want to see my baby," Paul said.

Anthony laughed and dug out his phone so he could e-mail the pictures. "How was your weekend?" he asked as he flipped through the pictures to find the ones he wanted to send. "You have a big holiday coming up soon too. Got any special plans?"

"July 14 is on a Tuesday this year, so I have to work," Paul said. "It should be a busy night, though. Maybe I'll meet someone interesting."

"You always meet someone interesting." Anthony found the pictures of Layla and sent them on to Paul. "It's a good thing I don't live in Paris. I'd be jealous."

Oh, fuck, he hadn't meant to say that.

"If you lived in Paris, maybe the people wouldn't be as interesting," Paul replied lightly. "Oh, she's getting so big! Her eyes are going to be green. I don't care what Matt and Robin say. I can tell."

Thank God for baby pictures and Paul's fascination with Layla.

"Nobody on either side of their family has green eyes," Anthony said. "Lots of blue on Matt's side, mostly brown on Robin's. No green. I think they're going to win this one."

"You'll see," Paul said. "And when I'm right and everyone else is wrong, I will graciously agree not to gloat."

Anthony laughed. "You're crazy. Good crazy, but still crazy."

PAUL ENDED the call with Anthony and slumped back on the couch. A boyfriend. Anthony had a fucking boyfriend. Okay, so he wasn't fucking him yet, but it wouldn't be long unless Steve was an idiot. He'd have to be to have someone like Anthony and not take him to bed every chance he got.

Not that Anthony didn't deserve more than that, because of course he did. He deserved to be savored, in every aspect of who he was. Paul had done his best to show him that while they were together. He did his best to keep showing him that, even if the distance between them made it impossible to savor him physically. He sometimes thought about suggesting phone sex—with Skype they could even have the visual added to the mix—but they'd parted as friends, and Paul found he enjoyed the novelty of having a friend. Not a fuck buddy. Not his brother or father nagging at him all the time. Just a friend. Someone he could talk to, hang out with—online, if not in person—joke with, talk rugby with, the whole package. He couldn't remember the last time he'd had a friend. Certainly not since his mother died and his entire life became wrapped up in the restaurant.

That didn't do anything for the severe case of blue balls he was left with after their weekly Skype calls or even after the less predictable e-mail or chat exchanges. The minute he saw Anthony's name pop up in e-mail or in chat, he started getting hard, and it only got worse the longer they talked. He'd consoled himself on the nights he didn't meet anyone interesting at the restaurant with the fact that Anthony wasn't getting any either. Now, though….

He looked down at his watch. It was already after midnight. By the time he took the Métro or a cab to le Marais, the bars would be closing. He could go out early tomorrow night and find someone to give him a helping hand, and still be home early enough to not be tired when he went in on Thursday. Or he could find someone and fuck him all night long and to hell with being tired on Thursday. The mood he was in, that's what it would take.

"WHAT IS up with you?" Florent asked when he finally cornered Paul between the lunch and dinner shifts two weeks later.

"What are you talking about?" Paul countered.

"You've been on a tear recently, taking someone home with you almost every night you work, sometimes even picking someone up at lunch. Half the time you come into work in the morning looking like you haven't slept at all. I don't know what's driving you, but it has to stop."

"That's not your business," Paul said, pushing past Florent and heading outside for a cigarette.

"It really is," Florent replied. "The regulars are starting to notice. So far, they've masked it as concern because you aren't looking well, and Papa has told them that you've been ill and are still recovering, but that's only going to hold for so long. Whatever is eating at you, you need to deal with it. Or if the restaurant isn't where you want to be anymore, that's fine, but you need to leave and do something else, because Papa and I won't let you destroy our reputation."

"Is that a threat?" Paul lit his cigarette with shaking hands. "Because you know how well I react to those."

"No, it's not a threat." Florent ran his hand through his hair and glared at Paul. "But I'm not going to stand by idly and watch you fuck away your life and our livelihood. I didn't say anything when it was once in a while because I know how many hours you spend here and I know how hard it is to meet people. I'm single too. I get that. This isn't once in a while anymore. What changed?"

Anthony found someone new. Not that Paul would tell his brother that.

"I'll be more careful," he said. "I don't want to damage the restaurant's reputation. This place is my life."

"I suspect that's part of the problem," Florent said. "I talked to Papa about hiring someone part-time so we could all have an extra day off and maybe a few half days where we only work lunch or dinner, but not both. He didn't say no."

"Which means he didn't say yes either," Paul pointed out.

"He's thinking about it," Florent replied. "That's more than he's ever done before. He threw himself into work after Maman died. I don't think he realized how much that cost us too."

An extra day, or even a couple of extra evenings, off would make it easier to go to le Marais and meet someone. It would make it less obvious to the people at the restaurant what he was doing. That wouldn't make sleeping any easier after his hookups left, but at least he wouldn't run the risk of the regulars realizing he was using the restaurant as a way to get laid regularly.

"I haven't been sleeping well," Paul admitted. "I don't know if an extra day off would make a difference, but it can't hurt if we can find someone good to help out. As long as two of the three of us are here most nights and we're all here on Friday and Saturday, it could work. Monday is usually quiet enough we could manage with just one of us here, so that we'd each have two nights off a week. That would be three evening shifts for the new person. If we did three lunch shifts, that would give us each a break then too. It would be a start. If the person's good, we could always look at adding more."

"Why aren't you sleeping?" Florent asked.

Paul shrugged. "I can't settle at night. It doesn't seem to matter what I do or don't do. I get one or two nights of good sleep a week. The rest of the time, I toss and turn until it's time to wake up."

"Is something different the nights you do sleep?"

"Not really. I think exhaustion just catches up with me and I pass out because my body can't stay awake anymore."

"Does the sex make any difference? Do you sleep better those nights?" Florent pressed.

Paul flushed. He didn't want to discuss his sex life with his brother. "No. Or not necessarily. Some nights it seems to help. Other nights, not at all. And no, I haven't found a pattern in the sex itself to explain it."

None of it was remarkable enough to remember in the morning. It was physical release, nothing more.

"Then why do it? What do you get out of it? You aren't looking for a relationship or you wouldn't be picking up someone different every time. It isn't helping you relax and sleep. It isn't making you happy. What's the point?"

"It feels good while I'm doing it," Paul said. "It's the only thing that feels good right now."

"Has it occurred to you that there might be a problem with that statement? You didn't used to be like this. The restaurant used to make you happy. You used to go to rallies and things on your day off. You used to care about things beyond your next fuck. And I'm not talking about years ago, either. This is recent."

"I'm not doing anything wrong," Paul said. "There's nothing wrong with sex. I'm not coercing anyone. I'm not taking advantage of anyone who isn't interested. We both get out of it what we wanted going in. There are never any promises broken or anyone disappointed in the morning. If it gets me through the night and the next day, that's not a bad thing."

"You're missing the point," Florent yelled. "Are you trying to be obtuse or are you really this stupid? This isn't about the sex. It's about why you need sex to get through the night and the next day, as you put it. No, you aren't hurting the men you're with. I've watched you do this enough times to know everything is consensual, but you're doing it to mask something that's hurting you. It doesn't solve the problem or you wouldn't need it again the next night."

Paul crushed out his cigarette. "This conversation is over. I will be more discreet at the restaurant if you talk Papa into hiring someone so we have two nights off a week. I'll get some sleeping pills so I don't look tired all the time. The rest is none of your damn business."

He stalked back inside and grabbed the tray of clean glasses with enough force to set them tinkling against each other. He took a deep breath to settle himself. Papa wouldn't appreciate it if he broke the stemware because he was annoyed with Florent.

Where the hell did Florent get off, questioning him that way? What Paul did with his own time was nobody's business but his own, and that included the meddlesome busybodies who were asking Papa about him too. As long as he came to work on time, gave good service, and didn't come on to someone who wasn't interested, he wasn't doing anything wrong. It wasn't like he picked someone up every night. He never took anyone home with him on Tuesdays. He had other plans that night. And if he picked someone up on Wednesdays, it wasn't from the restaurant. They were too busy on Fridays and Saturdays for him to put much effort into it, so unless he got lucky—like he'd done with Anthony—he went home alone most weekend nights. And Monday was too dead for there to be anyone interesting anyway. That meant Thursday and Sunday were the only really good nights to meet someone, but even then it only happened if there was an event at the parc des expos. Ludovic aside, he knew better than to flirt with the regulars. He wasn't stupid, despite what Florent clearly thought.

He pushed aside the thought that he always slept best on Tuesdays. It was just because he didn't have to get up in the morning. When he finally fell asleep, he could sleep as long as he wanted rather than having to set an alarm so he could get to work. It didn't have anything to do with talking to Anthony.

CHAPTER 13

THE LATE October sun shone directly through the windshield as Anthony drove east toward Raleigh for his monthly meeting with Patricia. Sometimes he wondered why he still bothered making the drive. They talked on Skype regularly and e-mailed daily, but he wasn't ready to give up the face-to-face meetings. They got so much more done when they were in the same room.

He didn't have a whole lot to put on their agenda today, just a couple of points to discuss about their performance in the UK and some thoughts about what might improve their traction in France and Germany, but beyond that, he was there to listen to Patricia's latest brilliant idea, whatever that might be.

He parked in the lot outside the office and headed inside. Danielle waved at him from behind her desk as he walked in. "No crutches today?" he asked, glancing around and not seeing the supports she usually needed to walk.

"Not anymore," she said with a huge grin. "The prosthetic came in, and my physical therapist says I need to stop relying on the crutches so I get used to walking with it. I have a cane just to be safe."

"That's wonderful!" He circled the desk to give her a hug. When she'd started working for Along the Spectrum Press six months ago, she'd been recovering from a car accident that had cost her a leg and her job in retail. As far as Anthony was concerned, hiring Danielle was the best decision Patricia had made in a month of Sundays. She had a knack for customer service and an attention to detail that made her the ideal administrative assistant, freeing up Patricia and Juana, the operations manager, to deal with long-term projects rather than day-to-day issues. "Let me see."

Danielle stood up and walked to the door and back. Anthony could see the unevenness in her gait, but she didn't hesitate or stumble. "That's amazing. I'm so proud of you. Next thing you know, you'll be running marathons again."

"I don't know about that, but there's a 5k run in March that has a 1k fun run for the kids associated with it. I'm going to enter. Even if I can't run yet, I damn well better be able to walk that far in six months," Danielle said.

"You'll make it," Anthony replied. "Let me know when it is. I'll drive over for the weekend and cheer you on."

"If you aren't in France, I'll hold you to it," Danielle said.

Of course, the Salon du livre was in March, and if he took any vacation time before or after the event, he might not be home then. He'd have to get the dates and plan around them if at all possible. It shouldn't matter whether he went early or stayed late. A week off was a week off.

"Danielle, has Anthony come in—Oh, hi Anthony." Anthony turned at the sound of his name. Juana Gutierrez, their operations manager, bustled into the reception area, such as it was, since they didn't have much foot traffic. "Patricia is waiting for you, but I want my hug first."

He bent to hug the diminutive woman who ran the company with an iron fist. He'd watched vendors underestimate her when they started trying to sell her a product. No one made that mistake a second time. "How are you?"

"Oh, I'm blessed, like always. Go on in. Patricia's expecting you. Danielle and I will take her calls until you're finished."

That was a surprise. While Patricia cleared her calendar of meetings for the day he was scheduled to be in town, she still took phone calls if something came in only she could deal with. She hadn't given him any indication of there being a problem.

He took a deep breath to settle his nerves. Patricia would have told him if there was a problem. She must have some new initiative in mind that she wanted to talk to him about. No reason to be nervous.

Her bright smile greeted him as he walked into her office. No matter what Juana thought Patricia needed to talk to him about, Patricia wouldn't be smiling that way if it was bad. He gave her a hug.

"How was the drive?" she asked.

"Two hours, the same as it always is," Anthony said. "At least it's a pretty drive."

"Yes, it is," Patricia agreed. "How is everyone in Winston-Salem?"

"Everyone's fine. Layla is growing like a weed. Matt and Robin dote on her more each day, which I would have sworn was impossible except I see it every time I go over," Anthony said.

"And Steve?" Patricia asked.

Anthony shrugged. "We decided we were better off as friends. He's a lot of fun, but that's as far as it went. We still go out and do things together because he's good company and better than going out alone if the guys are busy, but we aren't dating anymore."

"You're okay with that?" Patricia asked. "The last time you were here, I thought things were going well."

"It was a mutual decision," Anthony said. "I'm not messed up over it. Not like I was with Doug."

"That's good. It makes this a little easier to ask. How would you feel about moving to Paris for a year or two?"

Anthony stared at her for a moment, trying to determine if she was serious. Her expression never changed. Whatever had prompted this brainstorm of hers, she was completely serious about it.

"Oh please, don't throw me into the briar patch," he said with a grin.

She laughed, as he'd intended. "That won't work on me, Brer Rabbit. I know how much you love Paris. Don't say yes yet. Really think about it. This isn't a couple of weeks and someone feeds your fish while you're gone. This is twelve months or more. You have your mother to think about. Matt and Robin and Layla. You won't be here for her birthday, or if you are, you'll have to fly here to do it. Obviously we'd cover your moving expenses since we're sending you there, but you'd still have to break your lease or find someone to take it over for you. It's a big decision."

She was right, of course. She was always right. "Tell me what you want me to accomplish while I'm there," he said. "If I say yes, what would I be doing that I can't do from here?"

"The problem we have with trying to get our books into the French and German markets is not having anyone on the ground," Patricia said. "We need someone to meet with printers, distributors, diffusers, even bookstores. We need someone to manage stock. All the production infrastructure we have in place here needs to be recreated there. The back-end work of translation can still be handled as it has been since we started, but once the files are ready, I need someone who can push them through the rest of the process and not just stop with throwing them up on Amazon. We knew all this before we went to the Salon du livre, but my hopes for finding a way to do all this remotely didn't pan out. I could look into hiring someone in France—and that's one of your goals, actually, to find someone to take over for you once everything is in place so you can come home—but I didn't get where I am by blindly placing my trust in people

I don't know. I need someone who understands who we are and what we stand for and how we do business to set things up."

Anthony ran back through the meetings he'd had at the Salon du livre. He'd spent his evenings with Paul, but the days had been full of productive, thought-provoking meetings. He had the contacts to do what Patricia was asking, and he didn't think it would take more than a year, although it might take that long to find someone interested in taking over the running of it once it was set up.

"I'm the most logical person to do it," Anthony said. "I speak French, and I know the company as well as anyone but you and Juana. My mother no longer knows who I am when I go to visit, and her heart condition has worsened. They're moving her to hospice care in November. I'm going up to see her for a few weeks around Thanksgiving, but I expect that to be the last visit. In a lot of ways, I hope it's the last visit. I want her not to suffer anymore."

"We can delay it until she passes," Patricia said. "The only rush is my own impatience to see this happen. We could do it six months or even a year from now if you want to wait."

"If I thought my being there would make any difference, I'd consider it," Anthony said, "but all that's left is the shell. My mom was gone a long time ago."

"That doesn't make it any easier."

"No, but I'm hardly there as it is. When she was healthy enough to move her, the doctors advised against it because they said she'd do better in a familiar place, and now it's too late. Winston-Salem may as well be Paris, as often as I see her. If I lived in town and could go by every day, it might be different, but I don't."

"You could work from up there," Patricia said. "As much as I enjoy our monthly meetings, we really could do them via Skype so you could be there with her. Even if she doesn't know you, that doesn't mean your presence isn't a comfort on some level."

Anthony had thought about it more than once, but when he visited in September, she hadn't given any sign of being aware of anyone's presence—his or the nurses'. It truly had reached the point where death would be a mercy. "I wouldn't be able to go to France before Thanksgiving anyway. I remember when I went as a student and had to get a long-stay visa. It'll take at least three weeks, and could take as long as six, before I get the visa even if I apply tomorrow. I'm leaving for Michigan in two weeks. Let me see how things stand when I get up there and let you know then, if that's okay. I want to do it, obviously, but moving there for an extended period of time is more complicated than tossing a few changes of clothes in a suitcase and getting on a plane."

"Juana has been looking into what we need to do to sponsor your visa. You're right. It isn't that easy. I'll have her start processing the paperwork. That way it will be ready when you are, whether that's in January or in June or later. You'll have to find a place to live."

"I could see if Paul would be willing to look at some places for me," Anthony said. "We're still talking every week."

Patricia arched an eyebrow at him. Anthony sighed and rolled his eyes. "Yes, I know what you think of that, but I'm not carrying a torch for him or vice versa. We've become friends. I *like* him, Patricia. I genuinely enjoy talking to him, and it has nothing to do with sex because we aren't having any."

"Not even phone sex?"

"No, not even phone sex. We've both been seeing other people. I can't even think of a conversation we've had that resembles flirting, much less phone sex," Anthony said in exasperation.

"As long as you aren't setting yourself up for more heartbreak."

"I'm not," Anthony promised. "We're friends."

"Think it through, weigh all your options, and make the decision that's right for you," Patricia said. "When you're ready, let me know what you've decided. Now, since you're here, I have a list of other things for us to talk about."

ANTHONY HANDED Matt his drink and set his own on the coaster before picking Layla out of her bouncy seat. "How's my precious girl today?" he asked as he kissed her forehead. She cooed at him.

"Thanks for coming over," Matt said. "I'm glad Robin still has her stitch and bitch with her friends, but Layla had a bad night last night, and I had a crazy day at work, and I couldn't face the evening without some adult company too."

"I'm happy to come over anytime," Anthony said. "You know that."

"I do, and I'm forever thankful for it." Matt took a long swig of iced tea and leaned against the back of the couch with his eyes closed. "How was your week? You went to Raleigh, right?"

"Yes," Anthony said. He juggled Layla into one arm so he could take a sip of his own drink. She reached for the glass, but he kept it out of her reach. "Not yet, sweetheart. You have to be a little bit older before you can have anything besides Mama's milk." He set the glass down. "Patricia had a proposition for me."

"Oh really?" Matt drawled, cracking open one eyelid. "Since when do you like women?"

Anthony threw a pillow at him. He knew they were called throw pillows for a reason. "Not that kind of proposition. She offered me the chance to move to Paris for a year or two on the company's dime to set up a branch for Along the Spectrum."

"Wow, that's quite a proposition," Matt said, opening both eyes and sitting up. "What did you tell her?"

"We agreed I'd think about it until after I get back from Michigan and make a decision then," Anthony said. "Mom's condition isn't going to improve. I came to terms with that a long time ago, but if she really is reaching the final weeks, I might delay until after she passes. This isn't a now-or-never proposition."

"What does Paul think about it?" Matt asked.

"I haven't told him yet," Anthony said. "I met with Patricia yesterday, and I won't talk to Paul until Tuesday. Besides, it's not definite yet."

"Are you really considering saying no?" Matt pressed. "I don't mean 'not right now.' I mean 'no, never.' Because I know all about your love affair with Paris. You'd never stop kicking yourself if you didn't go when your mom's situation allows it."

"It's a lot to think about. I'd have to give up my apartment, hopefully find someone to sublease it until the lease expires in June, or else deal with the expenses of breaking the lease. I'd have to figure out what to do with my aquarium—or the fish, anyway. I can store the aquarium. I'd have to store most of my stuff because there's no point in paying to ship it to France, even if I'm staying for a year or two. And then there's you and Robin and Layla. Yes, it's an opportunity I'm not likely to get again, but I have a life here."

"And we'll still be here when you get back," Matt said. "You've managed to keep a friendship going with a fling in Paris through e-mail and Skype. I'm pretty sure we can do as well or better after fifteen years. And you'll be able to come home. It's not like you'll be trapped there. You could come home for Layla's birthday or your mom's funeral or Christmas. You'd have to buy the plane ticket, but you could come."

"I wouldn't be able to come over spur of the moment to give you a break."

"So Cary would come, or Will or Sam or one of Robin's friends, or I'd man up and deal with Layla by myself," Matt said. "She will get older and start sleeping through the night, and it will get easier. It's your decision, bro, but the only reason I can see not to do it is your mom, and that isn't going to be a problem for much longer if the doctors are right. You've been saying for over a year now that it's time."

"It is. My aunt even finally agrees with me, and you know she disagrees with me on principle," Anthony said.

"Then let's hope you're both right and she lets go soon," Matt said. "And when she does and you have her estate in order, you should go to Paris. It'll be for a year or two, and then you'll come home, and it'll be just like it always was. What are you going to do about Paul?"

"What about Paul?" Anthony asked. "I'll tell him I'm moving there, obviously, but other than asking for help finding a place to stay and maybe doing stuff together when he has time off, I don't see what he has to do with anything."

"Oh, maybe the fact that when you were in Paris last time, you spent every free moment in bed with him?" Matt said.

"Not every free moment," Anthony protested. "We spent the day in the city before I came home."

"That doesn't change my point," Matt said. "You were pretty gone over him when you got home eight months ago."

"I was, and since then we've become friends, we've both seen other people, and we've moved on. I haven't been moping around because I'm here and he's there. It didn't work out with Steve, but you can't tell me you think that's because of Paul."

"No, I don't think it was because of Paul, and you're right about having dated Steve for a couple of months. I just don't want you to go back with expectations, only to find Paul isn't everything you remember."

"But that's the beauty of it," Anthony said. "I've spent the past eight months getting to know him in a way I didn't before. He isn't everything I remember. He's so much more in many ways. And in others he's less, and that's okay too, because I know *him* now, not some imaginary construct. I'm not going back with any illusions or expectations because there aren't any to have."

"I can't decide if that's incredibly mature or incredibly naïve," Matt said. "But I'm obviously not going to change your mind. I met him that night last month when you were still chatting with him when I came by, so I can see why you'd find him attractive. And from everything you told me, he seems like a genuinely nice guy, but that doesn't mean he's the right guy for you any more than Steve was."

"I know that," Anthony said. "He smokes, his schedule is hell, and he picks guys up at the restaurant because that's easier than having a relationship. I could live with the smoking and even the schedule, since mine is flexible to some degree, but I am looking for a relationship. Paul was perfect for a hookup in Paris. He's not interested in being the man I bring home to introduce to my family and friends, and that's fine. He's still my friend."

CHAPTER 14

THE SKYPE icon blinked at Paul, alerting him to Anthony's call. He clicked to accept it and grinned as Anthony's face appeared on the screen. The smile faded when he got a good look at Anthony's expression, though. He'd known Anthony was going through a rough patch with his mother, but this was more than just a rough patch.

"Hey, you don't look so good."

"Hi, Paul. Yeah, it's been a shitty week. We moved Mom to hospice care because she's obviously dying, but my aunt has been fighting it, insisting she get more care than just keeping her comfortable as she dies. It all came to a head this morning. They took out the feeding tube, so now we just wait."

Paul closed his eyes against the remembered pain of losing his mother. "I'm so sorry. I know that doesn't help at all. I wish I could do something to help."

Anthony's smile was forced, but it was there. "I got through the day by reminding myself I would get to talk to you tonight. It gave me something to look forward to amid all the nastiness and recriminations. I get that my aunt is losing her sister, but it's not like I don't have a stake in this too. This is my mother we're talking about."

"You don't have to explain that to me," Paul said. "My mother died of cancer about fifteen years ago. She stayed lucid until the end, which is a blessing, I suppose, but that only meant that she was part of the decision-making around ending her treatment and moving to palliative care. It didn't make any part of it easier. My father still hasn't recovered. Not really."

"I don't think it's something you recover from," Anthony said. "I think it's something you learn to live with because you don't have a choice. The silver lining is that I'll be able to accept Patricia's offer sooner rather than later."

"What offer is that?" Paul asked. "A promotion? Don't forget you promised to come see me in March."

"How would you feel about me coming a little sooner than that?" Anthony asked. "Like the middle of January?"

"January is dead. I can take vacation then, although why you'd want to come to Paris in January is beyond me," Paul said, pushing down the tremor of excitement. Anthony had a boyfriend. If he came to visit, it would be as friends, nothing more.

"It wouldn't be for a vacation," Anthony replied. "Patricia wants me to move to Paris to set up a regional office for Along the Spectrum. It would be a year commitment, maybe more, depending on how long it takes to get everything set up and find someone local to run it for us."

Paul stared mutely at the screen. Not a vacation, no immediate time limit. He took a deep breath and reminded himself Anthony was seeing someone else. "What does Steve think of this?"

"I haven't asked him," Anthony said. "We aren't dating anymore. We're fine as friends, but the rest wasn't what either of us wanted. When we both preferred watching the game on TV to sex, it was pretty obvious."

So many comments sprang to Paul's mind, about Steve's prowess as a lover, about his mental acuity in letting someone like Anthony get away, about how insatiable Anthony had been with Paul, but he bit them all back. Anthony didn't need those kinds of comments right now. "Mid-January gives you some time to plan. Have you thought about where you're going to live? You're welcome to stay with me as long as you need to."

"That's really generous of you," Anthony said. "I don't think it matters where in the city I live. I'll still be working from home, but it will put me in Paris so I can meet with printers and distributors and the rest. The Métro will get me to those meetings anywhere in the city, and if they aren't in town, I'd have to take the train or rent a car anyway. I've been doing some browsing on a real estate website, and I've found a couple of interesting options. Would you be willing to take a look at them for me?"

"Sure," Paul said, "but I don't know your tastes or your needs. I meant it when I said you could stay with me for a few weeks. That would give you time to see them yourself and make sure it fits what you need."

"I suppose I could set up my laptop in your living room for a few days," Anthony said. "It's not ideal working conditions, but Patricia won't expect me to be at top productivity while I'm moving. I wouldn't want to cramp your style, though."

Paul rolled his eyes, even as he ignored the pinch of sadness at Anthony's subtle dig. "If I get that desperate, I'll go to their place instead of bringing them back to mine, but I can go a couple of weeks, you know. I'm not that desperate."

Anthony chuckled. "We already know your bed is big enough for two, unless you're planning on making me sleep on the couch."

"I won't make you sleep on the couch," Paul said. "I won't even hog the covers."

Anthony shook his head, but he was smiling. "Good, because I'm not cuddling with you to stay warm."

"Aw, why not?" Paul teased. "It's not like there's much we haven't done already."

"Yeah, but that was when it was nothing but sex," Anthony said. "You're my friend now, and that's far too important to me to mess up by fucking around. I don't care what people say, friends with benefits never works. The friendship always suffers, and I won't risk that."

As much as Paul liked the idea of being too important to risk in Anthony's opinion, he couldn't stop the thread of disappointment. Sex with Anthony had been in an entirely different class than with any of the men he'd slept with since then.

"When do you think you'll come? I'll see about getting that day off. We finally found another waiter Papa will trust in the restaurant, so my schedule is a little more flexible than it used to be. Not a lot because we seem to be busier than ever, but someone can cover for me the day you get in."

"I don't have a ticket yet. You're the first person I've told that this is actually happening. Matt and I talked about it when Patricia first proposed it, but it was dependent on my mother's condition, which is why I didn't say anything to you before now. Until I knew it was happening for sure, I didn't want to get anyone's hopes up, including mine. There's no reason I can't get a ticket to come in on a Wednesday, though. That way you don't have to mess up anyone's schedule. I can get settled, and then when you're at work the next day, I can start looking at apartments. I don't suppose I can find anything furnished?"

"Probably not," Paul said. "Most of the furnished apartments are really studio apartments aimed at students, and they're livable, but not much more. You'd be better off finding a place you like and furnishing it from Ikea or somewhere. Not fancy but what you need rather than whatever junk a landlord has tossed in to give students somewhere to sleep. Assuming you aren't having your things shipped over from home."

"I wasn't planning on it. It seems like a lot for a temporary move, even if it is for a year," Anthony said. "I'd have to turn around and have it shipped back home when I get everything set up and turn the new office over to someone else. I guess if I buy anything worth keeping, you can help me find someone to give it to, or even somewhere I could donate it."

"I'm sure we'll think of something," Paul said. "We might have some stuff in storage that you could use to get started too. I'd have to talk to Papa, of course, but since it's just sitting in the cellar collecting dust, I don't see why you couldn't use it."

"That would be fantastic," Anthony said. "Patricia is paying my moving expenses, but that doesn't mean I want to send her a huge bill if I can help it. She's already going to have to pay for my plane fare and extra baggage fees for the stuff I need to bring with me. It's not like I can throw a couple of changes of clothes in a suitcase like I do for a conference."

"I'll make sure to bring the car when I come to pick you up," Paul said with a laugh. "We won't want to carry all that luggage on the train."

"It won't be that much," Anthony said. "Two good-sized suitcases and my carry-ons."

"I'll bring the car," Paul repeated. "You'll be tired. You won't want to deal with the train, no matter how much you think it would be okay, and this way you won't have to pay for a taxi. Because I know what time flights from the US arrive, and you really don't want to sit in a cab for two hours because you arrived at the height of rush hour."

"So you'll sit in traffic for two hours instead?" Anthony asked.

"At least we'll be together," Paul replied.

"PAPA, I was thinking about the bed and the desk we put in the cellar a few years ago," Paul said when he got to work on Thursday morning. "They're still there, aren't they?"

"They are," Papa replied. "But I don't see how the desk would fit in your apartment, and you already have a bed."

"They aren't for me," Paul explained. "I have a friend who'll be moving to Paris in January from the United States. He'll be here for a year, so he'll need a place to live and furniture and all, but it isn't a permanent move. He doesn't want to pay to ship his stuff over only to pay to ship it back in a year. He can buy some things at Ikea or elsewhere, but I thought it would be nice if he had one or two nice pieces too, and we aren't using them."

"I didn't know you had any friends overseas," Papa said. "Where did you meet him?"

"Here in Paris, in March, when he was here for the Salon du livre," Paul said. He'd hoped to avoid the interrogation, but that clearly wasn't in the cards. "We hit it off while he was here and have stayed in touch. I offered to let him stay with me for a few weeks until he can find an apartment and get it ready to live in, but he needs space to work, and my apartment doesn't really provide that."

"Was he the blond who came in with the beautiful black woman every night?" Papa asked.

Paul should have known Papa would remember Anthony and Patricia. He remembered everyone. It was what made their restaurant such a return draw for tourists and regulars alike. "Yes, that's Anthony and his boss, Patricia. She runs a publishing company, and she's trying to expand their sales in France. That's why they were here in March, and it's why Anthony's moving here now. He didn't give me all the details, but they wouldn't mean much to me anyway. Publishing isn't my field."

Papa harrumphed but didn't ask any more questions. "I suppose he can use them. They're just gathering dust. But I want them back when he leaves."

"Of course, Papa. It would be a loan. He understands that," Paul said.

Papa didn't look convinced, but he waved Paul off. "You have work to do. We'll discuss it more when he gets here."

Paul disappeared gratefully into the cellar to refill the stock of wine behind the bar. They went through more glasses of the house wines than bottles of other vintages at lunchtime, but it paid to be ready, and anything they didn't use at lunch would be snatched up at dinner.

Florent met him at the bar when he came back up the stairs with a case of wine in his arms. "What has Papa in a mood? You weren't here yesterday for him to have gotten complaints about you."

"He hasn't gotten any complaints about me since we hired Gaël," Paul said. "I asked about borrowing some of the furniture in the cellar for a friend who's moving to Paris in January."

"A friend," Florent repeated. "By which you mean Anthony, because you don't have any other friends. Why's he moving to Paris?"

Paul repeated the explanation he'd given Papa.

"Good, maybe now you'll be in a better mood if you have someone to go home to instead of going home to an empty apartment all the time," Florent said.

"It's not like that," Paul said. "We're friends. I'm sure I'll see him on my days off, if his schedule allows it, and I'm sure he'll come in for dinner sometimes, because he's said more than once how much he enjoyed the food here and wishes he could find something as good at home. But that's all. At least after he finds an apartment. But that won't take more than a week or two."

Florent looked at him oddly. "You don't think it's odd that you've stayed in touch all this time? I watched you together that week, you know. I've never seen you act like that with anyone, not even with Gilles before everything went sour."

Paul made a moue of disgust at the mention of the one man he'd dreamed of spending his life with. "That's because Anthony's actually a decent human being."

"You thought Gilles was too, once upon a time," Florent said. "Even if you don't remember it now, you thought he hung the moon."

Then Maman's illness had gotten worse, Gilles had gotten more demanding, and when Paul chose to be at his mother's deathbed rather than in his lover's bed, Gilles dumped him. Paul had washed his hands of relationships from then on. "Well, I was wrong, wasn't I? Look, I know you're trying to help, but I have a chance at something with Anthony that I haven't had in a long time. I have the chance to have a friend. I can get sex when I need it. I don't need to mess up my friendship with Anthony by trying to get it from him."

Anthony had made it very clear he wouldn't be giving it anyway, so better to correct those assumptions before they had the chance to take root.

"Has it occurred to you that you could be messing up your chance at more with Anthony by getting it elsewhere?" Florent asked.

Maybe, if he'd had the slightest hint that Anthony would be interested, but Anthony hadn't given any hint, and Paul had learned his lesson with Gilles.

"He's no more interested in a relationship with me than I am in a relationship at all," Paul said. "I appreciate you trying to look out for my happiness, but in this case, you're looking in the wrong direction entirely. Although that might explain why Papa was in a bad mood, if he thought I was asking to borrow the furniture as a way to get in Anthony's pants again."

"I could see it being a concern in his mind," Florent agreed. "But he agreed, so I'd let it go. No reason to make it worse by trying to change his mind."

"God no. If I did that, I'd end up with a lecture on how I shouldn't sleep around so much, and how it reflects badly on me and on the restaurant, and do I really want to get a reputation. Like anyone really cares." Paul rolled his eyes. "By the time I leave with someone, the customers have all gone home, so they don't have to see it, and every waiter flirts a little with customers. It's part of the job to give attentive service and engage the patrons. I'm not the only one who's gotten numbers. I've seen more than one in your receipts too."

"The difference is that I put them in the trash," Florent said.

"But nobody sees that either," Paul said. "It all happens after they've gone home."

Florent shrugged. "When is Anthony moving to Paris?"

"January, sometime," Paul said. "He doesn't have his ticket yet, but he said he'd let me know when he does. He's going to fly in on a Wednesday so I can pick him up. No reason to make him lug his bags through the Métro or pay for a taxi. His mother is dying. He needs to stay and settle that first."

"Tell him I'm sorry," Florent said. "I didn't get to know him, because he was always at your table, but I know how hard that is."

"I will," Paul said.

"Paul, Florent, the tables aren't ready and the restaurant opens in ten minutes. Stop talking and get to work!"

Paul and Florent exchanged guilty glances and hurried to get everything ready for the lunch rush. The rest could wait until later.

CHAPTER 15

ANTHONY FIDGETED in his seat as the plane taxied toward the terminal at Charles de Gaulle Airport. The flight hadn't been bad, and he'd been able to get some sleep, but nothing could change the fact that his body still thought it was two in the morning. He stretched as much as he could in the seat and rolled his ankles. They weren't as swollen as they could have been. The business-class seat had footrests so he could elevate them somewhat, but his feet still felt hot and itchy, testament to too much time spent sitting still. He'd have to take a long walk if he could stand the cold. The exercise would reduce the swelling faster than anything else. It might help with the general fatigue too, although that was from far more than one night of broken sleep. He'd settled his mother's estate to his aunt's satisfaction, but grief and dealing with her had taken a toll on him that would require more than a little exercise and good night's sleep to heal.

He checked again to make sure he had his passport handy. Immigration wasn't usually a problem going into France, but it had been years since he'd come as anything more than a tourist there for a few days, either for pleasure or for work. This time he was coming to stay, and he expected a closer examination of his documentation. The lady in the consulate in Charlotte had assured him all his paperwork was in order, but until he was through immigration—and probably through the trip to the prefecture to get his *carte de séjour*—he wouldn't be able to relax completely.

Only knowing Paul would be waiting for him when he made it through customs and immigration kept him from jumping out of his skin. He might have to navigate immigration on his own, but once he passed that hurdle, Paul could help him with the rest. They'd already browsed through apartment listings online together and made a list of likely places for Anthony to live. Most of them were in Montparnasse or south toward the parc des expos because Paul knew those areas best to advise Anthony on good neighborhoods to live in, but Anthony didn't mind. Living near his one friend in Paris when he'd be working from home and all his business contacts would be other companies, not colleagues, would not be a bad thing. He'd be able to see Paul more often when he had time off.

The plane parked at the gate, and then Anthony was too busy dealing with his carry-ons, immigration, and his two big suitcases to think anymore. He walked through customs with a sigh of relief.

"Anthony!"

Anthony looked around until he found Paul leaning casually against the wall outside customs. He waved to show he'd seen Paul and started in that direction. Paul pushed off the wall and came to meet him, kissing him on each cheek rather than shaking hands as Anthony expected.

"It's good to see you. Let me take one of your bags."

Anthony turned over the handle of the lighter of his two suitcases. "It's good to see you too."

"How was your flight?"

"Uneventful," Anthony said, "which is always the best thing you can say about a flight."

"Very true," Paul said. "Do you need anything before we head into the city? A cup of coffee? A trip to the restroom?"

"No, I'm fine. We had breakfast on the plane, if you can call it that," Anthony said. "That will hold me until we get to your place. I might take you up on a cup of coffee when we get there, though. Four hours of sleep is better than none, but it's not really enough."

"You can take a nap this afternoon if you want," Paul said. "I didn't have anything planned except the usual Wednesday chores, like groceries, but I can do that by myself if you want to stay in and rest."

Anthony shook his head, ignoring the tendril of anticipation at the thought of sleeping in Paul's bed. He and Steve had had sex, but they'd never slept in the same bed. It had never felt right. He hadn't slept next to anyone since his week with Paul. "If I do that, I won't sleep tonight and it'll take that much longer to get over the jet lag. I'd rather make myself stay awake and sleep well tonight, maybe a little earlier than usual, but still at bedtime, not in the middle of the afternoon. I'll go shopping with you. That'll keep me awake."

"You're certainly welcome to come along. I mostly buy staples like coffee and then eat at the restaurant, but you won't want to come there for lunch and dinner every day, so this way you can pick out some things for lunch yourself instead of me picking things I think you might like."

"I probably won't come every night because I can't justify spending the money when you have a kitchen and I'll have one once I find my own place, but I will come sometimes. I wasn't kidding about missing the food," Anthony said.

"Is that all you missed?" Paul asked.

"About Paris? No, the list of things I miss about Paris would take the whole trip into town and I'd still be talking," Anthony said. He was dodging the question, and Paul clearly knew it, but Anthony wasn't going there. He and Paul were friends, nothing more, and no amount of meaningless flirting on Paul's part could change that.

"I'm hurt," Paul said. "You didn't miss me?" He batted his eyelashes at Anthony in such an exaggerated fashion that Anthony couldn't help but laugh.

"I never said you wouldn't be on the list of things I miss about Paris, but we talked almost every week I was gone. I haven't had good French food in ten months. Not the same thing."

"That's better," Paul said. They reached the car and piled Anthony's luggage in the back of the *deux chevaux*.

"I didn't know they still made these," Anthony exclaimed.

"They don't, but Papa won't give his up," Paul said, "and since it still runs fine, there's no reason to. It's not like we use it all that often."

"If it's not broke, don't fix it?" Anthony said as he climbed into the car.

"Exactly."

Traffic was as horrific as Paul had warned Anthony it might be. The périphérique was at a standstill. Paul turned on the radio. "I know you said you didn't want to nap this afternoon, but why don't you try to get a little more sleep now? It's only eight thirty. That's not an unreasonable time to still be asleep. I don't usually get up until nine. It'll give you a little more energy for the rest of the day."

Anthony wanted to stay awake, but Paul needed to concentrate on driving, not entertaining Anthony, and with traffic as bad as it was, it could take an hour or more to get to Paul's place. "Okay, but wake me up if there's anything you need me to do."

"I will," Paul promised.

Anthony used his coat to pillow his head as he leaned against the window and closed his eyes. The music and the vibrations from the car lulled him into a light doze. He must have fallen asleep eventually because Paul turning off the car startled him into wakefulness.

"Here we are," Paul said. "I even found a parking spot out front. Everyone's already left for work, I guess."

Anthony yawned and stretched as much as he could in the little car. "How long did I sleep?"

"About an hour," Paul said. "Once we got past the accident on the périphérique, traffic got a lot lighter. Let's get your bags upstairs, and then you can have a shower and some coffee and we can think about lunch. We could grab crêpes before we go shopping."

"That sounds perfect." The cold air was a shock to Anthony's system when he climbed out of the car to get his luggage. He blinked a couple of times as his eyes started watering. "I knew it was colder here than in North Carolina, but knowing and feeling aren't the same thing."

"Go inside and warm up," Paul said, offering Anthony the keys. "I can get your bags."

"No, it was the shock of going from the warm car, that's all. I'm going to live here. I have to get used to it." Anthony grabbed his carry-ons and one of the suitcases from the back of the car. Paul took the other one and they headed inside. The entryway of the building wasn't warm, but it was warmer than the open air, especially with no wind to cut through his jeans. Wool pants might be in order for the next couple of months.

"There's no way we're going to fit in the elevator with all my luggage," Anthony said.

"You should fit with your bags," Paul said. "I can take the stairs. I usually do, for the exercise. I'll meet you upstairs."

They juggled Anthony and the suitcases into the elevator, although Anthony wasn't sure he'd be able to get out without help. He pushed the button and waited as the elevator clunked and clanked and made its way slowly to the fourth floor. He rested his head against the wall and congratulated himself for not jumping Paul the minute he saw him. For all that they wanted different things out of the person they were with, Paul hadn't grown less attractive in the time they were apart. Familiarity didn't always breed contempt. His own awareness aside, the conversation had been easy, the way it had always been on Skype and in their e-mails. Anthony could do this. He could crash at his friend's place for a week or two until he found and furnished a place of his own without it turning into anything more.

The elevator dinged and the door slid open. Before Anthony could reach for the outside door to push it open, Paul pulled it back with his usual quirky smile. "Give me your briefcase and one of the suitcases. That'll give you room to maneuver the other suitcase out of the elevator."

Anthony did as directed and then retrieved the rest of his stuff out of the elevator as well. Paul unlocked the door and gestured for Anthony to precede him. "You know where everything is. Take your stuff into the bedroom. We can figure out from there what to unpack and what to leave in the bag."

Anthony headed down the hall into Paul's bedroom. Nothing had changed since he'd last been there, not that he expected it to have done so. He pushed his suitcase into a corner and set his duffel bag next to it.

Paul came in right behind him with the other suitcase. "I cleared some space for you in the armoire," he said. "You can hang a few shirts and trousers up if you want." He pushed past Anthony to open the door of the armoire, his hip brushing against Anthony's as he did. The bedroom was tiny, barely big enough for two without the addition of Anthony's things. It didn't mean anything. Paul wasn't offering anything. He was squeezing past Anthony, nothing more.

"Thanks," Anthony said. He cleared his throat when the word came out raspy. "I really appreciate you upending your life to make room for me."

Paul turned back to face Anthony, so close Anthony could feel the heat of his body through his clothes. "It's nothing. You would have done the same for me if I were moving to North Carolina. There's space in one of the drawers too."

He started toward the dresser, but he either misjudged the space or caught his foot in the strap of Anthony's duffel and stumbled. Anthony reached out to steady him without thinking, his arms going around Paul's waist. Paul grabbed Anthony's shoulders reflexively, meeting Anthony's gaze, and the heat Anthony saw there undid all his good intentions. He didn't know which one of them moved first, but Paul met his kiss with as much frenetic energy as Anthony channeled into it.

They toppled onto the bed, a tangle of arms and legs and desperately seeking hands. Anthony groaned when Paul grabbed his ass and focused his efforts on getting inside Paul's shirt without breaking the kiss. Why hadn't they stopped to take off their coats at the door?

Paul twisted out of his coat without pausing in kissing Anthony. Anthony wasn't sure he could manage the same feat of gymnastics, but he would do his best because pulling away even long enough to strip was out of the question. He managed his coat, but before he could try to figure out the rest of his clothes, Paul rolled him onto his back and pinned him to the bed. He bucked up against Paul's weight, the movement rubbing their bodies together. They groaned in unison, laughing into the kiss at their own desperation.

Paul pinned Anthony to the bed and ground down into the cradle of Anthony's hips. Anthony groaned again and stuck his hand down the back of Paul's pants in retaliation. Paul yelped at Anthony's cold palm, but he only rocked faster against Anthony's aching cock.

It shouldn't feel this good, Anthony thought wildly as he raced toward his climax. They hadn't even managed to get undressed. It didn't matter, though. Paul set his blood on fire like nobody's business, and nothing, not even Paul's cold hands pulling his shirt free and skating over his stomach, could cool his ardor. If anything, the contrast spurred him on. He squeezed his handful of Paul's butt, urging Paul to move faster. Anthony needed a shower and clean clothes anyway.

They rutted together wildly, assuring Anthony that Paul was as desperate as he was. Paul wormed his hand between them and closed it over Anthony's cock through the fabric of his jeans. It wasn't enough when he wanted skin on skin and Paul's hands and mouth everywhere and Paul inside him, fucking him into the mattress or maybe riding him into oblivion. It wasn't enough and yet it was so much more than he'd let himself admit to needing that it shattered him. His release tore through him, stealing his breath and nearly his consciousness. He struggled to make his body cooperate so he could do something for Paul, but as always, Paul seemed to take more pleasure in Anthony's release than in anything Anthony did to him. He rubbed against Anthony a couple more times before groaning deep in his throat and giving a whole-body shudder as he came.

As the last of the tension in Paul's body faded, he rolled to the side and pulled Anthony into his arms. Anthony went with the movement because it felt too good not to, but a niggling voice in the back of his mind wondered if Paul had planned this. He'd *said* all the things Anthony expected to hear about being friends and being perfectly capable of finding sex elsewhere if he wanted it since Anthony wasn't offering. But there'd been the kiss at the airport. On his cheek, yes, but French men generally didn't exchange *les bises* with other men unless they were family. The stumble that led to them kissing seemed real enough, but Paul could have stood by the door and simply told Anthony about the space in the armoire and the dresser without entering the small space with him. He'd brushed against Anthony a time or two even before he caught his foot in the strap of the duffel.

"That was unexpected." Paul nibbled on Anthony's earlobe. "Not unwelcome, but definitely unexpected."

So maybe it hadn't been planned, but planned or not, Anthony wouldn't be just another one of Paul's hookups. "We shouldn't make a habit of it."

"No, we probably shouldn't," Paul agreed, "but damn. You barely touch me and it feels better than anything I've done with anyone else since you left."

Paul's words sent fresh heat curling through Anthony's belly. He wanted to think their fling had been as special to Paul as it had been to him, but Paul had made it clear he wasn't interested in romance. Sex, sure, but nothing that lasted. "I guess I'm just good that way."

Paul laughed. "You certainly are. Do you want a bath?"

"Yes, but you can go first if you want. It's your apartment."

"Aww, you're not going to share with me?" Paul teased.

"Despite what just happened, I'm your friend, not your lover," Anthony said firmly. "Take your bath and then I'll take mine, and then we can go shopping and do whatever else you'd planned for the day."

"The only thing I'd planned was helping you get settled," Paul said. He had an odd look on his face, but Anthony was too tired to parse the meaning of it.

"Please, Paul. Go take your bath or let me go take mine. I'm running on too little sleep and too much adrenaline. I'm going to say the wrong thing without meaning to, and I don't want to spoil our reunion with a fight that could have been avoided."

"Go ahead. You remember where everything is?"

Anthony nodded as he dragged himself out of bed. He grabbed his toiletries kit from the outside pocket of his suitcase, pulled out a change of clothes, and headed into the bathroom. He turned the water on as hot as it would go and stripped down, wondering how everything had gone so wrong so quickly.

WHEN THE door to the bathroom closed, Paul cursed under his breath and sat up. He'd planned to be so good and show Anthony that they could be together and be friends without it turning to sex, and this was exactly why he'd wanted to do it that way. He hadn't started it—Anthony had reached for him at the same time Paul had reached for Anthony—but he hadn't stopped it either. Now Anthony was in the bathroom, angry at him, while Paul sat out here angry at himself. He hadn't even had the good grace to undress Anthony before rutting all over him like a wild dog. No wonder Anthony was annoyed. It had been so long since Paul had a real lover that he'd forgotten how to act with one. Not that Anthony wanted to be Paul's lover. He'd made that very clear, despite the way he'd grabbed Paul's ass.

This was why he didn't do relationships. Relationships meant emotions, and emotions were messy. When emotions got involved, people developed expectations and that meant trying to live up to them, something Paul never could do, and when he didn't, it led to scenes and recriminations and general unpleasantness. He'd apologize to Anthony when he came out, make it clear he was entirely to blame, and that it wouldn't happen again. And then he'd stick to that, because that was the expectation, and he'd be damned before he let Anthony down again.

The door opened and Anthony came out, still rubbing a towel over his damp hair. God, he looked good. He'd kept his promise and grown in his beard, and it was as alluring as Paul had known it would be. Not jumping Anthony again was going to be the hardest thing he'd ever done, but it was the one thing Anthony had asked of him. "I'm sorry. I shouldn't have let things get carried away. It was out of line, and it won't happen again."

Anthony sat down on the bed next to him and stared at the towel. "I'm pretty sure we're both responsible. I could have said no too, and I didn't." He looked up and met Paul's gaze. "Tell me the truth. Did you plan it?"

"No, of course not," Paul said hotly. "I wouldn't do that to you."

"I didn't really think you had, not after I calmed down, but I had to ask. For the record, I didn't plan it either. It's not all that surprising, given our history. Every other time we've been in this room together, we ended up in bed having sex. Would you rather I get a hotel until I find an apartment?"

Paul pondered that for a moment. In some ways it would be easier. Anthony was right about proximity and their history in Paul's bed setting a pattern of behavior that they'd fallen back into too easily. "That would be a serious waste of money," he said. "We're both adults. We can keep our hands to ourselves until you can find a place of your own. Or we can discuss it rationally before we decide not to keep our hands to ourselves. I really did mean it when I agreed with you about the friends with benefits idea not being a good one, and staying your friend ranks up there with the restaurant in my priority list. I know I'm a bad bet, but I want this to work."

"Hey, that's my friend you're insulting." Anthony nudged Paul's shoulder with his own. "Water under the bridge, okay? We got it out of our systems. Now we move on."

Paul looked into Anthony's dear face and guileless eyes and nodded. "Deal."

CHAPTER 16

MONDAY NIGHT a week later was as dead as always, but Paul found he didn't mind as much because Anthony was sitting in "his" booth in the back corner of the restaurant. Paul took care of the other two tables in his section, both groups in town for the current convention at the parc des expos. They'd been in on Friday too, so he was glad to see that they'd come back in. They'd sat in Florent's section the first night, but as busy as Friday had been, he and Florent hadn't worried about whose table was whose and simply did what needed doing next.

After he took their orders, he went to check on Anthony. "How was your day?" he asked, shaking Anthony's hand. He'd been careful since the first day not to cross any line that could constitute coming on to Anthony in any way. If he wouldn't do it with one of the regulars in the restaurant, he wouldn't do it with Anthony.

"Productive," Anthony said. "I made several appointments to see apartments tomorrow. We'll see what they look like in person, but the photos on the website look promising, and they're within my price range and in areas you recommended."

The sooner Anthony found something, the sooner he'd move out. Paul pasted a smile on his face anyway. "That's good news. If you like any of them, we can look at them again on Wednesday when I'm off. Do you know what you want for dinner?"

"I want the charcuterie plate, but if I eat that by myself, even the half *planche*, I won't eat dinner. Unless you want to share it with me."

"If Papa got wind of that, I'd never hear the end of it," Paul said with a grin. "But I bet I can get the chef to put a piece or two on a plate for you. Since you're a regular now and all."

"That would be great," Anthony said. "It's one of those things I can't find in the US. Not of the same quality, anyway. Okay, so whatever the chef can put together for me and then the duck. Of all the things I ate here last year, that was my favorite."

Paul grinned. "A lot of people say that, particularly because it isn't flavored with fruit this time of year. I think you had it with cherries, didn't you?"

"No, just a balsamic reduction sauce, I think," Anthony replied. "Whatever it was, it was delicious, and I've been waiting to have it again."

"I'll let Nicolas know what you want. Do you want wine with it? We're walking home."

"Trying to get me drunk?" Anthony teased.

"Would it do me any good?" Paul teased back.

"Not a bit."

"Then no, not trying. Just suggesting that the half bottle of Côtes du Rhône that we happened to get in this week and that isn't on the menu yet would go very nicely with the duck and not be too much for one person," Paul said with his best professional smile.

Anthony snorted, and Paul broke, laughing all the way to the kitchen.

He gave Nicolas Anthony's order and checked on his other tables. When everything appeared under control, he checked on the bar and went down to the cellar to bring up one of the half bottles in case Anthony wanted it. As long as he charged for it, Papa wouldn't care that he brought it out before it was on the menu. Florent was at the bar when he came back upstairs.

"I took the escargots to your small table and a charcuterie platter to the big table," Florent said. "There was a little plate of charcuterie too, but I figured you'd want to take that to Anthony."

"Thanks," Paul said.

"You're happier now that he's back," Florent said before Paul could walk away. "I'm glad. I wasn't sure if him being here would make things better or worse."

Paul flashed Florent a grin as he went to get Anthony's appetizer. As promised, Nicolas had put a slice each of the four different kinds of meat on a small plate, still artfully arranged but the right amount for one person who wanted to enjoy his dinner. He waved his thanks and carried it out to Anthony, who was absorbed in something on his tablet. "What're you reading?"

"An article on trends in publishing in Asia," Anthony said. "Nothing fun, I'm afraid. Patricia sent it to me. She wants my opinion on it. And since I'm still getting settled in, I didn't have a chance to read it earlier.

If I talk to her about it tomorrow, then I can take Wednesday off to spend with you and work on Saturday or Sunday instead."

"Then I won't disturb you," Paul said. "Do you want the wine?"

"You aren't disturbing me. It's dry, slow reading, lots of statistics and interpretations, but of course each person they talk to has a different explanation of the statistics. The interruption is welcome. And yes, I'd like the wine."

"You should finish the article before your duck comes," Paul said, comforted by the thought that Anthony wanted him around. "You wouldn't want to spoil your meal."

Anthony grinned. "Nothing could spoil my meal tonight, not even work reading. I'm in Paris, at my favorite restaurant, with my favorite waiter. What could be better?"

"When you put it that way…," Paul said. "I'll get your wine."

He retrieved the bottle he'd stashed beneath the bar and checked in the kitchen. One of Florent's orders was ready, so he helped carry that out, then took Anthony his wine.

"All done with my reading," he said as Paul opened the bottle.

"Good. Taste this and tell me what you think. We opened a bottle when the shipment came in so we'd know what it tasted like to be able to recommend it, but you're the first customer to try it," Paul said.

Anthony took a sip of the splash Paul had poured. "This is really nice. Not quite as good as the Hautes-Côtes de Beaune I had with Patricia, but really nice."

"It's a different region and not the same grapes, but it's a decent substitute if a half bottle is what's needed," Paul agreed. He poured Anthony a glass. "I'm going to check on Florent and take a smoke break, but I'll be back before your duck is ready."

"I'll be here," Anthony promised.

Paul checked with Florent, but Florent waved him off, so he stepped into the alley and lit a cigarette. Having Anthony in the restaurant was both a blessing and a curse, a vivid reminder of all they'd done together the week Anthony had been a regular and weren't doing now. But also of how much closer they were in so many ways. He knew things about Anthony he hadn't known a year ago, and Anthony knew things about him. Maybe not everything, but a lot, and that would only deepen as they spent more time together. Anthony might not always be able to take

Wednesdays off, but even if he couldn't take the whole day, they could still have lunch or dinner together once Anthony moved out.

He took another deep drag on his cigarette. The nicotine burned through his system. He was smoking more since Anthony came back, he realized idly. Probably because, the first morning aside, he hadn't had sex since then. Nicotine was a safe substitute, one Anthony didn't disapprove of.

He missed the physical release of it, but not as much as he expected. Sitting around in the evenings talking to Anthony was relaxing in its own way. He'd miss it when Anthony found his own place. For all that it hadn't even been a week, he had gotten used to sharing his space with Anthony. He sighed. Anthony had made it clear he couldn't stay, and Paul would respect that. He had lived alone for years. He could go back to it in a couple of weeks. He crushed out the butt of his cigarette and flicked it into the trash can. He needed to get back inside and check on Anthony's meal and then see if Florent needed a break.

MOST OF the customers had left, with only Anthony lingering to walk home with Paul, when Florent caught him alone behind the bar. "I can set up for tomorrow if you and Anthony want to go on home. I can sleep late since it's my day off, and I imagine you're eager to spend time with him."

"Thanks," Paul said, "but I'll stay and help."

"Is something wrong? You've been in such a good mood since he came back."

"No, nothing's wrong," Paul said. "Just thinking about some things."

Florent grabbed a dish towel and started helping Paul with the clean glasses. "What things?"

Paul almost rolled his eyes. He should have known Florent wouldn't let it go. "Anthony and how nice it's been having him at my place, and how much I'm going to miss him when he finds his own apartment."

"You don't miss having the apartment to yourself?" Florent asked. "After Gilles, you always said you'd never put yourself in a situation where you couldn't kick the other guy out if you wanted to."

"That doesn't mean I don't get lonely sometimes," Paul said. "Sometimes it would be nice to wake up in the middle of the night and have someone to snuggle with."

"I thought you and Anthony were just friends," Florent said. "Are you doing a lot of snuggling?"

"No, but I also haven't woken up in the middle of the night since he's been back," Paul admitted. "It's nice to be able to sit around and talk before bed. We have a glass of wine, talk about our days, and unwind a little before going to sleep."

"Have you thought about asking him to stay?" Florent asked. "Or if not, about suggesting he look for a place big enough for two? If you can each afford a one-bedroom apartment, you can afford to share a two-bedroom apartment."

"It's not like that," Paul said.

"I didn't say it was," Florent replied. "If you're lonely, a roommate could help. I'd offer except we spend too much time together already."

"I'll think about it," Paul said. "If I'm sharing an apartment with Anthony, it would feel weird bringing someone home with me."

"You said you'd go to the guy's place if you met someone while Anthony was staying with you," Florent reminded him. "It wouldn't be any different if you and Anthony were roommates."

Except that for all he'd said it, Paul preferred being on his own turf.

"Then again, I haven't noticed you checking anyone out this week either. Did no one catch your eye?"

No one who was more interesting to him than Anthony.

"No," he said around the constriction in his throat. "I'd rather spend the time with Anthony."

Florent gave him a pointed look. "Maybe you should do something about that, then. Before he gets away. He's still sitting back there, waiting for you. That ought to tell you something."

It told Paul all kinds of things, although not the things Florent was suggesting. "He understands I can't leave you with all the work. It was the same when he was here in March."

"It's Monday night, and most of it's done. Go home and unwind. Get a good night's sleep. You can make it up to me another time."

A glance around showed that Florent was right. They'd managed most of the setup for the next day, and the little bit left wouldn't take Florent more than half an hour. "Leave the tables. I'll come in early and set them in the morning. Anthony has appointments to view apartments, so we'll be up and about early."

"Good night," Florent said with a wave of his hand.

Paul grabbed his coat and went to collect Anthony.

"You're done sooner than I expected," Anthony said with a smile. "I was composing my thoughts for Patricia."

"Do you need more time? Because I can always find things to do around here if you want to finish up."

"No, we can go. I can do this tomorrow while you're at work before she gets up. That's the advantage of my boss being six hours behind me. I don't have to prepare for a meeting the night before," Anthony said. He pulled on his coat and tucked his tablet in his briefcase. "It's been a long day. I'm ready for bed."

"You didn't have to wait for me," Paul said. "I gave you the spare key for a reason."

Anthony smiled. "I know, and I've been using it, but I wanted to stay, and I used the time to get some work done, so it wasn't wasted. If I'd gone back to the apartment, I'd have fallen asleep, not gotten to spend the evening with you, and not gotten as much work done, so it was a good evening all around."

Anthony's words gave Paul a modicum of hope that Florent's suggestion could work. If nothing else, Anthony seemed to look forward to Paul's company as much as Paul looked forward to Anthony's. Then again, Anthony didn't know many people in Paris right now. Once he had his own place and started going out, professionally or personally, he might feel differently. Paul was just a waiter. A good one in a good restaurant that he would eventually co-own with his brother—please God, not for many, many years or only because Papa retired—but still a waiter. Anthony's job put him in the position of meeting businessmen from all over the world.

Then there was his schedule. Sure, Anthony didn't seem to mind it. He'd been awake every night when Paul got home, even the first night when he was still so jet-lagged, but he wasn't really working yet, so it didn't matter if he slept late in the morning and stayed up late at night. At some point his schedule would change, and he'd have nine o'clock appointments and wouldn't want to stay up talking until one or two in the morning like they were doing now. That had been one of the things Gilles hurled at him when they ended their relationship. Anthony would be nicer about it because he was a much nicer man than Gilles had been, but that didn't mean it wouldn't cause problems eventually.

"You're awfully quiet," Anthony said. "Is everything all right?"

"Yes, sorry, just thinking about something Florent said," Paul replied. "Nothing important. Tell me about the apartments you found."

Anthony accepted the excuse and happily described the different apartments he was interested in as they walked. "I've been looking mostly at two-bedroom apartments so I can set the second room up as an office. Most of them also have a nice living room where I could invite people over for dinner or drinks or whatever. That probably isn't as important as I'd like to think it would be, but it's nice to have the choice. The one I really liked from looking at it online doesn't have an elevator, but the exercise would be good for me since I spend most of my time sitting in front of a computer."

"Where is it?" Paul asked.

Anthony grinned. "Rue du Hameau."

"You're kidding me," Paul said.

Anthony shook his head. "No, honest. Right down the street. There's another one on boulevard Victor, but it's more expensive and a little smaller. Maybe it's newer? Or there's some amenity that I didn't see when I read the ad? Not overly expensive, but more than the one that looked better on the website."

"And that's why you always have to see them in person. The real estate ads put everything in the best light," Paul agreed. "It could be something nicer about the one on boulevard Victor or it could be a problem in the one on rue du Hameau, or it could be the location, although I'd rather live on a side street than on boulevard Victor."

"Me too," Anthony said, "but if the bedrooms face the courtyard instead of the street, there might not be too much noise. I'll have to see tomorrow."

They reached the apartment and headed inside. "I know you had wine with dinner, but do you want another glass?" Paul asked.

"Sure, but just half. I wouldn't want to break our routine," Anthony said. "I've told you all about my day, but you haven't told me about yours."

"There's not much to tell," Paul said. "It's Monday. Nothing much ever happens on Monday, which is why Papa takes today off."

"Have you convinced him to take a second day off?" Anthony asked. "You did tell me you'd hired another waiter part-time, right?"

"Yes, Gaël. Even without Papa, we don't need him on Mondays. He's been coming in on Thursdays through Sundays. Papa likes him, but not enough to take a second day off. He has finally agreed that Florent and I could not always work lunch, though, so that's good. I'll probably take Friday lunch and let Florent have Thursday lunch off. That way I'm not taking all my time off at once."

"Let me know for sure. I'll make sure to leave lunch free on Friday. Once I have my own place, we'll have to plan a little more to see each other. I can schedule my appointments when I want to and plan my work hours around that as long as everything gets done. We can have lunch together on Fridays in addition to whatever we do on Wednesdays. Unless you have other plans, of course. I know I'm not your only friend in Paris."

If only that were true….

CHAPTER 17

ANTHONY HEARD the key in the lock and smiled. Midnight, as usual. In the ten days he'd been staying at Paul's place, Paul's schedule hadn't varied once by more than ten or fifteen minutes when he'd been working, and they'd spent his night off together. Anthony couldn't help the little thrill at the thought that Paul would rather come straight home and spend time with Anthony than find a guy with a nearby hotel room. It probably wasn't that. Paul was probably just being a polite host.

"Hi," he called when the door opened. "I'm in the kitchen."

He poured a glass of wine for Paul and topped off his own glass. He'd have to get Paul to finish the bottle. There wasn't enough to save.

"Hi." Paul took the glass of wine Anthony held out to him with a grateful smile. "How was your day?"

"Fine, but you look like it was a rough night," Anthony said.

"No more than the typical Friday," Paul replied. "You've eaten there on Friday. You know what it's like. No chance to breathe, much less sit down. I didn't get a break tonight like usual."

"No wonder you're edgy. You didn't get your cigarette," Anthony said. "You can go smoke one now. I can wait."

"I had one on the walk home," Paul said, "but thanks. I just need to wind down, and that'll take some time."

A nice, sweaty bout of sex would speed up that process. Anthony pushed the traitorous thought away. They were friends, and not the kind with benefits.

"I signed the lease on the apartment down the street today. I can move in on Monday, so I'll be out of your hair soon. You'll be able to get back to your regular routine and blow off steam without me around if you want," he blurted out, to hide how flustered the thought had made him.

"You still have to find furniture," Paul reminded him, "unless you're planning on sleeping on the floor. We can move in the bed frame from the cellar, but you'll need a mattress. And really, there's no rush. I've enjoyed having you around. It's nice to have company without any demands and with someone whose schedule is flexible enough to accommodate the craziness of my life."

Anthony frowned. "Is that why you're still single? You think no one will work around your schedule at the restaurant?"

"One of the reasons," Paul replied. "The last guy I dated made it very clear what he thought of my dedication to the restaurant on more than one level."

"Bastard," Anthony said. "Your dedication to the restaurant is one of your best qualities because it says so much about you and what you truly value. If he couldn't see that, you're better off without him. I've known you less than a year, and most of that online, and I can see how much it means to you."

Paul smiled and took a sip of his wine. He twirled the glass in his hand, making Anthony wonder what he was thinking.

"I'll miss having you here when you move," he said finally. "I haven't lived with anyone since I could afford my own place, not even with Gilles—the ex I was just talking about. It's been nice."

"It has been," Anthony said, "but your apartment really is too small for two people, and I can only work for so long without a proper office to keep records and everything. Besides, I know I'm keeping you from bringing home any likely prospects. Kind of hard to have sex if I'm asleep in the only bed."

"That isn't why I haven't hooked up with anyone this week, you know," Paul said. "I haven't found anyone who interested me, that's all."

"That never seemed to be a problem before. Different clientele coming in to the parc des expos this week?" Anthony asked.

Paul shook his head. "I don't know. I didn't pay attention." He ran his hand through his hair. "Listen, Anthony, I know this is probably out of line, but I didn't look because I didn't want to. I wanted to come home and talk with you. We've done everything backward from the minute we met, and I know what we said about being friends and that being more important than being fuck buddies, but what if I want more than that?"

Anthony took a sip of his own wine to cover his shock. Of all the things he'd ever expected Paul to say to him, that wasn't even on the list. A part of him wanted to shout hell yes and jump into bed as quickly as possible. Sleeping next to Paul every night and not touching him had been its own brand of torture. The more rational part of his brain provided all the reasons why this was a bad idea. "Don't take this the wrong way," Anthony said, "but I met you when you cruised me at the restaurant. We had a week of amazing sex that we knew from the beginning would be nothing more than sex, and then I've spent the last ten months listening to you talk about all the other men you slept with the exact same way. Whether it was for a night or a week, it was still the same kind of meaningless hookup. And that's fine. There's no reason you shouldn't have done that. We didn't make any kind of promises to each other, and I wasn't celibate either, but it makes it a little hard now to accept that you suddenly want a relationship."

Paul's face fell. "Of course, I won't mention it again."

"Stop," Anthony said, a little unsettled by how easily Paul was put off, but he pressed on. It wasn't a bad idea necessarily, just one that would take some getting used to and some negotiation on both sides. "I didn't say no. I said it's not something I can just say yes to without thinking about it and without some proof on your part that I can trust you. I didn't come to France looking for a romantic relationship, with you or anyone else. I came to do a job."

"I know that," Paul said. "If you'd come back because of me, you wouldn't be moving into your own apartment on Monday."

"Actually I would be," Anthony replied. "If you're serious about this, it's even more important for me to move out."

"How do you figure that?" Paul asked. "Wouldn't it make more sense to live together?"

The question drove home to Anthony just how little experience Paul must have had with relationships. "Eventually, maybe, but not right away. We each need our own space so that when we fight—and everyone does sometimes—we can get away from each other for a while. We've never dated. We've had sex, we've exchanged e-mails and talked on Skype, and we've spent this week in each other's pockets, but that's it. It takes more than that to make a relationship work."

"Does that mean you're willing to try dating?" Paul asked.

Anthony considered it. He liked so many things about Paul, and the only thing he didn't like might not be as much of an issue if they were dating, but the leap of faith that would entail was daunting with Paul's track record.

"I'm willing to entertain the idea," Anthony said. "Let me get settled in my apartment and get my job on track, and we can see how things go. I want to trust you, but it's hard under the circumstances. And no sex right away. We already know we're compatible on that level. It's all the other levels we need to find out about."

He expected Paul to laugh or ask how long he expected that prohibition to last or anything really to break the tension, but instead Paul nodded solemnly and took another sip of wine. "If you can wait until Wednesday, I can borrow the car again and we can go shopping for furniture. Some places will deliver, but Ikea doesn't, so we may need the car, depending on what you find where."

Anthony clinked their glasses together. "Deal."

"WELL?" FLORENT asked when Paul walked into the restaurant the next morning. "What did he say?"

Paul grimaced. The last thing he wanted to talk about was his conversation with Anthony.

"I'm sorry," Florent said. "I really thought he'd say yes."

"He didn't say no," Paul replied. "He just didn't say yes either."

Florent frowned. "What does that mean?"

Paul sighed. How to explain to Florent that he'd fucked up completely by sleeping around the way he had and telling Anthony about it? He'd been so intent on proving he'd moved on after Anthony left that he hadn't paused to consider how it might look if Anthony ever came back. Oh, he could say it wasn't his fault, that he hadn't known a relationship with Anthony would ever be possible beyond another hookup if Anthony came back for the Salon du livre again. Even so, he'd chosen quite deliberately to share those experiences with Anthony. To make him jealous, to make him envious, to make himself look good? It didn't matter. The damage was done.

"My choice in men since he left makes me untrustworthy," Paul said bitterly. "We hadn't made any promises. He acknowledged that, but even so."

"He sees a pattern of behavior and doesn't know if he's enough of a reason for you to change it," Florent said with a nod. "You've certainly told me often enough that you weren't interested in a relationship. Even if you didn't tell him that in words, your actions said it for you. That doesn't mean you haven't changed your mind. People do all the time, but it'll take time for him to trust that you have changed your mind, and in doing so, your behavior."

"He said he's willing to see how things go," Paul said. "I really want this to work. I'm happier with him, even if all we do is drink a glass of wine and talk, than I can remember being in a long time."

"Did you tell him that?"

"Not in those words, but yes."

"Maybe you need to use those words," Florent said. "And then a lot of other words, like about why you felt the need to sleep with as many men as you did, not just after he left but all along. And why you don't feel that need now. You don't still feel that need, do you?"

Paul started to say no because he hadn't felt the urge to look this week, knowing Anthony was at his apartment waiting for him, but he could feel the familiar restlessness building under his skin. He could ignore it for now, but he knew the pattern. It would build and build, the nights getting longer and darker, until he cracked.

"Paul?"

"No, it's fine," Paul said. "It was easy, that's all."

Florent searched his face. "If you say so. Anthony wants to trust you. Having sex with someone else behind his back is the fastest way to ruin that."

"I know that," Paul snapped. "I already said I wasn't going to do that anymore."

"If there's anything I can do, let me know."

There wasn't, but Paul appreciated the thought. He had to suck it up and prove to Anthony that he was committed to making a relationship work. How hard could it be?

THREE NIGHTS later when he let himself into his empty apartment, having spent the day getting Anthony settled in his new place down the block, Paul regretted ever asking the question. Anthony had been the picture of gratitude all day as Paul drove him from store to store, helping him pick out furniture and arrange delivery or else load the pieces into the car and cart them up the stairs to his apartment. Every muscle in his body ached from the work, but that wasn't the problem. While he was at Anthony's place, sitting next to him on the couch, the muscle ache had been an almost pleasant reminder of the time they'd spent together. Anthony looked so happy with his purchases and his new space. He had an ultramodern office with all the bells and whistles he could possibly want and next to it a quaint bedroom that could have come from any country hotel in France. Also, from what he'd said, exactly what he wanted. The living room furniture was generic Ikea, comfortable but utilitarian. Anthony had cooked dinner as a thank-you for Paul's help and the evening had been absolutely perfect.

Until it had come time to leave. Anthony had thanked him again but showed him the door. Even the promise of meeting for lunch on Friday wasn't enough to ease the feeling of being sent home without so much as a kiss for his troubles.

Paul hadn't done anything wrong, so why did it feel like he was being punished? He shut the door to his apartment and grabbed his cigarettes. It was way too cold to be out on his balcony, but he stood there anyway as he lit up and took a deep drag. The nicotine settled him a little. He exhaled the smoke slowly and stared up at the night sky. With the lights from the city, he couldn't see many stars, but the crescent moon broke the black canvas. He couldn't crack after less than a week, and especially not on the first night he was alone. That wouldn't help his cause at all, no matter how justified his annoyance might feel. He tried to look at it from Anthony's point of view; sweet, kind, loving Anthony, who wanted a relationship and didn't do sex for the sake of having sex. Except for his one week with Paul. He was turning even his one week of meaningless sex into a relationship. No, Anthony didn't understand how little Paul's hookups had impacted his life. They weren't important. Not like Anthony was important.

Paul tried to think back to before everything went wrong with Gilles, when he still believed he might find someone to spend his life with, whether that person worked in the restaurant with him, as his parents had done, or whether they found a way to work around the schedule issues. He'd grown used to his interactions all having a physical side, usually only a physical side. Back then, though, he'd known how to be patient, known that a kiss on a first date wasn't a given and that relationships took time to develop, both emotionally and physically. He and Anthony had done everything backward. To Paul, it was a case of closing the cage after the bird had escaped, but Anthony was insistent. No sex for now. Paul still hadn't asked how long that prohibition would last. He wasn't sure he wanted to know. It might make the waiting even harder.

Still, he could learn patience again. The one round of sex they'd had since Anthony's return, as rushed and simple as it had been, had been more fulfilling than any longer, more involved session he'd had with anyone since Anthony left. It would be worth the wait.

He finished his cigarette and stepped back inside. Out of habit he shut the *volets*, leaving his bedroom cloaked in complete darkness. If Anthony were there, he'd be ensconced in bed with the lamp on, reading on his tablet or perusing the newspaper. He'd look up at Paul and smile when he closed the *volets*. He wouldn't pat the bed or lift the covers invitingly, but the smile would be welcoming in its own way, an acknowledgment of Paul's presence and an assurance of his own. Paul might not get laid, but he wouldn't be alone, and that was just as precious.

But Anthony wasn't there, so Paul stumbled through the darkness until he could reach the switch on the wall and flip the light on. He got ready for bed and climbed between the cold sheets. Anthony might not have cuddled with him to stay warm, but he'd still added body heat to the bed.

Paul tossed and turned, trying in vain to get warm. After several long minutes, he got up again and pulled on a pair of socks and a sweatshirt. He had to work tomorrow, which meant sleeping tonight.

The extra layers of clothes helped him warm up, but sleep still eluded him. He cursed under his breath and went to the bathroom for an aspirin. Maybe that would help with the ache in his muscles and let him sleep.

CHAPTER 18

PAUL GRABBED the seven-hour lamb from the kitchen and carried the plate out to the customer in the front room who had arrived late in the evening and taken their last empty table. Once, Paul would have given him a little extra attention to see what kind of reaction he would get, but he couldn't do that now. He'd promised Anthony he wouldn't sleep around anymore. If he broke his promise after less than two weeks, Anthony would never trust him.

"Here you are, the seven-hour lamb," Paul said, with a smile for the customer.

"Thank you," the man replied. "This place is a real find. I'm glad I came in tonight."

The tone of his voice struck a chord in Paul, but he pushed it aside. Tomorrow was Friday and he had a lunch date with Anthony. He didn't need to do this tonight. "We're glad you found us."

"The concierge at the Mercure recommended you," the man said. "I love traveling, but sometimes it's hard to find what you're looking for."

"Are you in town for the home show at the parc des expos?" Paul asked before he could stop himself. He didn't need to encourage the man. He was already too interested in Paul.

"Yes. And this year my colleague canceled at the last minute, so I'm here alone. It's not all bad, though. I found you."

Paul frowned.

"Your restaurant, that is."

"Enjoy your meal," Paul said before beating a retreat with a sick feeling in his stomach. He caught Gaël's eye and mimed smoking. Gaël waved in acknowledgment so Paul grabbed his coat and escaped into the alley. He'd been trying to be so good. He hadn't flirted with anyone since Anthony had moved out. Had he done something tonight without realizing it? The customer had clearly taken his attentiveness as a sign of interest, although he'd backed down when Paul hadn't reacted to the obvious invitation. But he couldn't deny the momentary thrill he'd felt at realizing he'd caught the man's attention without even trying. With the slightest effort, he wouldn't have to go home to an empty apartment. For one night he wouldn't have to face the smothering darkness that left him edgy and unable to sleep.

And tomorrow he'd have to face Anthony and admit what he'd done, which would cost him any chance at winning Anthony's trust. It wasn't worth it. One night of fleeting peace couldn't replace Anthony.

He finished his cigarette and went back inside to find Florent.

"I need you to take over table two for me," he told his brother.

"Why?"

Papa walked by and looked at them oddly. "I'll explain later. Switch tables with me. It doesn't matter which one. Please."

"Fine, take the table in the back corner," Florent said. "But I want that explanation later."

Paul nodded and went to check on his new table, making sure not to meet the other customer's gaze as he went by. The table he'd acquired from Florent was a group of older gentlemen, Papa's contemporaries or even a little older. They'd expect exemplary service, delicious food, and quality wine. Paul could give them all three without doing anything to endanger his relationship with Anthony.

He managed to avoid Florent's searching stare for the rest of the evening, but when the last customer left—the one Paul was avoiding, he noticed—and they started getting things ready for the Friday lunch shift, Paul's luck ran out.

"Here," Florent said, tossing a pile of napkins on the table. "Sit down and help me fold those."

"I should work on the bar," Paul protested.

"Gaël did that already," Florent said. "His tables cleared out early so he did prep work for tomorrow. What was the deal with the table you foisted off on me?"

"I made a promise to Anthony," Paul said.

"Yes, I know. You haven't broken it. You're sitting here with me and no one's waiting for you."

"No, but he would have waited if I'd given him the slightest sign of interest," Paul said.

"Did you?"

"I don't think I did, but if I didn't, then why did he come on so strong when I brought his dinner?" Paul asked. "Maybe I've done it so often and for so long that I don't even know I'm doing it. I was being polite and making conversation—or that's what I thought I was doing—and suddenly he was talking about being alone in town and how lucky he was to have found me. I must have looked surprised because he covered and said he meant the restaurant, but that's not what he meant, Florent. I spent enough years watching for exactly those kinds of signs. I know what I saw. I don't know why he saw it in me."

"I don't either, but the important thing is that you didn't act on it," Florent said. "You're trying to break a long-standing habit. It's natural to be tempted, to act without thinking, but you caught yourself before you made a mistake."

"I was tempted," Paul admitted. "I went outside for a break, and all I could think of for a minute was that it would feel so good and Anthony would never know. Then I told myself it might feel good while it was happening, but it wouldn't last, and it would ruin the chance of making a go with Anthony."

"But that's good," Florent said. "Don't you see that? You didn't give in to the impulse. You thought it through and made the right choice."

"What happens when I don't?" Paul said. "It's only been two weeks. What happens when the impulse gets stronger and I lose sight of Anthony?"

"Do you really think that will happen?"

"I don't know," Paul said. "I want to say no, but I'm back to not sleeping well, to feeling this itch under my skin that never goes away. Right now I tell myself it's temporary, but what if it's not? What if it doesn't get any better and I break?"

"I can't believe I'm about to ask this, but when did you usually close the deal with your hookups?" Florent asked.

"What? I'm trying not to do that anymore, remember?"

"I know. That's why I asked. When are you most vulnerable to making a bad choice?" Florent elaborated.

"When I take the check," Paul said. "Because that's when they have to choose to wait for me."

"Then it's simple. I'll take the checks to all your tables from now on, or at least the ones with any likely candidates," Florent said. "You can do all the prep work at the bar and we'll call it even."

Relief swept through Paul, taking the tension that had hounded him all evening with it. He had a plan. A real and concrete plan to make sure he didn't do something stupid without realizing it. If he didn't take the checks, he couldn't arrange for a customer to wait for him until he was finished for the night.

"Thank you."

"I want you to be happy," Florent said. "If this is what it takes, it's easy enough to do. If there's something else I could do, tell me. We'll make this work."

Paul took a deep breath. "Tomorrow will be easier anyway. I'm having lunch with Anthony."

"You need to have sex with Anthony," Florent muttered. "That would settle you."

Paul flushed. "When he's ready. Not that it's any of your business."

Florent muttered something else under his breath that Paul didn't understand, but he let it go. He didn't want to know.

PAUL BUZZED Anthony's apartment at precisely eleven the next morning. He'd been ready an hour earlier, too excited to stay in bed even though he hadn't fallen asleep until after three, but Anthony liked to work in the morning before they had lunch, and Paul wouldn't interfere with that.

"Hello?"

"It's Paul."

"I'll buzz you up. I need a couple more minutes before we go."

The buzzer rang to unlock the front door. Paul pushed it open and climbed the stairs to Anthony's apartment. The apartment door stood ajar, so he tapped on it as he walked in. "I'm here."

"I'm in the office. Make yourself at home. I'll be out in a minute."

Paul smelled coffee so he peeked into the kitchen. Anthony had a pot on the hot plate of the brewer. Paul poured a cup and carried the carafe into Anthony's office. "There's a little coffee left. Do you want it?"

"Yes, please," Anthony said. "It's been a morning and it's only eleven. I'm sorry I'm not ready to go yet."

Paul was a little disappointed that Anthony's job was cutting into their time together, but he pushed it aside and poured the remaining coffee into Anthony's cup.

"Thank you," Anthony said. "I'm writing the last e-mail now, and then I'm closing it until you have to go to work."

"I'll wait in the living room," Paul said. He rinsed the carafe and set it by the sink so it would be ready when Anthony wanted more coffee.

He went back into the living room and sipped at his coffee, letting the hot liquid warm him through. The walk to Anthony's apartment wasn't long, but the temperature had hit a record low the night before, and it was still bitterly cold outside. Even with his scarf pulled up around his ears, he'd felt the wind like a knife. When he'd planned his suggestion for the afternoon, he hadn't counted on it being quite this cold.

"Okay, sorry about that," Anthony said as he came into the living room with his coffee in hand. He crossed to Paul and gave him a quick kiss. "Thank you for refilling my coffee too. I have the radiator turned up as high as it will go, and I still can't get warm."

The kiss, as fleeting as it was, warmed Paul far more than the coffee. "You're welcome. I was going to suggest walking down to the Japanese restaurant on rue de Vaugirard for lunch and then stopping at the bookstore on the way back. The owner is a regular at the restaurant, and I thought I could introduce you, but I'm not sure we want to walk all that way in this weather."

Anthony shivered. "As much as I love Japanese food, today is a hearty stew kind of day. Maybe we could save that for next week if it's warmer? I think I have everything we need for a beef stew. We could stay in and cook, and maybe that would help warm up the apartment too."

"That sounds much nicer than walking in this cold," Paul agreed. "The bookstore isn't going anywhere. I can introduce you to Jean-Charles another time. Do you have a recipe in mind or is this a dump everything in the pot kind of stew?"

"Definitely the dump everything in the pot kind," Anthony said. "I'm no gourmet chef. Unless you have a recipe hidden up your sleeve."

Paul shook his head. "I just serve the food. I don't make it. Papa kicked me out of the kitchen a long time ago."

Anthony laughed. "Then let's get started."

Paul grabbed his cup and followed Anthony into the kitchen. Anthony pulled out a package of stew meat with the label of the local butcher, a bunch of carrots, some leeks, a bundle of celery, two potatoes, and a head of garlic. "What else do we need?"

"Do you have any red wine? Nothing fancy, just something to add to the broth," Paul asked.

"Let me look," Anthony said. Paul started peeling the carrots while Anthony went to check his wine selection. Whether he had wine or not, the carrots had to be chopped. "Will this do?"

Paul looked at the label and nodded. "Perfect. Nothing fancy but good enough to add some nice flavor to the stew. Now, we need beef stock, and do you have any mushrooms? We could almost make a bœuf bourguignon."

"Yum," Anthony said. "My favorite winter dish. You're sure you don't mind helping me cook? It's not exactly a fun date."

It was the perfect date, as far as Paul was concerned. "We're spending the afternoon together. That's all I care about."

Anthony's smile lit up the kitchen, and Paul felt the restlessness inside him settle at the sight. As momentarily gratifying as it might have been if he'd given in last night, it couldn't replace the look on Anthony's face right now.

"WHAT'S GOTTEN into you tonight?" Florent asked when Paul snapped at him for the fourth time in ten minutes. Paul knew he was out of control, but he couldn't seem to rein himself in.

"Nothing," he said sharply.

"It's not nothing," Florent insisted. "Did you and Anthony have a fight?"

"No." Paul turned away and summoned his best smile for the man sitting alone in the booth he'd come to think of as Anthony's. Fuck that. If Anthony could blow off their usual dinner for someone else, Paul could too.

He took orders from all his tables and dropped them off with Nicolas. As he headed to the bar to make the aperitifs for his customers, Florent came at him again. "What are you doing? I haven't seen you like this since Anthony came back. You're on the prowl. I thought you wanted Anthony to trust you."

"He should have thought about that before he blew me off for Wednesday," Paul said. He poured the drinks and then poured a shot of whisky for himself. He tossed it back and glared at Florent before stalking off to deliver the drinks.

He smiled and flirted with the man in the back corner and made sure everyone else had everything they needed. He successfully avoided Florent for the next hour, but when he went to take his break, Florent followed him outside.

"Why did he break your standing date for Wednesday?" Florent asked.

"It doesn't matter," Paul said. "It's Gilles all over again."

"Paul, why did he break the date?"

"He's having dinner with some guy named Pierre from Hachette," Paul sneered.

"Listen to yourself. He's in publishing. Of course he's going to have business dinners with publishing people," Florent said. "If you lose it every time he has a business function to attend, you're never going to stay sane."

"It's on Wednesday. I wouldn't care if it were on Tuesday or Thursday or any other day."

"He may not have had a choice," Florent said. "You realize that, right?"

Paul glared at him. It didn't matter. Paul had turned his life upside down for Anthony. He'd done everything Anthony asked, contenting himself with the occasional kiss, not flirting at the restaurant, everything, and it hadn't mattered. "I don't care anymore."

"Like hell you don't," Florent said. "You care too much. Go home. Gaël and I will cover for you. I won't let you mess up the best thing that's ever happened to you because you're too stupid and probably too drunk to realize what you're doing."

Paul didn't want to go home. He wanted to get laid. He wanted to forget Anthony. He wanted to feel free again for a few hours. He wanted….

"No, I changed my mind," Florent said. "Because if you leave like this, you'll end up going to a club where I can't stop you. You're on bar duty the rest of the night, and you're coming home with me. Tomorrow when you've calmed down and you're sober, we'll talk about it again."

"Fuck you."

"That's Anthony's job, not mine," Florent said.

"If only," Paul muttered, but he headed back inside to the bar. He'd put on a smile for anyone who came in wanting a drink, though most people wanted dinner as well, and he'd do what Florent said because he'd never hear the end of it otherwise. He'd deal with the rest later.

CHAPTER 19

THE BUZZING of the speaker system on his door surprised Anthony. He wasn't expecting any deliveries, and Paul had to work the Tuesday lunch shift, so it couldn't be him. "Yes?" he said into the speaker.

"It's Florent, Paul's brother. We need to talk."

Anthony pressed the button to release the lock on the door to the apartment building so Florent could come in. He opened the door to his apartment, as well, and waited. If something was wrong, Paul would have called, he assured himself. He didn't need to worry. Florent probably wanted Anthony's help in surprising Paul for his birthday or something like that.

Florent greeted him with a handshake and a curt nod.

"Would you like some coffee?" Anthony asked. "I haven't been out this morning, but I know how cold it's been."

"Yes, thank you," Florent said. "It was a bit of a walk to get here. I came from home, not from the restaurant."

"What brings you to visit?" Anthony asked as he walked into the kitchen to get coffee for Florent and refill his own cup.

Florent didn't answer until Anthony brought both cups into the living room and sat down.

"How much has Paul told you about his hookups?" Florent asked.

"Not much," Anthony said. "That they happened. That he's not doing it anymore. What else is there to say?"

"That's what I was afraid of," Florent said, running a hand through his hair. "Has he told you about Gilles?"

"His ex-boyfriend?" Anthony asked. "He said they broke up because Gilles wasn't willing to work around Paul's schedule at the restaurant, which is a pretty shitty reason to break up, if you ask me."

"Definitely," Florent agreed. "Did he say anything else?"

"Not really. I got the impression it was a while ago, and he didn't make it sound like all that big a deal beyond his concern about his schedule meshing with someone else's."

"Yeah, well, he's an idiot who doesn't know a good thing when it bites him in the ass," Florent said. "He said something to me last year, when he was sleeping around more than I'd ever known him to do before. He said there wasn't anything wrong with sex if everyone understood it was just sex, and it got him through the night and the next day. I don't claim to understand my brother as well as I'd like to, but that isn't a healthy attitude."

"No," Anthony said softly, "it's not."

"Here's the thing that worries me. He's stopped sleeping around because you asked him to—not that I think you should have done differently—but he's also not sleeping with you, because you're here and he's at his place. How is he getting through the night now?"

"What do you mean?" Anthony asked.

"I don't think you can see it," Florent said. "He's different when you're around. When you're there, he's the brother I've always known— witty, a little crass at times, but bright as a summer day. When you aren't there, though, that all disappears. Oh, not usually on Thursday since he'll see you at lunch on Friday, but by Monday when he's barely seen you if you haven't come into the restaurant for dinner, all the wittiness starts to crack, like a veneer over something much darker and not nearly as pleasant, and that's when I start worrying about him. I don't see him on Tuesdays, but then he sees you on Wednesday and everything is back to normal or mostly normal on Thursday. He's turned his life completely upside down to try to win your trust, but it's costing him dearly. And then you canceled your standing date for tomorrow."

"It was the only day this month the rights manager from Hachette could meet with me," Anthony said. "I want to spend time with Paul. I look forward to Wednesdays as much as he does, but I was sent here to do a job. I thought he understood that."

Florent frowned. "See, that's where the problem is, because for all you say you look forward to Wednesdays as much as he does, you look forward to them. He *survives* because of them. He hasn't flirted with another man since you came back, much less picked someone up. He's done everything you could have asked, but he's doing it on the promise of a future that hasn't materialized yet, and if it doesn't soon, he's going to slip because I'm not sure his sleeping around was just a bad habit. I'm afraid it turned into a coping mechanism."

Anthony's eyes closed as the words tore into him, ripping into his heart like bullets. "And I made it worse by insisting on having two places to live and on waiting to have sex again until I was sure I could trust him."

"Maybe, but you also make things better," Florent said. "You have to or you'd have seen how worn he is. He can do this, but he needs your support, not just passively in that you're glad he's not sleeping around. He needs you to be there proactively, to help him through the long nights if that's what he needs. I don't pretend to know all of what's bothering him, but I know something is, and if you want your relationship to work, you need to find out what it is and help him deal with it."

"Thank you," Anthony said. "I can't miss the meeting tomorrow. To cancel at the last minute like this… that's not a signal I can afford to send to a company like Hachette."

"Go to the restaurant tonight," Florent said. "I don't know what he'll do without me to keep an eye on him otherwise."

Anthony must have looked skeptical, because Florent frowned. "I'm serious, Anthony. The way he was acting last night, if I hadn't been there, he would have broken his promise to you. He was that out of control. I kept him from making a mistake he would have regretted, but I'm off tonight, and if I go in, it'll make Papa more suspicious than he already is. If you're there, he'll hold it together, and then you can go home with him afterward. Talk it out, fuck it out, I don't care, but get him through the night. You can sort the rest out later."

"Is it really that bad?" Anthony asked.

Florent rolled his eyes. "Yes, it's really that bad. You know what? I have a better idea. What's on your calendar for today? Because I don't have anything planned for today except kicking your ass for being as big an idiot as my brother. We'll go to the restaurant right now, I'll take Paul's shifts today, and you can hash it out now. He can work tomorrow when you have to be in meetings anyway."

Anthony ran through his to-do list for the day. Most of it was just going back over his notes for his meeting tomorrow, but he had them memorized already. Florent's urgency was catching. "Are you sure you don't mind?"

"I wouldn't have suggested it if I minded," Florent said. "Does that mean you'll come?"

"Yes, let me get my coat and scarf."

Anthony's mind raced as he shut down his computer and grabbed his coat and scarf from his bedroom. He hadn't meant to build Paul an insurmountable obstacle. He'd wanted to see that Paul was serious about their relationship, that he wasn't setting himself up to get his heart broken again. If what Florent said was true—and really, what did he gain by lying?—Anthony had done far worse. Yet at the same time, Florent's words suggested the change in Paul's behavior was far better proof of how seriously Paul took his promise than Anthony had realized.

He only hoped Paul would talk to him as honestly as Florent had. Anthony would do what he could to help—he hadn't realized Paul was hurting as badly as Florent claimed—but Paul would have to tell him how.

"Okay, I'm ready," he said, coming back into the foyer where Florent had also dressed again for the winter weather. They walked the two blocks to the restaurant quickly, heads bent against the biting wind. When Anthony would have walked in the front, though, Florent caught his arm.

"Come around back. Stand in the kitchen and watch him for a bit, see what I'm talking about, and then I'll get him and bring him into the back. The customers don't need to see his reaction, whatever it is. I really hope he'll be so happy to have the day to spend with you that he'll agree and be done with it, but after last night, I'm not sure."

Anthony nodded and followed Florent through the kitchen entrance off the alley where they usually took deliveries. From his vantage point near the door from the kitchen to the restaurant, he could see the bar and the front room of the restaurant. He saw Gaël first, but a moment later, Paul came toward the bar. Anthony hadn't wanted to believe Florent, but seeing Paul drove home how right Florent had been. Paul had dark circles under his eyes, like he hadn't slept in days, and everything about the way he held himself felt wrong, like every muscle was tense and the only thing keeping him from flying apart was his clenched jaw and white-knuckled grip on the tray in his hand. "How did I not see this?"

"Because when he's with you or expecting to be with you or has just been with you, he's not like this," Florent said. "This is what happens when you haven't been around."

Anthony nodded, queasy at the thought of how badly everything could have gone wrong if Florent hadn't intervened. "I'll wait out back if you can get him into the alley."

He paced the cold stones as he waited, trying to keep warm and work off the tension that built with each passing second. He'd hoped Paul would jump at the offer of the comfort Florent claimed Anthony brought him, but apparently not, if the time it took before the door opened and Paul came out was any indication. He was dressed to leave, at least.

"Why didn't you tell me?" Anthony blurted out before he could think better of it.

"Not here," Paul ground out. Damn Florent and his nosiness. Paul didn't want to have this conversation with Anthony at all, but he wasn't about to have it in the freezing alley behind the restaurant.

Anthony acquiesced immediately. "Your place or mine?"

It didn't matter. It wouldn't be a comfortable or easy conversation no matter where they had it. "Mine." At least that way he'd be on his own turf.

Anthony nodded and started toward the street before pausing and reaching for Paul's hand. Paul almost pulled away, in too churlish a mood to want the sign of affection, but the look on Anthony's face stopped him. Whatever Florent had said—and Florent had given him few enough details before sending Paul out back—it hadn't driven Anthony off. Paul took Anthony's hand and smiled despite his irritation when Anthony tucked both their hands in his coat pocket. If he didn't know better, he'd swear Anthony had never been through a real winter before.

"I thought it got cold in Michigan."

"It does," Anthony said, "but I haven't lived there for fifteen years. I'm out of practice."

Paul chuckled. "It'll warm up soon. Then it'll get hot and you'll have to deal with not having air-conditioning."

"I haven't been warm since I got here," Anthony said. "Actually that's not true. I was warm the nights I slept at your apartment with you."

Paul pulled his hand away. "You need to not say things like that."

"Sorry."

They walked the rest of the way to Paul's apartment in tense silence. Florent hadn't related much of his conversation with Anthony, only that he'd told Anthony Paul was on the verge of cracking if something didn't change, but Paul knew Florent's opinion on the whole situation. He'd made that clear more than once to Paul. If he'd shared any of that with Anthony, Anthony no doubt thought the worst. He'd have to clear that up before they went any further.

"What did Florent tell you?" he asked when they reached his apartment.

Anthony didn't answer. Instead he pulled Paul into his arms and kissed him. The turmoil that had raged through Paul from the moment

Anthony said he'd have to work on Wednesday reared its head. He returned the kiss desperately. He wanted Anthony with a need born of privation and fear, but he couldn't give in to it. That's what had landed them in this mess in the first place. He pulled back and took a deep, gulping breath of air to steady himself. "Are you trying to make this harder for me?"

"No, of course not," Anthony said. "I'm trying to show you I'm here for you, whatever you need. You look like you haven't slept in days, and Florent said—"

"Forget about what Florent said," Paul interrupted. "He's a nosy busybody who should spend his time worrying about his own love life instead of poking around in mine."

"I haven't done a very good job of giving you a love life," Anthony replied. "I was so afraid of how much it would hurt if you slept around behind my back that I didn't see what it was doing to you to make me trust you."

"It wasn't an unreasonable request," Paul said. "You shouldn't have to worry about whether I'll cheat on you. If this is what it takes to prove it to you, then I'll do it."

"No, I shouldn't, but you shouldn't be as frazzled as you are. I didn't know it was taking this much of a toll on you," Anthony said. "Why didn't you tell me?"

"Because there was nothing to tell," Paul said. "I'm not having sex with anyone else like you asked me to, and I'm not having sex with you—like you asked—so I'm a little on edge. It's perfectly normal."

"This is more than a little on edge," Anthony insisted. "Florent said you've been behaving erratically. You have dark circles under your eyes like you haven't slept. You're tense in a way I've never known you to be. I can't help if you don't tell me what's wrong."

If only it were that easy, but how could he explain the way the darkness and emptiness closed in on him when he was alone in bed at night? How could he make Anthony, who had always wanted a relationship, understand that even meaningless sex was better than being alone? He could say the words, but they wouldn't compute in Anthony's romantic soul.

He shrugged. "I'm fine."

"You're not fine," Anthony said, crowding into Paul's personal space. "Let me help."

Images of pulling Anthony into his arms and off to bed, of losing himself in the warmth and welcome of Anthony's body assailed him, but they'd done that and he'd nearly lost Anthony because of it.

"You can't," Paul said hoarsely.

"Why not?" Anthony pressed. "What do you need? What did you get out of the anonymous fucks that I'm not giving you?"

Paul snorted. "Sex? Companionship? A body to hold through the night?"

Anthony stepped back and walked to the door that led down the hall to Paul's bedroom. "Are you coming?"

"I don't want a pity fuck," Paul snarled. "I haven't fallen that low."

Anthony grabbed Paul and kissed him hard, his teeth colliding with Paul's as he ravished Paul's mouth. "The list of things I'm feeling right now is too long to count, but pity isn't one of them."

Paul wanted to ask what those things were. It was important, he thought fleetingly, before the pent-up desperation from weeks of abstinence and loneliness wiped every thought from his head that didn't involve getting Anthony naked in his bed.

CHAPTER 20

PAUL ALL but shoved Anthony down the hall, not that Anthony fought him in the slightest. "Get undressed," he ordered as they crossed the threshold to his bedroom. Another time he'd linger and strip Anthony slowly, worshipping each piece of skin as it was revealed, but not today. Fortunately Anthony didn't seem to have any more patience than Paul. He tore his sweater and T-shirt over his head and reached for the buckle of his belt while Paul stared.

"You too," Anthony demanded. "I want all of you."

Anthony could have anything he wanted if he just kept looking at Paul with that expression on his face that was surely reserved for heroes and demigods, not for screwed-up basket cases like Paul. Paul toed off his shoes as he undid the buttons on his shirt. That dealt with, he stripped off his pants, underwear, and socks in one smooth motion. When he straightened, Anthony had removed his own jeans and stood completely, mouth-wateringly naked in front of Paul.

Paul lunged, toppling them both onto the bed. Anthony caught himself on Paul's shoulders to slow the fall. Paul turned his head to press a kiss to one bicep, but that was the limit of his patience and tenderness. Despite Anthony's complaint about always feeling cold, his skin burned against Paul's.

Mindful of Anthony's meeting tomorrow, he didn't attack Anthony's neck the way he wanted because he would inevitably leave marks. He fell on Anthony's chest instead, biting and sucking at his nipples: one, then the other, then back to the first. Anthony cried out, but Paul could detect no pain in the sound nor feel any rejection in the way Anthony clung to him and arched beneath him.

As good as Anthony's skin tasted, that wasn't the flavor that had haunted his dreams. He worked his way over Anthony's abdomen, leaving a trail of reddening bite marks as he went, until he could reach Anthony's growing erection. He stroked it a few times, reveling in the way Anthony hardened beneath his touch. His own cock nagged like a toothache, but he ignored it. He smelled the musk that signaled Anthony's desire, and that aroused him far more than anything he might do to himself right now. He buried his face in Anthony's bush, rubbing his nose through the wiry curls. He wanted to drown in the scent and feel of Anthony, to embed it so deeply in his heart and mind that he could endure any number of lonely nights and busy days. Anthony might not believe him—and given Paul's track record, Paul wouldn't blame him if he didn't—but this was all Paul needed. To be with Anthony, to be able to touch and be touched in return, to know that he wasn't alone or wouldn't be for long when they were apart.

Anthony panted hard above his head, the sound of his harsh breathing all the encouragement Paul needed to turn his head and lick his way up the thick shaft to the darker tip. He tongued the slit, tasting the bitter fluid gathered there. Anthony bucked against his mouth with a sharp cry. Paul opened his mouth wider and let Anthony's cock slide over his tongue, wringing another shout from Anthony. How many of those delectable sounds could he pull from Anthony's mouth before he came? He looked forward to finding out.

He hovered over Anthony's erection at first, focusing on the sensitive head and letting his hand work the rest. He curled his tongue so he could play with the tendon that made Anthony thrash and moan and spurt with each pass. He could spend hours teasing Anthony this way, his cock heavy on Paul's tongue, the smell of desire surrounding him, Anthony's gasps and moans filling his ears and his heart. He doubted Anthony had the patience, though, and truthfully Paul needed more. Moving his hand, he plunged his mouth down the length of Anthony's cock. The head hit the back of his throat, and he swallowed to avoid gagging. He hit bottom and stayed there as long as he could, letting the constriction drive Anthony wild. When the need to breathe became urgent, he pulled back, only to dive down again as soon as he sucked in more air. Anthony bucked up to meet him, nearly choking Paul with his frantic thrusts. He pinned Anthony's hips to the bed with one arm, but the angle was awkward.

Releasing his prize, Paul pushed up on his knees to make it easier to keep Anthony where he wanted him. "Don't move," he ordered, bringing more of his weight to bear in keeping Anthony in place.

"How am I supposed to do that with you sucking me like that?" Anthony asked huskily.

"Try." Paul didn't wait for Anthony to reply, lowering his head and taking him deep into his mouth again. The angle made it easier to deep-throat Anthony. He bobbed his head, keeping as much pressure on the tip as possible.

"Fuck," Anthony shouted. "Paul…." The rest of Anthony's words were lost in Paul's inability to translate the English in the midst of his passion, but the tone told him all he needed to know.

With the hand not holding Anthony still, he reached for his own erection, stroking it in time with the movement of his head. If it wasn't quite as fulfilling as sinking into Anthony's ass would be, neither of them had the patience at the moment that proper preparation would require. Next time, Paul promised himself.

He'd been saying that every time since the first night he and Anthony met.

The tenor of Anthony's cries changed, warning Paul of his impending release. He could have pulled back, but he wanted everything Anthony had to give. He released his hold on his own cock in favor of palming Anthony's sac. Anthony tensed beneath him and shot his load into Paul's mouth. Paul swallowed every drop, massaging Anthony's balls to prolong his climax as long as he could.

When the flood finally stopped, Paul let Anthony's cock slip from his mouth and reared up on his knees. He studied Anthony's recumbent form as he jerked his own erection sharply, chasing his release. Anthony's blue eyes were closed, his handsome features lax, every line of his body proclaiming his satiation. Smugness filled Paul along with his desire. He had done this. He'd left Anthony a boneless heap on his bed. Then Anthony's eyes flickered open, and their gazes met and held, so much warmth and affection in their depths that Paul couldn't look away. He shunted his hand faster, so close to coming that it hurt.

"Now," Anthony said, in French this time. "Come all over me."

What little control Paul had held on to shattered at the provocative words. He threw his head back as his orgasm tore through him. His release spurted all over Anthony's belly and cock, painting pearly streaks across his pale skin.

"I love the way you look when you come," Anthony said.

Paul shivered at the word love on Anthony's tongue. It wasn't in the context he wanted to hear, but it was too soon. They'd only barely begun something that looked like a real relationship instead of the sex they'd had before or the friendship they'd developed in the months they'd spent on different continents.

Anthony reached for him, and Paul let himself be pulled into Anthony's embrace. He pillowed his head on Anthony's shoulder and took a deep breath, soaking in Anthony's closeness. It wouldn't last, but he would savor it for as long as he could. And maybe, if he was lucky, Anthony would agree to another round later, or if not today, then soon. He closed his eyes and let the moment stretch.

He must have dozed because the shadows had lengthened on the walls when he opened his eyes again.

"Feeling better?" Anthony asked.

Paul nodded against Anthony's chest.

"We should talk."

So much for a peaceful afternoon.

He started to sit up, but Anthony tightened his arms around him, holding him in place. "You don't need to get up. We're both perfectly comfortable right here. You said you needed to be held, so lie still and let me hold you."

Paul frowned a little but subsided against Anthony's side. "What do you want to know?"

"I didn't mean to set you a Herculean task," Anthony said. "I didn't understand what a drastic change I was asking you to make."

"I know that," Paul said. "I didn't want you to know."

"Why not?"

"Why not?" Paul repeated. "Because it makes me look bad. Not even able to get through a week without craving sex, willing to get it from a stranger because no one wants me more than once.... That's not exactly something I want to admit to the man I hoped to spend the rest of my life with."

"I want you more than once," Anthony said, "and I did back when we first met too. And don't say that was convenience or that it was just sex, because you know as well as I do that it wasn't. However it started, it was already something real before I left or we wouldn't have kept in touch."

"All the more reason not to want to look bad in front of you," Paul muttered.

"You still haven't told me why," Anthony said.

Paul closed his eyes and tried to find a way to explain it. "Sometimes it feels like the walls are closing in on me, and there's this itch under my skin, this need that doesn't go away. I can ignore it for a while, but eventually I have to do something about it or I feel like I'm going to go crazy. Sex settles it for a while. And before you ask, I tried jerking off. It's not the same. It's not the physical release, or not just that."

"What else is it?" Anthony asked.

The thrill of the hunt, the power trip of making a man come apart beneath his hands, the knowledge that he still had what it took to attract someone, even if he didn't want to keep him.

"Or better yet, is there anything else that has the same effect?"

That was a far easier question to answer.

"You," Paul said. "I don't feel that way when we're together. It's when you aren't around that I get edgy."

"No matter how we structure our life together, there will be times I won't be around," Anthony said. "I'll still have to go to BEA in New York, to the Frankfurt Book Fair, probably to the London Book Fair, and depending on what other markets Patricia decides to expand into, there may be others. Even if I make the move to Paris permanent and we move in together and have the otherwise perfect life, travel is part of my job."

Paul had hoped in the quiet privacy of his deepest dreams that Anthony would stay in Paris permanently, but to hear it said so matter-of-factly as a real possibility took his breath away. He hugged Anthony more tightly, as if he could keep him there by force of will alone. "I know," he said. "I won't keep you from doing your job."

"That's not what I was worried about," Anthony said. "I'm worried about how you'll fare if I'm gone for a couple of weeks. We saw each other on Friday. It's only Tuesday. And no, we wouldn't have seen each other tomorrow, but I hadn't canceled our lunch for Friday. It would have only been a week, and yet you were in bad enough shape last night that Florent came to find me today. So either the benefits don't last very long or just being together isn't really enough. Either way, my trips would almost certainly have me away that long or longer. How are you going to cope while I'm gone?"

"I don't know," Paul said honestly, "but I'll find a way. I won't cheat on you while you're gone. I swear."

Anthony tilted Paul's head up for a kiss. "I know you won't. That wasn't why I asked. I'm worried about *you*, not about whether you'd sleep with someone else. If you didn't this past month when I didn't realize what was going on, you won't when you can count down until I come back. But I don't want to come home to find you a wreck either."

Paul considered the question, but everything he came up with was conjecture. "It might help if we talked on the nights we can't spend together. I never even looked at other men on Tuesday nights when you were in the US because I knew you'd call when I got home, and talking to you was better than anything I could have done with them." He laughed bitterly. "That probably should have told me something."

"Maybe," Anthony said, "but that assumes you were looking for a message, and neither of us was at the time. I could call you when I get home tomorrow night. We could see how it goes since you have to work on Thursday."

Paul nodded. "I'd like that."

"Then that's what I'll do," Anthony said. He rolled so they were facing each other, noses practically touching. "I didn't mean for you to doubt my commitment to making things work between us."

"I know that," Paul said.

"Good," Anthony said. "Because somewhere between last March and now, I fell in love with you. It's about time I said it. I know it's not a magic cure, but maybe hearing it will help a little too."

Paul's breath clogged in his throat. Anthony loved him. He opened his mouth, only to close it again, words escaping him. He probably looked like one of Anthony's fish.

The thought startled an inappropriate laugh out of him. "We have to buy you an aquarium," he said at Anthony's quizzical look. "As often as you talked about your fish, you wouldn't be happy without one."

"How about we wait until we figure out where we're going to live first?" Anthony said. "Moving an aquarium without losing fish is hard work."

"I love you too," Paul said.

CHAPTER 21

"CAN YOU believe it's been a year since our first trip to Paris?" Patricia asked when Anthony joined her at their booth to set up for the Salon du livre, which opened the next day. "You did make reservations for us for tonight, right?"

"Of course I did," Anthony said as he leaned in to kiss her cheek. "And no, I can't believe it's been a year."

She studied his face for a moment, then nodded decisively. "You're happy here. That's good. I wasn't sure when you first told me how complicated things had gotten with Paul."

Things weren't perfect, but they had gotten better since the day Florent had come knocking on his door. In the intervening three weeks, they'd talked on the phone every night and seen each other more often than in Anthony's first month in Paris. Some nights they had sex, but not always. Often they simply lay together and talked late into the night. Anthony had given thanks for his flexible schedule more than one morning when he'd gone back to sleep after Paul left, only to wake up and start his work day at one or two in the afternoon.

"We're making it work," he said when it was clear Patricia was waiting for an answer. "I wanted to talk to you about that, actually."

"While we're setting up the booth," Patricia said.

Anthony grabbed a box cutter and started opening boxes. They had a smaller space in Paris than they did at BEA in New York, but they still had books to set out and displays to create.

"How much would it complicate your plans if I stayed in Paris permanently instead of just for a year like we originally planned?" he asked as he handed her books for the big display rack.

"I send you to four big events a year right now," Patricia said. "Three of them are in Europe, and one of them is in the city you're planning on living in. It'll save me money to have you here because I'll only be paying for one transatlantic flight a year instead of three. Are things that serious?"

"Maybe not yet, but they're heading that way," Anthony said. "We have some things to think about, like where we want to live. Paul owns his apartment, but it's really too small for both of us, especially with me working from home. I'm renting my place because I thought it was temporary when I signed the lease. There's enough space for both of us, although a bigger place wouldn't be bad either. But it's stupid to sell Paul's apartment only to live in a rented one. So we'd need to look at buying one together, but that's a bigger commitment than either of us is comfortable making after only two months." Especially considering the missteps and near missteps of the first month, but he didn't mention that to Patricia. She didn't need that level of detail about his sex life. "And then there's the question of whether I'd be able to stay."

"Why wouldn't you?" Patricia asked. "I thought France issued resident visas to spouses of French citizens."

"Now you're getting way ahead of the game," Anthony said. "We aren't ready to get married yet." He hoped they would be eventually. He loved Paul and would gladly spend the rest of his life with him, but Paul had to be ready to make that commitment too. "I wasn't sure how you would take it if I told you I wanted to stay."

"Skyping with you isn't as much fun as seeing you in person, but that's not a reason to make you come back to North Carolina," Patricia said. "We've done fine the past two months with having our meetings that way. We can compensate by building in a few days before or after the big book fairs if we have things that need to be taken care of face to face."

"Thank you," Anthony said. "I'm not sure what I would have done if you'd said no."

"I wouldn't be much of a friend if I said no," Patricia replied. "Yes, I have a business to run, but it doesn't help me or anyone else if I'm a hardass for no reason. I'll get Juana to start looking into the tax situation for you. I don't know if you'll owe US or French taxes or both."

"God, I hope it's not both," Anthony groaned. "I'd like to have some money to live on."

Patricia laughed. "We'll figure it out. Let's get this booth done. I want dinner."

"GOD, I'VE missed this," Patricia said when Paul brought her a *kir royal* without her even having to ask.

"You have no restaurants with good service in North Carolina?" Paul asked. It was so odd to hear Paul speaking English. Anthony knew he spoke it, but they always spoke in French, except when Paul had him so wrung out that his brain couldn't distinguish between the two languages anymore and English slipped out without him realizing it.

"None like this," Patricia said. "None I go to often enough to make it a regular thing and get to know the people there. It's mostly big chain restaurants around where I live."

"That is no good," Paul said. "We will take good care of you while you're here."

"I know you will," Patricia said. "Can I talk to you about reserving a table for a business dinner for a couple of nights or do I need to talk to your father about that?"

"It would be better to talk to Papa if you want something specific," Paul said. "I can bring him to the table."

Paul disappeared and came back a few minutes later with his father. Maurice had warmed up to Anthony somewhat when he realized Anthony was there to stay, not only in Paris but also with Paul, but he made sure to be on his best behavior whenever he was in the restaurant.

"*Madame?*" Maurice said.

"I'm sorry, I don't speak any French."

"It is no problem, *madame*. Paul says you wish to reserve a table?"

"For tomorrow night and Friday night," Patricia said. "We are hosting dinners for some business partners. It will mostly be a social occasion, a chance to talk informally, but the right atmosphere and service will matter."

"Of course. We will put you at the large table in the front, where you will have plenty of space, and I will oversee your dinner myself. It will be the perfect experience for you."

Anthony didn't grimace, but he wanted to. If Maurice was personally overseeing everything, he wouldn't get more than a glimpse of Paul. Not that he would have flirted overtly with Paul during a business dinner, but they could have shared the occasional smile or exchanged conversation when Paul came to check on the table. As it was, he'd be lucky to even get to say hi.

"I appreciate it," Patricia said. "We had such a wonderful experience eating here last year that I couldn't imagine having these dinners anywhere else."

Maurice gave a recognizant bow. "We are pleased to hear that. Enjoy your dinner tonight. I'm certain Paul will take good care of you."

"He always has," Patricia said.

PAUL NEARLY groaned out loud when he rounded the corner to the back room of the restaurant and saw Ludovic sitting at one of his tables. He did not need this tonight. The Salon du livre had kept Anthony incredibly busy. He hadn't seen Anthony since Friday night, when he had dinner in the restaurant with Patricia and a group of business contacts, but they hadn't had time to do more than steal a quick kiss in the cellar. Paul had been tempted to pull Anthony into one of the restrooms, but it hadn't been just Patricia waiting for him this time, and Paul wouldn't be part of Anthony making a bad impression on people they wanted to work with. Anthony texted every night, but usually to say he was falling asleep trying to wait for Paul to get home and he'd try again the next night. Except it had been seven nights, and they still hadn't managed to connect more than through a few texts. Paul was reaching the end of his rope, and seeing Ludovic's assessing smile as he approached pushed him one step closer.

"Paul," Ludovic said, "good to see you. I was hoping you'd be working tonight."

Paul's stomach tied itself in knots. He didn't need this, not when he was already on edge from not talking to Anthony in a week. He could feel the itch under his skin intensifying even as he wondered how he could ever have been attracted enough to Ludovic to want to sleep with him once, much less more than that. "Tuesday is Florent's day off."

Ludovic raised an eyebrow. "Does that mean I got lucky and tomorrow is your day off?"

"It is my day off, but I already have plans," Paul said. He thought about mentioning his boyfriend, but he didn't want Ludovic to touch that, even with words.

"I wasn't interested in tomorrow as much as I was in not worrying about keeping you up tonight," Ludovic replied.

It hadn't even been good sex. What the hell had he been thinking?

He hadn't been, of course, which was the problem. He'd been missing Anthony and desperate to prove their week together hadn't meant any more to him than it seemingly had to Anthony. He'd been lonely and afraid he always would be, and he'd let his libido run away with his good sense.

He wouldn't make that mistake again.

He could shut Ludovic down, send Gaël over and let him deal with him, but Paul knew Ludovic's type. He'd end up complaining about something out of spite, and Gaël would bear the brunt of Papa's displeasure when Paul was the problem. He could tell Papa and let Papa deal with Ludovic—however much they sometimes clashed, he never doubted for an instant that Papa would shield Paul from this if he asked—but he'd have to see that look of disappointment Papa got on his face when he had to face Paul's past indiscretions.

Even Anthony sometimes earned him that look, although Papa was beginning to accept that Paul was serious about Anthony and that Anthony was serious about him in return.

No, the best thing to do was to suck it up and deal with Ludovic. When the evening was over—or tomorrow at the latest—he'd be able to talk to Anthony, and that would make the hassle worth it.

"Would you like an aperitif?" he asked instead of answering Ludovic's question.

BY THE time Paul slipped out for his smoke break, his hands were shaking from dealing with Ludovic and missing Anthony and the growing restlessness under his skin. He'd been doing so well. He hadn't expected this week—and tonight, especially—to be so hard. He took a long drag on his cigarette and waited for the nicotine to settle him. It was Tuesday. They weren't all that busy. Maybe he could duck out a little early. If he knew he'd see Anthony before bed, it would make the rest of the night easier.

He hated what it said about him that he needed the hope of seeing Anthony to make it through the night, but he wasn't above admitting he couldn't do it on his own. Trying to do that had gotten him nothing but a string of one-night stands. Relying on Anthony had gotten him… well, everything. As hard as the month after Anthony's return had been, the past three weeks had been paradise. Nothing was worth giving that up for, certainly not some random hookup from his past. So why couldn't he let it go and treat Ludovic like he did any other customer?

That was the part that was driving him mad. He wasn't tempted. He looked at Ludovic now and wondered what he'd been thinking, and yet he was on edge, prowling around the restaurant like he'd done at the height of his promiscuity. He took another drag on the cigarette to see if it would settle him. He needed to calm down so he could go back inside and do his job. He and Anthony had already planned to spend tomorrow together. They hadn't decided what they were going to do with their day together. That would depend on how exhausted Anthony was from the four days of the Salon plus the two extra days of meetings he'd set up for Patricia while she was in town. Paul knew he'd spent most of that time playing translator for her, an exhausting occupation by itself, but on top of that, he'd had ten-hour days at the Salon and dinner meetings afterward. Not the recipe for being energetic tomorrow.

Feeling calmer with his thoughts focused on Anthony, Paul pondered their options. It had warmed up enough that they could go out somewhere, maybe have a picnic like they'd done last year the day after the Salon du livre. It could become their tradition. A picnic in one of Paris's many parks the day after Patricia went home.

Of course that assumed Anthony stayed in Paris permanently. He'd said he was going to talk to Patricia about it, but they hadn't had time to talk since then for Paul to know if Anthony had managed to discuss it with her, much less to know what she'd said. That was probably playing into the way he was feeling, he realized. It hadn't occurred to him until Anthony said it that Patricia might have an issue with him staying in Paris permanently, and that if she did, they might have some hard decisions to make. Not tomorrow or next week, since Anthony still estimated it would take him a year or more to do everything Patricia had sent him to Paris to do, but eventually.

He could text Anthony and ask about that, even if he didn't ask about anything else. If he knew that, maybe he would have an easier time tonight. It felt selfish, though, to disturb Anthony's dinner—and his last night with Patricia—to get a reassurance that could just as easily wait until morning. Anthony would answer as quickly as he could, and he wouldn't say anything to Paul about the interruption because that's the kind of man he was, but Paul was trying to be the kind of man who deserved someone like Anthony.

Anthony would laugh at that and say something about having picked Paul knowing his faults as well as he knew his more stellar traits, but Paul wanted more than that. Anthony had this idea of him that Paul wanted to live up to.

He finished his cigarette and glanced at his watch. He still had a few minutes before he had to go back inside. He pulled out his phone to check the weather report for tomorrow.

Clear and cool, but the sun would make for a nice change after the drizzle they'd had for the past few days. Perfect weather for a picnic. Now he only needed to decide which park to take Anthony to. They could go back to parc Monceau or they could go farther afield. The bois de Boulogne wouldn't be in full bloom yet, but they could walk there for hours. If Anthony wasn't up for walking, they could go to the jardin de Luxembourg or even to the champ de Mars near the Eiffel Tower. The flowers there were always stunning. Of course they'd have the tourists to deal with, but there were always tourists in Paris, even in the lesser-known corners of the city. Not as many, but they were still there.

He'd stop at the bakery, the charcuterie, and the crémerie in the morning and then see how Anthony was feeling. If he was up for a walk, they'd go to the bois de Boulogne. If not, they'd find a park within the city.

Feeling better now that he had a plan, he headed back inside to face the rest of the evening.

BY THE time his second break rolled around, Paul had had it, with himself, with Ludovic, with the restaurant, with everything that kept him from being with Anthony right now. He'd hoped focusing on Anthony and his plans for tomorrow would help—and it had worked for a short time—but as the hours dragged on, it spun in the opposite direction, only adding to his need to be with Anthony now. The only good thing to come out of the evening—or even the last few days—as far as Paul was concerned was the knowledge that going with someone other than Anthony didn't hold any appeal to him. He was jealous of the people who got to spend time with Anthony while he was stuck at the restaurant, but not to the point of wanting to turn to someone else for consolation or revenge.

He doubted that knowledge would help him sleep tonight. He needed to talk to Anthony. He pulled his cell phone out of his pocket to text Anthony.

Please don't go to sleep early tonight. I need to talk to you.

A few seconds later his phone beeped that he had a new message.

Call when you get home. Even if it wakes me up.

Paul frowned. He didn't want to wake Anthony up, but he wasn't sure he'd manage to sleep tonight if he didn't find a way to settle.

I love you, he texted back.

I love you too.

The reminder helped. Whatever screwed-up need had him jumping out of his skin every time Gaël brushed past him and flinching each time Ludovic flirted with him, Anthony still loved him. Another two hours at the most and he would be home and could call Anthony, and maybe then he could sleep.

CHAPTER 22

PAUL WAITED only long enough to wave good-bye to Papa before he called Anthony. The phone rang three times before Anthony answered.

"Hello?"

Damn, he'd woken Anthony up, because usually Anthony answered the phone in French, but that sleepy hello had definitely been in English. He'd hoped Anthony wouldn't be that tired.

"Hi," Paul said. "I didn't mean to wake you up."

"It's okay," Anthony said, in French this time, although Paul smiled to hear the American accent creeping back in. Anthony spoke French so well and with so little accent most of the time that Paul could almost forget it wasn't his native language… until moments like this. "I told you to call whenever you got home."

"I'm still walking home," Paul admitted, "but I didn't want to wait any longer to talk to you. I talked to you more when you were still in North Carolina than I have this week."

"I know. I'm sorry," Anthony said. "I knew it would be chaotic, but I didn't expect it to be quite this busy. Last year we didn't know anyone—and no one knew us—so when the Salon ended, we'd come to the restaurant for dinner and that would be the end of it. The downside of beginning to make ourselves known in the industry, I guess."

"But that's a good thing," Paul said. "That's what Patricia sent you here to do."

"Yes, it's a good thing," Anthony said. "We're in demand now, as a partner through sublicensing, and as a customer for printers and distributors. It just meant six really busy days. But that's over. I'm looking forward to tomorrow."

"Me too," Paul said. "The weather's supposed to be nicer tomorrow. I thought we could have a picnic somewhere."

"Like we did last year?" Anthony said, and Paul could hear the smile in his voice.

"Yes, although we don't have to go to the same park. There are plenty of other places we could go instead."

"Surprise me," Anthony said. "Unless you'd rather I surprise you."

"No, I'll pick a place," Paul said. "Now that I know you like the idea." He let himself into his apartment building and climbed the stairs because he would lose reception on his phone if he took the elevator.

"Somehow I doubt that's the reason you texted me earlier," Anthony said. "If it was, you would've just asked me if I wanted to have a picnic tomorrow. What's going on?"

"I missed you," Paul admitted. "It wasn't a good night."

"I'm sorry," Anthony said. "I know it's been hard on you."

It shouldn't have been. It was only a few days, and Paul had known they were coming. He'd prepared for them, and he was going to see Anthony tomorrow. "It's that itch under my skin. I couldn't get rid of it tonight." The moment the words left his mouth, he realized how that could sound to Anthony. "I didn't do anything stupid, even though I could have. I texted you instead, but that only made it worse."

"Paul, calm down," Anthony said. "I trust you. I know you wouldn't go with someone else just because I couldn't be there tonight."

"But I could have," Paul said softly. "One of the customers tonight was someone I know, someone I slept with a couple of times. He made it quite clear he was interested in a repeat." He shuddered, just thinking about it. "I didn't want to do it. I didn't want him, but it started the restlessness up all over again. I'm supposed to be better than this."

"Hey, stop that," Anthony said. "Bad habits don't go away just because we want them to. Ask anyone who's ever tried to stop biting their fingernails or change their diet. It takes time and effort and sometimes backsliding. You didn't take him up on his offer. You called me instead. I'd say that's progress."

Paul was only halfway convinced. "I hate that I can't get through a week without feeling this way if you aren't around. What's going to happen when you have to go to London or New York or somewhere farther away?"

"I don't know," Anthony said, "but we'll figure it out when it happens. What do you need tonight?"

An image of pinning Anthony to the bed flashed through his mind, but he pushed that aside. He couldn't ask Anthony to get dressed and come over this late. He could wait until tomorrow night for that.

"Talking to you helps," Paul said, and it did. He was calmer than he'd been when he left the restaurant. Not completely calm, maybe, but better. He could hold on through the night until he saw Anthony in the morning. They might not leave Anthony's apartment right away if he couldn't settle the rest of the way, but he could make it through the night. He *would* make it through the night.

"Good, so talk to me," Anthony said.

Every topic of conversation fled Paul's mind. "Um… what was your meeting tonight?"

"It was with one of the publishers who's been courting Patricia for acquisition of rights. Terribly boring unless you're one of the authors whose books were being discussed. And that's not talking to me, that's me talking. Talk to me."

"About what?" Paul asked.

"Anything. About your day, about this customer who annoyed you, about what's going through your head right now. About our plans for tomorrow. Whatever you need to talk about."

"He looked at me like I was on the menu," Paul said. "Like he could pay for me the same way he paid for dinner. I hope I never made anyone feel the way he made me feel tonight."

"I can't speak for everyone, but you never made me feel that way," Anthony said.

"How did I make you feel?" Paul asked on impulse. He'd never given it much thought before tonight because he'd always been careful to make sure his conquests were willing, but now he wondered. Was his reaction simply because he hadn't wanted Ludovic's attention? Or had he managed to send some people away feeling as dirty as he felt right now?

"Oh, it's going to be that kind of conversation, is it?" Anthony teased. "Is that what you need tonight? For me to tell you in great detail what you do to me every time you touch me? Or maybe what you need tonight is for me to make love to you for a change?"

Paul groaned at the husky words. He hadn't intended for this to devolve into phone sex, but now that Anthony had started it, he couldn't say no. "Yes," he said hoarsely.

"Yes to which part?" Anthony teased.

"Any of it," Paul said. "All of it."

"Then unless you made it farther into your apartment than the living room, you'd better get undressed and into bed," Anthony said. "I'm already several steps ahead of you."

"You sleep in sweats and a T-shirt when you're alone," Paul said. "You told me you needed it to stay warm."

"It's not cold tonight," Anthony replied. "I was wearing boxers. Now I'm only wearing a smile. What are you wearing?"

"I'm still dressed from the restaurant," Paul said. "Jeans and a button-down, like always. Give me a minute. I'll take them off."

"Just your shirt," Anthony said. "That is, if you're giving me control tonight."

Paul hesitated. He took care of his lovers. Even at his worst, he'd always prided himself on that. He made sure they came first. Then he worried about his own release. "I…."

"You don't have to," Anthony said. "But if you don't, I want something in return."

"What?" Paul asked, because surely that would be easier than what Anthony was asking.

"Tell me the fantasy you've never told anyone else," Anthony said. "The one you never acted on for whatever reason. What do you *really* want?"

Images of Anthony beneath him, fucked so hard, so raw, so thoroughly that he couldn't think, couldn't speak, couldn't move, flashed through his head. Paul swallowed hard as he balanced the vulnerability of giving Anthony control against the risk of sharing his deepest fantasy. He took a deep breath. "Are you touching yourself?"

"Now I am," Anthony said. "I started getting hard the minute I heard your voice. You're not the only one who's suffered from our time apart."

"Stop," Paul said. "We aren't rushing tonight."

"When do we ever not rush?" Anthony quipped. "You've had me naked and in bed within minutes of arriving at your place almost every time we've had sex. And before you start worrying, no, I'm not complaining. It's incredibly arousing to know you want me that much."

"We aren't rushing tonight," Paul insisted. "That's my fantasy. To take my time and get so much of you that I can go more than a minute without craving you again."

"You can try," Anthony said, "but I'll never get so much of you that I don't want more."

Paul's eyes closed at the thought of Anthony taking all he had to give and still wanting more. "Is it warm enough in your room to kick the covers off? I want to look at you as well as feel you."

"It's always warm enough when you're looking at me," Anthony replied. Paul resisted the urge to snort at that. Anthony had pulled the covers back over them more than once when they'd been making love because he'd said it was too cold. For the purposes of his fantasy, though, Paul would indulge his imagination.

Now to decide what he wanted to do with the buffet of delights spread out in front of his mind's eye. "You're so beautiful," Paul said. "I can see you lying there, naked and hard, just waiting for me to take care of you."

"You always take care of me," Anthony said huskily. "Such good care of me."

Paul didn't feel like it at the moment, with the itch still under his skin and the memory of Ludovic's slimy stare fresh in his mind, but he accepted Anthony's compliment. He'd erase all thought of everything but what he and Anthony were building together. "I start at your neck. The Salon du livre is over. No one will care if you have love bites tomorrow or even later in the week. There will be no one to see them, and if they do, they'll be jealous that someone loved you so well."

"Let them see," Anthony said. "I'm not ashamed of you."

"I'd kiss and bite every inch of your neck," Paul said. "You'd be writhing on the bed, begging for more after the first bite, and I'd give it to you."

"Every bite goes straight to my dick," Anthony said with a groan. "I don't know how that's possible, but I love it."

"You're so responsive." Paul loved the way Anthony reacted to his love bites, whether they were on his neck and shoulder or lower, across his chest and stomach to his upper thighs. "I'll cover every inch of you in hickeys tonight. Could you come just from that?"

"Try me," Anthony said. If Paul were there, he would, but of all the things he dreamed of doing to Anthony, that one would be hard to simulate over the phone. Anthony could pinch at his skin in imitation of Paul's teeth, but it wouldn't be the same.

"Another night," Paul said. "When I'm there with you to do it for real. Get your fingers wet. Suck on them until they're dripping."

He listened for the sound of Anthony's mouth wetting his own fingers. He wasn't sure he'd be able to hear anything, depending on where the phone was in relationship to Anthony's mouth, but he waited until Anthony whispered, "Ready."

"For what?" Paul asked. He knew what he wanted, but Anthony had said he was ready. If Anthony had something in mind, Paul would give it to him in a heartbeat.

"For whatever you have planned," Anthony replied. "Tonight is about what you need."

Paul shook his head, though Anthony couldn't see it. He wanted to give Anthony what he needed. He wasn't a selfish lover, even if he was at times a selfish man.

"Tell me what you're thinking," Anthony urged.

"I'm thinking I'm going to wreck you," Paul said. "When I'm done with you, you won't know anything but my name."

Anthony moaned. "I can't wait. Tell me what you'll do to me."

"When I've covered you in bite marks and you're begging to come, I'll flip you over and start on your back. Is your back as sensitive as your chest?"

"No, but that doesn't mean you shouldn't take your time," Anthony replied. "It might not be as sensitive, but everything is sensitive when you touch me."

There it was again, that assurance that Anthony would enjoy anything Paul chose to do. It was a heady thought. How far could he push it?

"I already know how sensitive your ass is," Paul said.

"Leave it covered in hickeys," Anthony begged. "I don't want to be able to sit at my computer tomorrow for feeling you."

"I'll do more than just bite it," Paul growled. "I'll eat it out and then fuck it so deep you'll be feeling it for a week."

"God, yes," Anthony moaned. "Want that."

"Not yet, though," Paul said. "You can still talk. You don't want it bad enough yet."

"You should do something about that," Anthony goaded.

"I will," Paul promised. "Touch your hole. That's my tongue working you open, all wet and hungry for you."

"You did that to me the night we met," Anthony said. "I don't think I'd ever been rimmed that thoroughly. Certainly not enough to come from it."

"I'll do it again, anytime you want," Paul said.

"I always want it. I always want you," Anthony said, "but tonight it won't be enough, will it?"

Paul could make it enough. He could strip off his jeans and boxers and jerk off to the thought of Anthony playing with his own ass, imagining it was Paul's tongue. He could find his release and push the demons at bay for a few more hours. Tomorrow they'd see each other in person, they'd make love, have their picnic, and probably make love again because once wouldn't be enough, no matter how tonight ended. He didn't have to do this.

"Will it?" Anthony pushed.

"No," Paul ground out.

"Then take what you need."

"Do you have lube?" Paul asked. "Because you're going to need it."

"Just waiting for you to ask for it," Anthony replied. "Do I need to pull out my toys?"

"Oh, fuck," Paul groaned. "You don't have a dildo there. I helped you move. I'd know if you had one."

"You didn't unpack all my bags," Anthony said. "Or maybe I bought it after I moved. I had to have something to get me through the nights when you weren't here."

"Tomorrow, you're showing me every sex toy you own," Paul said. "And then you're going to use them on yourself while I watch."

"Worry about that tomorrow," Anthony said. "What about tonight?"

Paul's head whirled. He couldn't think past the image of Anthony with a dildo up his ass. "Those fingers up your ass are mine. Your ass is mine. Nobody touches you but me."

"Nobody but you," Anthony promised. "It's always you. If you're not with me, I imagine you are. If I use my toys, I imagine it's you."

"Get one," Paul ordered.

He waited through the rustling on the other end of the line. "Got it," Anthony said breathlessly.

Paul thought about asking him to describe it so he'd know what Anthony was using when he was alone, but that would break the fantasy of it being Paul seeing to Anthony's needs.

"I wouldn't take you right away," Paul said. "I need you stretched and open for me, so empty you can't stand it a minute more."

"Tell me what to do."

"Get yourself ready, as loose as you can, because I won't have the patience for slow once I get inside you. But don't touch your prostate. I don't want you coming yet," Paul ordered. "Tell me what you're doing."

Anthony huffed out a breath of laughter. "You want me to finger myself open, imagining it's you, and then you want me coherent enough to talk? Not asking for much, are you?"

"Tell me what you're doing," Paul repeated.

"I've got two fingers inside me," Anthony said. "They feel so good. They go deeper than your tongue, although not deep enough. I keep scissoring them, to get my sphincter to loosen for you. You'll slip right in when you're finally ready to fuck me."

Paul was so far past ready, but Anthony was still talking. Of course he'd ordered Anthony to keep talking, so maybe that wasn't a fair assessment.

"Are *you* ready?"

"So ready," Anthony said. "Please, Paul."

That husky whispered word broke the last of Paul's control. "Now," he said. "I need you now, hard and deep and a little rough. I need you wrecked with it."

Anthony's cry carried through the phone. Paul closed his eyes and let his imagination take over, Anthony's hand on a dildo driving deep into his ass, Paul between Anthony's legs, replacing the toy with his own erection, pounding deep and hard until Anthony was sobbing with need, begging Paul to let him come. He'd find Anthony's sweet spot and nail it until he came, and then he'd fuck him all the way through it, dragging it out until Anthony couldn't take any more. He'd pull out and suck him until he was hard again and start all over again.

"Paul!"

The sound of his name on Anthony's lips brought Paul back to the moment. Had he said those things aloud?

Anthony's breathing was harsh through the phone. "Damn," he said finally. "How do you make me come that hard when you aren't even here?"

"Talent," Paul quipped.

Anthony laughed as he'd intended. "Think you can sleep now?"

Paul took stock of himself. He was still fully dressed and hard as a rock, but the itch beneath his skin was gone. "Yeah. Thank you."

"I should be thanking you," Anthony said. "But, Paul?"

"Yeah?"

"One day, when you least expect it, all those things you just described… I'm going to do them to you."

Paul swallowed hard. Could he do that? Could he give up control enough to let Anthony take over that way?

"Not tomorrow," Anthony continued, "but one day."

"One day," Paul agreed.

"Sleep well. I'll see you in the morning."

"I love you."

"I love you too."

The phone beeped to let him know the call had ended. Paul stared down at it and wondered what the hell he'd just agreed to. Worrying about it now wouldn't change anything. He stripped down, climbed between the sheets, and fell asleep almost instantly.

CHAPTER 23

"I SHOULD call Matt," Anthony said as he snuggled deeper into Paul's arms.

"We're lying in bed naked, and you're thinking about Matt?" Paul asked. "Should I be worried?"

Anthony chuckled. "I love Matt like a brother, but he's as straight as they come. You don't have anything to worry about. I need to tell him my stay in France got extended indefinitely. I'm not close enough to anybody else at home for them to care, but Matt needs to know. I can e-mail my aunt—not that she'll care—but Matt deserves more than that."

"Yes, he does," Paul said. "I know how much he means to you, and I know how much you're giving up to stay here with me."

Anthony rolled Paul onto his back and pushed up onto his elbows so he could look down into Paul's face. "None of that. I'm not 'giving up' anything. I'm changing my career path a little, but not significantly since I'll still be able to do my job from here. I won't see Layla as often, but that just means I'll have to make the most of the times I do see her. In exchange I get to spend my life with you. And don't ask me if you're really worth that. It's not a hard choice. Yes, I'll miss Matt, but we'll keep in touch even if we don't see each other every week. I'm not going to lose him because we don't live in the same town anymore."

"Do you want me to stay while you talk?" Paul asked. "Or would you rather not have an audience?"

"That's up to you," Anthony said. "I'm not going to tell him anything you don't already know."

"That wasn't why I offered to stay," Paul replied. "I thought you might like the support."

"Thanks, but I'll be fine," Anthony said. "Matt won't be awake yet, and I don't want to make you late for your shift. There's no reason to make your father more annoyed with me than usual."

"He's not annoyed with you," Paul said. "He likes you."

"You could've fooled me," Anthony grumbled.

"He didn't know what to make of you at first," Paul admitted, "but he came around. He needed time to realize you were different, that you weren't just someone else I was sleeping with, especially given how we met."

As closely as that corresponded to Anthony's original fears, he couldn't really blame Maurice for his concern. He just wasn't convinced he'd come around as much as Paul thought he had. "Okay, then there's no reason to make him annoyed at you."

Anthony puttered around the apartment after Paul left while he waited for it to get late enough to call North Carolina on a Saturday morning. He'd managed two loads of laundry and all the dishes when he couldn't stand it anymore. Nine o'clock—three o'clock in the afternoon for Anthony—was late enough for a man with an infant who still didn't sleep through the night. He grabbed his phone and dialed Matt's number.

"Hi, Anthony. I didn't expect to hear from you this morning," Matt said when he answered the phone.

"Hi. How's Layla?"

"Getting big. Switch to FaceTime and you can see her. Breakfast was messy this morning, but she'll be thrilled to see Uncle Anthony."

"Hold on a sec," Anthony said as he switched from a voice call to video chat. Matt's face appeared on the screen, and a second later, the view switched to Layla. Her bib was covered in red stains of some kind. "Strawberries?" he asked.

"Blueberries. Her favorite," Matt said. "So what's up?"

"You know how I said the move to France would just be for a year?" Anthony said.

"You aren't coming home, are you?" Matt said.

"Not for the foreseeable future," Anthony said. "I mean, there's immigration issues to work out, but they should be pretty straightforward since I have a job and everything. I really love him."

"I know. I'm only surprised it took you this long to admit it," Matt said. "I figured it would be inside a month, not almost three. Robin and I had a bet going."

Anthony grimaced. "How much did you lose?"

"Baby duty on the weekends for a month," Matt replied. "She's been enjoying getting to sleep in."

"I'm sorry. I'll take baby duty when I come visit next time," Anthony said.

"Are you going to be in New York in May like usual?" Matt asked. "You could come down a few days before or after that. It wouldn't quite be in time for Layla's birthday, but she's too young to know the difference."

Anthony weighed the possibility of seeing Matt and his family against the stress his being gone would put on Paul and their relationship. He hadn't expected the days of the Salon du livre to take the toll they had, but then again, he and Paul had had almost no contact in that time because he'd had to play translator for Patricia in the evenings. At BEA, he would be done when the show floor closed at five. Even if Patricia had meetings in the evening, she wouldn't need him at all of them like she had in Paris. He would be able to talk to Paul in the evenings or in the mornings on his way to the conference center when Paul was between lunch and dinner shifts. It would be easier for all that he'd be farther away. "If that's okay with you. I can send you the dates. It would probably be better to come after. That way I can actually take a few days of vacation instead of spending my time prepping for the show and my meetings," he said. "Let me talk to Paul and Patricia and make sure that suits, but pencil me in."

"Are you happy?" Matt asked.

Anthony smiled. "Yes."

"Then I'm happy for you. I always figured if you ever left Winston-Salem, it would be for France. Layla expects weekly calls, though. She might only get to see you in person once or twice a year, but she loves her uncle Anthony."

"Every Saturday morning," Anthony promised. "And you and Robin are welcome to come visit anytime too. I don't have a guest room at the moment, but we'll work something out."

"Not this year, but we'll definitely come," Matt said. "Robin has always wanted to visit Paris."

"I can't wait. I want you to meet Paul in person," Anthony said, relieved that Matt had taken his news so well.

"YOU'RE AWFULLY quiet tonight," Paul said as they finished dinner on Paul's night off a couple of weeks later. "What's on your mind?"

"Just thinking," Anthony said.

"About what?"

Anthony shrugged, not sure how to put into words the thoughts that had been running through his head. His mother's birthday was coming up. He'd been too wrapped up in Layla's first Christmas—and it had been too long since he and his mother had celebrated Christmas together—that he hadn't felt her loss as keenly then, but distractions were harder to find on her birthday.

"My mom's birthday would have been in two weeks," Anthony said. "Mostly I'm glad she's at peace now, but I still miss her at odd times."

Paul nodded sympathetically. "Maman has been gone for fifteen years. I'd tell you it gets easier, but I think it just gets less surprising that she's gone. Do you want to do something to mark her birthday? We always bake a cake for Maman. We could do the same for your mother."

"No, it's fine," Anthony said. "None of you knew her. There's no reason for you to go to that trouble for her."

"We may not have known her, but we know you, and it's no trouble. We own a restaurant. One more cake won't even be a ripple in our usual day," Paul said. "What day is it?"

"Two weeks from today," Anthony said.

"I'll talk to Papa and Nicolas tomorrow," Paul said. "We'll do it up right."

ANTHONY STARED down at the cake Paul set on the table. They'd had dinner at the restaurant even though it was Paul's night off, and Paul had disappeared into the kitchen when they were done eating. The chocolate ganache was shiny and smooth with strawberries on one side and mint leaves as garnish.

"It's beautiful," Anthony said. "She would love it."

"Good. Everyone will be over in a minute to cut the cake and help you eat it," Paul said. "Florent is getting a bottle of champagne and some glasses. We can't have a birthday party without a toast to the birthday girl."

Anthony fought back tears at the effort Paul and his family had put into helping him remember his mother. He'd have to find some way to thank them. He couldn't make them something—they were all better chefs than he was, even Paul, who claimed not to be able to cook. He'd have to think of something else. Not that he knew what. Getting them all together outside the restaurant was almost impossible given their schedules. Maybe between the lunch and dinner shifts, if he gave them enough notice that they could prep as much as possible ahead of time. He hadn't understood what Paul meant about his schedule getting in the way of his attempts at a relationship until he started dating him in earnest. Fortunately his own schedule was flexible enough to accommodate Paul's.

"Oh, and I have something for you too," Paul said. "To cheer you up."

"You've done so much already," Anthony protested. "The cake, the champagne, getting everyone together. That's more than enough."

"Don't worry, I'll enjoy this as much as you will," Paul said as he handed Anthony an envelope. Anthony opened it and gaped at the tickets in his hand. Paul was always doing little things like this, whether it was thinking of his mother's birthday or planning a picnic for Wednesday afternoon or bringing Anthony flowers for his office. They might have started their relationship all backward, but Paul had more than made up for it since then.

"These are for the Lyon-Stade Français match," Anthony said.

"I thought you might like to see them play in person," Paul said. "It's one thing to cheer them on when you're watching them on TV. Going to a match is something completely different."

"I haven't seen them play in person since I lived in Lyon," Anthony said. "Paul, this is too much.'

"The tickets weren't that expensive," Paul said, "and like I said, I'll enjoy it too. It may not be Toulouse, but it should be a good match."

Before Anthony could say anything else, Florent arrived with the bottle of champagne and six glasses. Gaël, Nicolas, and Paul's father joined them a few moments later. Maurice took the champagne from Florent and popped the cork. He poured a sip into one flute and sniffed it before adding more and handing it to Anthony. He quickly filled the others and passed them around.

Everyone looked at Anthony, but words failed him so he simply lifted his glass. The others clinked their glasses against his solemnly and sipped as he did. With a lump in his throat, he cut the cake and passed that around too. The cake tasted as delicious as everything else that came out of the kitchen.

"Thank you," Anthony said finally. "My mother would have loved the cake and the champagne and all of you."

Maurice patted Anthony on the shoulder. "No thanks are necessary among family. I have to check on the other tables."

He walked off before Anthony could digest the words. Nicolas and Gaël left soon after, but Florent lingered.

"See? I told you he liked you," Paul said with a grin that broke the somber mood.

Anthony laughed. "So you did."

Florent patted Anthony's shoulder too. "He was never the most demonstrative man, and after Maman died, it got worse, but he would do anything for us. That includes you now."

Anthony was beginning to understand that. He'd have to make more of an effort to spend time at the restaurant with Paul's family. He might never help them run it, but he could be a part of it since it was such a part of their lives.

CHAPTER 24

IT WAS late by the time they got back from the rugby match, but it would be worth being tired tomorrow for the memory of the smile on Anthony's face now. Paul had spent as much time watching Anthony as he had the match. The tickets had definitely been one of his better ideas.

Anthony let them inside and hung up his light jacket. The mid-April days had warmed up but the nights were still cool enough to make a jacket a necessity. Paul hung his beside Anthony's and pulled Anthony into his arms. Anthony met him in a deep kiss, but when Paul would have started them down the hall to the bedroom, Anthony spun him so his back pressed against the wall.

"You take such good care of me," Anthony said against Paul's lips. "You feed me, you make every Wednesday special one way or another, you make love to me until I can't think…. Tonight I'm going to make love to you."

Paul's breath caught in his chest. He took care of his lovers. He made sure they found their release before seeing to his own. It was what he did. But this was Anthony holding him close and kissing him. Anthony, who loved him, even at his worst, who didn't care that he sometimes left his dirty clothes on the bathroom floor or forgot to wash out his coffee cup or used to sleep with other men. Anthony wouldn't question his ability as a lover if Paul took for once instead of always giving. He forced his lungs to work again and nodded his assent.

Anthony kissed him tenderly, the barest brush of his lips over Paul's. Automatically Paul leaned in to deepen the kiss, but Anthony pulled away. "I'm taking care of you, remember?"

"Am I allowed to do anything?" Paul asked, only half joking. He wanted to make Anthony happy, and that meant knowing his expectations.

"Relax and enjoy," Anthony replied. "I know that will be hard, but do it for me."

It shouldn't have been, except it went counter to the way Paul thought of himself as a lover.

"I promise it will be worth it," Anthony added before kissing Paul again, more deeply this time. Paul parted his lips for Anthony's tongue and told himself he was making Anthony happy and that was a pleasure in itself. His fingers twitched with the need to touch, but Anthony had said to enjoy.

"You're overthinking this." Anthony twined his fingers with Paul's and lifted them to his hip. "Trust me."

Of all the things Anthony could ask, that was the easiest. "I do."

"I know you do," Anthony said. "Come on." He led Paul to the bedroom and unbuttoned the three buttons at the top of his polo shirt. When he leaned in to kiss Paul's throat, Paul tipped his head back to give Anthony room to work. "I won't leave you covered in bruises. No need to give Florent and Gaël a reason to tease you at work tomorrow. It's gotten too warm for turtlenecks."

Anthony's words settled Paul's nerves. Anthony might be the one in charge tonight, but it was all the same concerns. "They can tease all they want, but Papa would give me the disappointed look that says I'm being unprofessional."

"We wouldn't want that," Anthony said. He mouthed at Paul's skin with barely a hint of teeth, enough to let Paul know he could mark him if he wanted but not enough to leave any trace behind. A surge of desire nearly outweighed Paul's need not to incur Papa's wrath. He pulled back enough to get his shirt over his head. "There are other places you can leave marks."

Anthony grinned at him with such anticipation that lust shot through Paul. "Oh, I was planning on it."

Paul groaned at the promise in Anthony's words and wondered where he'd be sporting bruises come morning. When Anthony first promised to turn the tables on Paul after Paul had admitted some of his deepest desires over the phone, Paul had described leaving bite marks all over Anthony's body so he would feel them for days. He'd never gone that far in reality, although Anthony usually had one fading mark or another, always left when he begged for more. He shivered from a mix of memory and anticipation. Whatever Anthony did, wherever he left hickeys, Paul would love every second of it.

Anthony didn't start with the rough, biting kisses he so loved to receive, though. Instead he licked and sucked more than he bit at Paul's skin, across his collarbone and down his chest to linger on one nipple, then the other. Paul cupped Anthony's head in his one hand while he steadied himself on Anthony's shoulder with the other. Surely that was allowed. He wasn't directing, just touching.

Anthony sucked a little harder until Paul gasped with it before straightening to kiss Paul full on the mouth again. "We'll be more comfortable in bed," Anthony said.

Paul reached for the button on his jeans, but Anthony stopped him. "Leave that for now. Just lie down and let me make you feel good."

"What about you?" Paul asked. He'd never be able to enjoy this if Anthony wasn't getting some pleasure from it as well.

Anthony grinned rakishly. "Don't even worry about that. I'm so turned on at the thought of finally getting to make love to you that I'll be lucky to last long enough to do all the things I want to do to you."

Paul relaxed a little at that. After all, he felt that way when he was the one guiding their lovemaking. It wasn't much of a stretch to think Anthony might feel the same, not now that it truly was making love and not just sex. He toed off his shoes and stretched out on the bed, reaching for Anthony as soon as he was settled.

Anthony followed him down and reclined beside him. "Now, where shall I start?"

Paul had a few suggestions, mostly revolving around Anthony shedding a few layers of clothes, but it was Anthony's show tonight, not Paul's. He would let Anthony lead.

Anthony's answer was with Paul's nipples again. He nipped and sucked at one while he played with the other with his fingers, driving Paul into a frenzy of need. He moaned at one particularly hard bite and arched off the bed.

"I love how responsive you are," Anthony murmured. "You're so hot like this. I could get off just watching you."

When Anthony returned to his obsession with Paul's nipples, Paul moaned a little more freely. Anything to make Anthony feel good too.

Eventually Anthony abandoned Paul's pecs for the sensitive patch of skin at the base of his ribs. "Tell me if it's too much."

Paul gasped as Anthony sucked hard enough to leave a mark. He gripped Anthony's shoulder hard, but to urge him on, not to stop him. No one would see this mark, but Paul would know it was there and would cherish the memory of Anthony leaving it on his skin. "More."

Anthony chuckled. "Now you know how I feel when you do that to me."

Paul was more interested in how Anthony felt to be doing it, but one look at Anthony's expression silenced the question before it could form. He had spent enough time studying all the ways passion manifested on Anthony's face. He didn't need words to recognize it now.

He palmed his cock through his jeans, but Anthony caught his hand and pinned it to the bed. "Tonight I'm taking care of you. You don't have to take care of yourself, and don't think I've missed how many times you've jerked off while I was too out of it rather than waiting for me. It's my turn."

Paul flushed, but he could hardly deny it. "Watching you gets me so worked up I can't wait."

"I get that," Anthony said, "but tonight you don't have to wait and you don't have to do it yourself. You just have to tell me what you want."

"And if I tell you what I want is to roll you onto your stomach and rim you?" Paul asked, because nothing made Anthony moan and shout like Paul's tongue up his ass.

"Then I'll tell you to hold that thought until tomorrow," Anthony said. "Tell me what you want me to do to you, and I'll do it. Otherwise lie back and let me take care of you my way."

Asking for anything specific felt too selfish so Paul subsided onto the bed and let Anthony do as he pleased. Anything he decided to do would feel good, and knowing it was what Anthony wanted would only make it better.

Anthony popped the button on Paul's jeans and slid down the zipper, brushing his knuckles along the line of Paul's cock as he worked. Paul bucked up into the caress, his body asking for what he would not.

"Lift your hips. Let me get your jeans off."

Another night Paul might have said something about how Anthony should have let him take them off before getting in bed, but tonight he simply did as Anthony asked and helped Anthony get his jeans off. Anthony tossed them aside and slid a hand up Paul's thigh to the leg of his boxers and then beneath, teasing Paul with a not-quite-there touch. "Please," Paul panted. "Touch me for real."

Anthony pulled his hand out from beneath Paul's boxers, much to Paul's dismay, only to pull the waistband down to his thighs. That was better. The suspense was killing him, though. When he made love to Anthony, he always knew the plan, whether it was a quick and dirty blow job or whether he spent hours buried in Anthony's ass. Leaving the decision in Anthony's hands now was unnerving.

Anthony ran the tip of one finger along the underside of Paul's cock, right along the thick vein. Paul moaned and bucked up into the touch, trying to get a firmer caress, but Anthony kept the contact light. It would have been maddening if not for the look of fascinated delight on Anthony's face. Paul wanted to scoff and make a comment about him never having seen a cock before, but he couldn't bring himself to spoil the mood. Anthony might be teasing Paul mercilessly, but he was getting as much pleasure from it as Paul was, and that was all that mattered. The rest would come. Anthony wasn't cruel. He might take his time and drive Paul mad with need, but he would also make sure Paul got what he needed out of their encounter.

"Do you know how many nights I've wanted to do this?" Anthony asked as he stroked Paul more firmly. "You get me in bed and worked up, and before I know it, I'm coming all over creation, and I never get the chance to return the favor."

"You have never left me unsatisfied," Paul gasped.

"That's because you're perfectly satisfied with your own hand after you've gotten me off," Anthony retorted.

It wasn't that at all, it was that he was so worked up from watching Anthony come apart beneath him that it only took the touch of his hand to finish him off.

"I'm with you and I'm satisfied," Paul said. "That's all I need."

Anthony scowled at him a little. "Not tonight. Tonight it's my turn."

"I already said yes," Paul reminded him. "You don't need to keep insisting."

Anthony met his eyes with a piercing stare. "I think I do. I think you get so caught up in trying to please me, whether it's in bed or with things like the rugby match tonight, that even now you can't relax and let this be about you."

Paul shook his head in automatic denial as another gasp escaped when Anthony stroked him again. "You're the one touching me, not the other way around."

"And if I know that brain of yours, you're still obsessing over whether I'm enjoying it," Anthony retorted.

"Is it so terrible of me to want you to feel good too?" Paul asked. It stung a little that he was so transparent, but that's what made them so good together. Anthony saw through his bullshit and called him on it when necessary. He hadn't expected now to be a time when it was necessary.

"It's not terrible at all," Anthony said. "I've thoroughly benefited from it, but I want to do the same for you. You're worried about being selfish, although you're the least selfish lover I've ever had, but in keeping the control all the time, you're keeping me from something I want too. It's not selfish to let me make love to you when I want it as much as I do. Even if I don't say it at every turn, I'm totally getting off on touching you and hearing you moan and seeing you react to my hands and mouth on you."

Paul let Anthony's words sink in, really sink in past the layers of hurt left behind by Gilles and his cruel parting words about how Paul needed to learn how to take care of a man if he wanted to keep one, past the years of only getting any praise from his lovers if he took control and pleased his partner first, past his fears of losing Anthony if a better deal came along.

He wanted desperately to believe Anthony, not because he was at all displeased with their love life but because it would mean being able to share the load at times, and wasn't that what a relationship was all about? Not being selfish, but each partner taking care of the other when time and need required?

He could do that. He could make a balanced relationship with Anthony work, especially if it meant having Anthony's hands on him like they were right now. Oh, fuck, and Anthony's mouth!

"You were thinking too hard," Anthony said with a mischievous grin. "I want you right here with me."

"Keep doing that and there's no chance of my mind wandering," Paul said huskily.

Anthony winked and returned his attention—and his mouth— to Paul's cock. Paul couldn't remember the last time he'd been on the receiving end of a blow job, but he pushed the thought aside because the last thing he wanted was to think about other men while he was in bed with Anthony. Besides, no matter when it was or who it was with, it wasn't as good as what Anthony was doing now. It couldn't possibly have been because Anthony loved him, and he loved Anthony, and that made all the difference in the world. He'd known sex with Anthony was different long before he'd been willing to put a name to what made it different.

He kept his head up so he could watch the stretch of Anthony's lips around his shaft, the bobbing of his head, but eventually the strain on his neck defeated his desire to see, and he let his head drop back to the pillow. Anthony took that as a sign he was doing something right and sucked Paul deeper into his mouth. Paul moaned and resisted the urge to thrust up into Anthony's mouth. He didn't want to choke Anthony.

Anthony, though, had no such qualms, pressing Paul deeper until the head of his cock slid down Anthony's throat.

"Fuck," Paul groaned.

Anthony hummed, the vibrations shooting along Paul's nerves, an electric shock of lust and want and need so strong he nearly came right then. He couldn't do that. He needed to hold on and take care of—

Anthony rolled Paul's balls in his palm and pressed on the spot right behind them. Stars danced in front of Paul's eyes, and he lost the fight for control. Anthony swallowed around him and finally came up for air, licking his lips as he met Paul's gaze again.

"I'm sorry," Paul said. "I should have warned you."

"Do you see me complaining?" Anthony asked. "My only worry now is how long it'll take you to be ready for more."

"More?" Paul squeaked.

Anthony grinned at him. "What was it you said on the phone after the Salon du livre? You wanted to wreck me so badly I wouldn't know anything but your name? You're still talking. I'm not done with you yet."

Paul moaned at the husky promise in Anthony's words. He didn't know how much he could take or how long it would take him to recover, but with enticement like that, he'd damn well give it his best shot. Paul shimmied out of his boxers and returned Anthony's grin. "Do your worst."

"Oh, I will."

Paul wanted to kiss the smirk off Anthony's face, but that would have required sitting up. Instead he lifted one knee so his foot rested on the bed. He cocked an eyebrow at Anthony in silent invitation.

Anthony's smirk faded into a look of pure hunger as he reached into the drawer next to the bed and pulled out condoms and lube. Paul clenched despite himself. It had been years since he'd bottomed for anyone, and that hadn't been the most fulfilling experience of his sexual career. He trusted Anthony implicitly, but that didn't stop him from closing his legs reflexively.

"Roll over," Anthony urged.

Paul did as Anthony asked, ignoring the nerves fluttering in his stomach. If he didn't like something, all he had to do was tell Anthony. Anthony would stop. Everything else was so much better with Anthony. This would be too. The sharp pinch of Anthony's teeth at the top of his crease surprised a cry out of Paul. He'd been expecting cold, lubed fingers, not Anthony's hot breath.

"What?" Anthony said when Paul pushed up on an elbow and looked back at him. "You thought I'd just dive in? I can't stand the taste of lube. If I'm going to enjoy this, it has to be first."

Paul subsided onto the bed and spread his legs. Anthony was taking seriously the business of turning all of Paul's favorite activities back on him. The blow job had been a success. That boded well for the rest.

Anthony swept his tongue up Paul's crack from balls to tailbone and back down again before zeroing in on Paul's entrance. Paul pulled one knee up to his side, opening himself as wide as he could for Anthony's exploration. Every nerve ending in his ass and groin zinged with pleasure and anticipation.

He lifted up against Anthony's mouth, wanting more contact. Anthony caught his hips with one hand to help support him and slipped the other beneath him to circle his cock again. Paul groaned sharply at the dual stimulation. Anthony was trying to kill him.

It took far less time than he expected for his cock to harden again. When he was fully erect and rocking back and forth between Anthony's hand and mouth, Anthony pulled back. Paul moaned in protest, but Anthony soothed him with a lingering stroke of his hand over the curve of Paul's ass.

"Not much longer," Anthony promised. "Let me slick you up a little and we'll be good to go."

Anthony must have tucked the lube beneath him to warm it up because his fingers were slippery but not at all cold when he pressed them against Paul's entrance. Paul tried not to tense up, but it took a moment for the muscles to relax after so long. Even the thorough rimming Anthony had given him could only loosen him up so much. Anthony played him like a symphony after that, the perfect crescendo of sensation until Paul could do nothing but shout Anthony's name amid the babble of meaningless sound that fell from his lips. He had promised to wreck Anthony, and now Anthony was making good on it.

When Anthony replaced his fingers with the head of his cock, Paul tensed up again, but he was too aroused to stay tight for long. He pulled up on both knees so he could fuck himself back onto Anthony's cock. Anthony froze and gave Paul that much control of the penetration as Paul worked Anthony slowly deeper. Finally he pushed back the last couple of millimeters and felt the rasp of Anthony's pubes against his ass. He dropped his head to the mattress and took a moment to simply breathe.

"Tell me when I can move," Anthony said. He stroked Paul's back tenderly, helping Paul relax even more.

"Now," Paul said when the burn of penetration had eased to a comfortable fullness. He braced himself for Anthony's thrusts, but the motion never came. Instead Anthony circled his hips, stirring his cock in Paul's passage without withdrawing at all. The constant stimulation on Paul's prostate left him gasping for breath and wondering why he'd waited so long to do this again.

A second climax began building at the base of his spine, right where the tip of Anthony's cock lodged within him, it felt like, electricity zipping up his spine and through his cock.

"Do you have any idea how good you look right now?" Anthony said. "I could stay right here forever and never get tired of looking at you."

Paul moaned. He wanted to tell Anthony that sounded perfect to him, but the words were more than his brain could process. He collapsed forward onto the bed, his face buried in the pillows, lifting his ass even more. The change in angle stimulated him differently, only adding to his breathless state. He shook his head, trying to make his mind work so he could beg Anthony for more, but nothing came out but a keening cry as Anthony finally lengthened his strokes and increased the power behind them.

With a shout, he came a second time. Anthony fucked him through his release, drawing out the spasms until Paul thought he'd black out. When any more would have been painful, Anthony pulled out, leaving Paul a quivering mess on the bed. He wanted to roll to his back and stroke or suck Anthony until he climaxed too, but that required more coordination than he currently had. He heard a groan, the long low one he'd come to associate with Anthony's orgasms, and then hot fluid landed across his back.

He'd done that to Anthony. Oh, not with his hands or his mouth, but watching him come, taking him apart—and he was well and truly wrecked, thank you, Anthony—had been enough to make Anthony come too.

He stayed where he was, slumped on the bed, as Anthony cleaned him up and rolled him out of the wet spot. When Anthony stretched out on the mattress next to him, Paul snuggled immediately into his embrace. Anthony kissed the top of his head. Paul smiled and tilted his chin up for a real kiss.

"Thank you," Anthony murmured.

Paul shook his head and kissed Anthony's shoulder. "Thank you for taking such good care of me."

"Does this mean you'll let me do it again some time?" Anthony asked.

"On one condition," Paul said.

"What's that?"

"When we finally find a place to move in together, we keep your mattress," Paul said. "If you're going to fuck me into a mattress, it should be the more comfortable one."

"You're on. How quickly can we start looking?"

Paul laughed and snuggled deeper into Anthony's arms. "The next day I have off."

"Who can you trade with so we can start looking tomorrow?"

"I could ask Papa about Monday."

Anthony considered that for a moment before shaking his head. "Next Wednesday it is."

"Papa likes you enough to say yes," Paul said.

"Maybe, but I'm finally in his good graces," Anthony replied. "I'd rather stay there. Two more days won't make that much of a difference as long as I know we'll start looking soon. I'm ready for you to come home to me every night."

So was Paul.

When ARIEL TACHNA was twelve years old, she discovered two things: the French language and romance novels. Those two loves have defined her ever since. By the time she finished high school, she'd written four novels, none of which anyone would want to read now, featuring a young woman who was—you guessed it—bilingual. That girl was everything Ariel wanted to be at age twelve and wasn't.

She now lives on the outskirts of Houston with her husband (who also speaks French), her kids (who understand French even when they're too lazy to speak it back), and their two dogs (who steadfastly refuse to answer any French commands).

Visit Ariel:
Website: www.arieltachna.com
Facebook: www.facebook.com/ArielTachna
E-mail: arieltachna@gmail.com

DANCE
OFF

ARIEL TACHNA & NESSA L. WARIN

On the reality show *Dance Off*, pro rugby player Olivier Gautier and Olympic swimmer JC Webster each have one goal in mind: to stay on the show as long as possible to earn his charity of choice maximum exposure and a larger donation. As the competition heats up, their goals expand to catching each other's interest, but Olivier is firmly in the closet and plans to stay there. JC is willing to be discreet, but not to hide forever.

Starting a romance with another man is challenge enough for any celebrity, but doing it under the microscope of reality TV—and one majorly intolerant costar—is even harder. Add in meddling dance pros, JC's overbearing family, and the need to play up chemistry with dance partners to win America's hearts, and JC and Olivier's time together is looking more and more like a recipe for disaster.

As the pressure to stay in the competition mounts, JC and Olivier must face their inevitable separation at the end of the show as well as decide whether a relationship as complicated as theirs can survive in the real world, outside the bubble of the set and practice studios.

www.dreamspinnerpress.com

ARIEL TACHNA
Home FOR Chirappu

Nikhilesh (Nik) Sharma hasn't been home to Alappuzha, India, since he came out to his family ten years ago. Now that his relationship with them is less strained, he's bringing his boyfriend Trent along to celebrate the winter holidays. As excited as he is to see everyone again, he worries the foreign culture, religious differences, and disapproval might shock Trent. At the same time, Trent worries Nik's big, close-knit family won't accept an American—much less a man—as Nik's partner and that his presence will impede the otherwise happy reunion. Whether the trip leads to misunderstandings that will drive them apart or to a new understanding that will draw them closer than ever, it's sure to be an experience they'll never forget.

www.dreamspinnerpress.com

THE PATH

ARIEL TACHNA

All his life Benicio Quispe has dreamed of being a guide on the Inca Trail. He gets his chance when the top travel agency in Cusco, Peru hires him. Alberto Salazar, his assigned mentor, fits Benicio's idea of a perfect guide, but he's also everything Benicio never dared to dream of in a boyfriend.

Alberto learned a long time ago to be discreet about his sexuality. It's a necessary sacrifice to keep the respect of the guides and porters whose help is critical in a successful hike. So he pushes aside his attraction to his new junior guide and goes on as usual. But when a group of old friends arrives to hike the trail again, they convince him a relationship with Benicio is worth pursuing. His newfound resolve is enough to get them on a first date, but no amount of courage can change the attitudes of their family and friends. The risks on the trail are easy compared to finding a path through the challenges keeping them apart.

www.dreamspinnerpress.com

Lang Downs: Book One

Caine Neiheisel is stuck in a dead-end job at the end of a dead-end relationship when the chance of a lifetime falls in his lap. His mother inherits her uncle's sheep station in New South Wales, Australia, and Caine sees it as the opportunity to start over, out on the range where his stutter won't hold him back and his willingness to work will surely make up for his lack of knowledge.

Unfortunately, Macklin Armstrong, the foreman of Lang Downs who should be Caine's biggest ally, alternates between being cool and downright dismissive, and the other hands are more amused by Caine's American accent than they are moved by his plight… until they find out he's gay and their amusement turns to scorn. It will take all of Caine's determination—and an act of cruel sabotage by a hostile neighbor—to bring the men of Lang Downs together and give Caine and Macklin a chance at love.

www.dreamspinnerpress.com

Sequel to *Inherit the Sky*
Lang Downs: Book Two

Twenty-year-old Chris Simms is barely keeping his head above water. After losing his mother and his home, he struggles to provide for himself and his brother. When homophobes attack him, he thinks his life is over, but then he's rescued by jackaroos from a nearby sheep station. He's as stunned to be offered a job there as he is to discover both the station owner and foreman are gay.

For Chris, Lang Downs is a dream—one that only gets better when Chris realizes the jackaroo he's crushing on, Jesse Harris, is gay and amenable to a fling. Everything goes well until Chris realizes he's falling for Jesse a lot harder than allowed by their deal.

Jesse is a drifter who moves from station to station, never looking for anything permanent. Convinced Chris is too young and fragile for a real relationship, he sets rules to keep things casual. Watching the station owner and his foreman together makes Jesse wonder if there are benefits to settling down, but when he realizes how Chris feels about him, he panics. He and Chris will have to decide if a try for happiness is worth the risk before the end of the season tears them apart.

www.dreamspinnerpress.com

ARIEL TACHNA
OUTLAST THE NIGHT

Sequel to *Chase the Stars*
Lang Downs: Book Three

Office manager Sam Emery is unemployed and out of luck. When his emotionally abusive wife demands a divorce, he contacts the one person he has left, his brother, Neil. He doesn't expect Neil to reject him, but he also doesn't expect the news of his divorce—and of his sexuality—to be met with such acceptance.

Neil takes Sam to Lang Downs, the sheep station Neil calls home. There, Sam learns that life as a gay man isn't impossible. Caine and Macklin, the station owners, certainly seem to be making it work. When Caine offers Sam a job, it's a dream come true.

Jeremy Taylor leaves the only home he's ever known when his brother's homophobia becomes more than he can bear. He goes to the one place he knows he will be accepted: Lang Downs. He clicks with Sam instantly—but the animosity between Lang Downs and Jeremy's home station runs deep, and the jackaroos won't accept Jeremy without a fight. Between Sam's insecurity and Jeremy's precarious position, their road will be a hard one—and that's without having to wait for Sam's divorce to be final before starting a new life together.

www.dreamspinnerpress.com

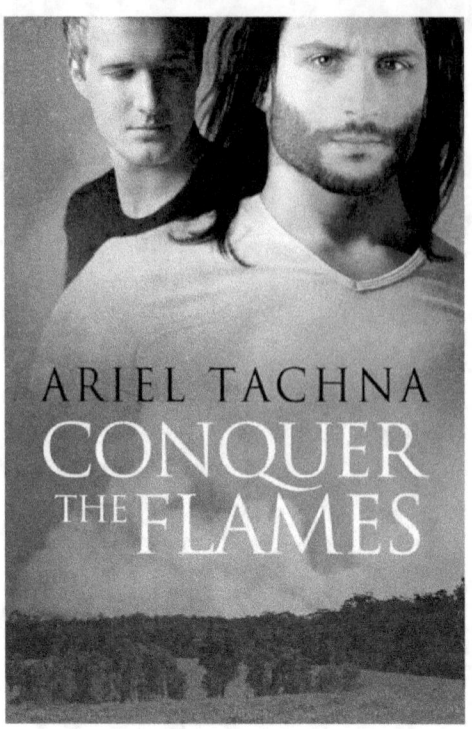

ARIEL TACHNA

CONQUER THE FLAMES

Sequel to *Outlast the Night*
Lang Downs: Book Four

Thorne Lachlan knows a thing or two about getting himself safely out of a blaze. For years he fought in the world's hot spots, a Commando with the Australian Army. Now, retired, he fights flames for the Royal Fire Service. When a grassfire brings him to Lang Downs, the next sheep station in danger, Thorne meets Ian Duncan and sparks fly that neither man can put out. But both men have ghosts from the past that stand in the way of moving beyond mutual attraction.

While Thorne longs for the home he could share with Ian at Lang Downs, he fears his own instability might make him a danger to others. And Ian's always believed that the foster care nightmare he escaped before coming to Lang Downs would make any relationship impossible. Trust doesn't come easily to Thorne or Ian until the fire's aftermath forces them to see past the scars keeping them both from healing.

www.dreamspinnerpress.com

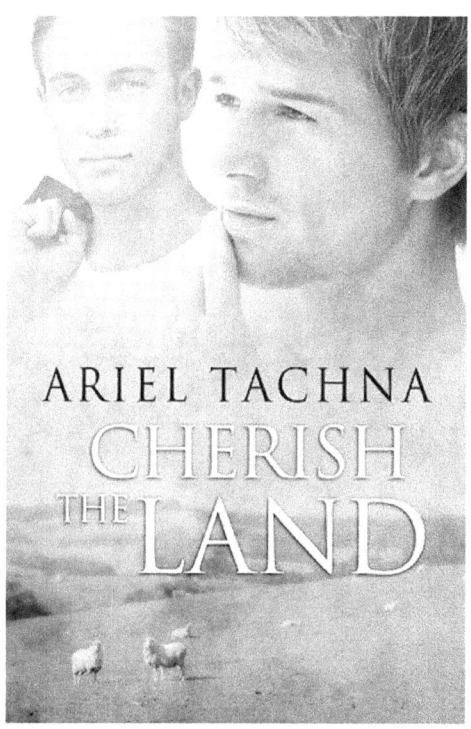

ARIEL TACHNA

CHERISH THE LAND

Sequel to *Conquer the Flames*
Lang Downs: Book Five

Seth Simms never wanted to be a cowboy, although to listen to his best friend, Jason Thompson, tell it, he isn't one. He just happens to have lucked out in coming to live on Lang Downs with his brother ten years ago. He found enough stability to finish high school and go off to university, but he never really believed Lang Downs would be the same haven for him that it had become for so many others. He's too messed up in the head. No one would accept someone with his issues.

All his life, Jason has had one goal: to come home to Lang Downs as resident veterinarian when they need his skills and jackaroo when they don't. And it means he gets to spend time with Seth during his occasional visits, even though his dream of going from friends to lovers is hopeless since Seth is straight.

When Seth unexpectedly comes home to stay, Jason takes it as the boon it is. But juggling a relationship with another jackaroo and his friendship with Seth isn't easy, and that's before Jason realizes how deep Seth's issues run and how dangerously Seth chooses to cope with them.

www.dreamspinnerpress.com

www.ingramcontent.com/pod-product-compliance
Lightning Source LLC
Chambersburg PA
CBHW070125260626
47160CB00004B/1620